For J x

Chapter One

Kate surveyed the room, trying her hardest to suppress her sense of awe. She didn't want to give anything away; after all, she was still undecided about the whole thing.

'Not bad, eh?' whispered the old man. She let out an involuntary nod. 'I know it all seems a bit opulent, but we spend so much of our lives here, waiting around. And I think it's the least we deserve, considering the service we provide. Wouldn't you agree?'

This time she refrained from responding. *This really is something else*, she thought. The walls were clean and clinical, like so many other workplaces, but apart from that, it all was very welcoming and exciting.

'Let's meet the troops, shall we?' said the old man, letting out a gentle chuckle. She liked him and trusted him – and yet for all his warmth and geniality, she couldn't escape the sense of sadness that surrounded him. Even when he smiled, his eyes seemed grey and empty. 'This is Nigel. Nigel, this is Kate.'

Nigel looked up, smiled weakly then returned to his newspaper. He was in an oversized recliner, which practically swallowed him up.

'Nigel's our oldest serving Intervener, except for myself, of course. So when I finally shuffle off this mortal coil, Nigel will be the Chief Intervener. And over here on the pool table, we've got Zak and Chris. What's the score, fellas?'

'Sixteen to him, ten to me. But I'm on the comeback trail, don't you worry!' Zak was much younger than the other men in the room, and there was a vitality, an infectiousness about him. Chris, on the other hand, remained stoic and did not acknowledge Kate's presence for the entirety of her visit.

'Pleased to meet you,' she said, giving them a quick wave. She looked up at the enormous screen, which took up almost the entirety of a wall. It was beaming out a daytime chat show that no one was watching. The room was filled with a variety of sources of entertainment, including a huge stocked bookcase, a shelf filled with board games and a grand piano.

'Which just leaves Sally. Not sure where she is – fellas? Where's Sal? Or need I ask?'

Nigel pointed towards the patio door without looking up from his paper. The old man led her out into the garden, where a woman who Kate surmised could have been no more than five years older or younger than her was kneeling down with a trowel in her hands. She looked up at Kate and smiled warmly. *She's prettier than me*, thought Kate, *but she seems all right.* She returned the smile.

'Sally's our resident gardener, as well as being an Intervener, of course!'

'Yeah – I keep asking the old sod to pay me double, but he's having none of it!'

All three of them laughed. She took off her gardening glove and thrust her hand towards Kate. 'Nice to meet you!' she said, her eyes positively twinkling.

Kate gazed in wonder at the virtual paradise that surrounded her. The garden was lusciously green and healthy; the flowers vivid and bright. It all looked so lovely in the afternoon sunshine.

'Gosh – it's beautiful out here!'

'Thank you muchly! Well, being an Intervener means spending a lot of time waiting around so – well, I like to come out here! It's my little project, if you will. Plus, it gets me away from the boys for a bit!'

'Oh, you love us really!' said the old man, putting his arm around her shoulder and squeezing her affectionately.

They seem nice enough, she thought. She had imagined a bunch of weirdos and misfits, like she would be the only normal one.

'I don't know if you're a smoker or not, but if you are then I'm afraid I have to insist on you doing it out here. It's just like any other workplace, really.'

'Oh, I don't smoke.'

'Hmm. Neither did any of this lot. Now, let me show you the sleeping quarters.'

He took her up the spiral staircase. Her feet sank into the thick carpet as she walked up. There were six doors. He led her into the first one. Just like the living room, its walls were whitewashed. It was much like a hotel room – comfy-looking but impersonal.

'Everybody has a room. They're all exactly the same – bed, wardrobe, TV, shower. The room is yours whether you live here or just work here. Sometimes you just want a little nap or some alone time – that's what it's here for. Any questions?'

Kate shook her head, but really she had lots of questions – *what did he mean, live here or just work here? What did Intervening actually entail?*

'We do, of course, have one more room to look at.'

He took her back down the stairs and through the double doors in the living room. In stark contrast to the rest of the house, the room was dark, foreboding and mechanical. Computers, wires and screens were everywhere. The biggest screen of all (even bigger than the TV in the living room) was green and, apart from the flashing words 'Awaiting Vision', totally blank. She felt a small chill down her spine. It all seemed real now.

'When you get your Vision, you sit down in that chair over there, pop the plates on, and if the signal's strong enough, your Vision will appear on the screen. The databases and satellites do the rest, then...well, off you go! Intervene! It's all very clever, really. When I started all those years ago, we had none of this. Once you got your Vision, it was up to you to figure out the time and location. If it was somewhere you didn't recognise, that was that. If it was somewhere you did recognise, you could be waiting hours for the reality to match your Vision. It was really quite tedious. Anyway, I've just about chewed your ear off here. The choice, my dear, is yours. If you decide to join us – welcome. You are about to use your gift for unimaginable good. We can negotiate your pay, but you must believe me when I assure you it will be generous. If not, then I beg of you – when you walk out that door, please never utter a word of what you have seen and what we have discussed to anyone. The world cannot know of the gift we bestow upon it. Now, how about a nice cup of tea for the road?'

'No thank you, Mr Waddington.'

'Please - it's Gordon. Whatever you decide - it's Gordon.' Kate left the building with a handshake. She had some serious thinking to do, and it began as her car pulled off the long gravel drive and back out onto the country lanes.

Chapter Two

'So how was the job interview, darling?' asked Pete as he kissed Kate's cheek. He wiped his hands on his apron and took it off. She slumped into her chair and kicked off her high heels.

'Yeah, it was okay. I still have to decide whether or not I'm going to take it.'

'Mummy!' screamed her daughter excitedly as she burst into the room. She jumped on Kate's lap and clasped her arms round her waist.

'Hi, Princess! Did you have a good day at school?'

'Yeah! I got all of my spellings right and my teacher said my painting was the best one in the whole class!'

'Wow! Well, mummy's very proud of you.'

The little girl picked up the remote control from the arm of the chair and flicked on the TV. The cartoon absorbed her attention.

'So were they any clearer about the pay?'

'Well, yes and no. I was told it would be an increase on my current pay, but beyond that, they were a bit vague.'

'What was the boss like? Has to be an improvement on the dragon you're working for right now, surely?'

Kate laughed. 'Yeah. She seemed nice enough.' She glanced at the TV, which was showing The Flintstones. 'Her name's Wilma.'

'And you'd be doing exactly the same job? Accounting?'

'Yep, pretty much! Except I'd be in charge of a smaller team. Think she said there were five of them.'

'Less work and better pay? Sounds good. And it's in the city?'

'Yeah. It's a new building. Very modern.'

'So what's stopping you?'

'Oh, I don't know. It's venturing into the unknown, isn't it? The grass isn't always greener, is it?'

Pete draped his arms around his wife's shoulders. 'Well, baby, whatever you decide to do, Lola and I will back you up all the way. Money isn't everything. We just want you to be happy, and maybe for Lola to see a little more of mummy! Now, how about I pour you a nice glass of wine and run you a bath? You can mull it over a bit more in the tub'.

Kate smiled and kissed her husband on the lips.

Chapter Three

Kate rang the doorbell. The old man answered.

'Ah, Kate, my dear! How lovely to see you again. Do come in. I trust you've made your decision, and I think I speak on behalf of the whole crew when I say we all hope it's a yes. It's been so long since we had a potential new Intervener, and we all think you'd fit in splendidly well.'

'Hello, Mr Waddington.'

'I told you, no need for formalities! Gordon will do just fine.'

'Of course. Sorry. Well, Gordon, the fact is that I'm still undecided. And the truth is that I'm curious.'

'As well you should be! What we do here is a truly curious thing! A phenomenon, no less.'

'Well, yes. I'd like to see how it all works. I'd like to give it a try. I've had...well, I've had a Vision.'

'You have? Today?'

'This morning!'

'Goodness, this is exciting! Well, let's waste no more time! Let's get you into the Vision Room!'

Gordon took her by the hand and led her towards the double doors.

'Everyone, you remember Kate! She's had a Vision!'

The gang – minus an absent Sally – mumbled their various greetings and pleasantries. Gordon sat her down on the leather chair in the Vision Room. Her measured determination quickly turned to apprehension – she was actually going to make that leap. She was actually, finally, going to turn her Visions into something incredible, something *real*. It was dizzying. She was, if the pamphlet and the people around her in the building were to be believed, going to save a life. She flinched a little as the old man placed the metal plates on her temples. They tightened slightly and automatically.

'Now, normally when any of us get a Vision, we hurry to the Electric Chair. That's just our nickname for it, by the way, before you start fretting! If possible, we try to project our Vision before it's even ended. That's not always feasible, however – I'm sure you will agree, a Vision can be an all-consuming thing and often one doesn't have the energy or the free will to do anything other than let it ride out. But the fresher the better. So please, don't be disheartened if it doesn't appear. This does not necessarily mean you don't have The Gift.'

'Well, I mean, should it be on the screen now?'

The giant screen continued to flash the words 'Awaiting Vision'.

'Patience, my dear. Projecting a faded Vision is a two-step process. First you must relax your mind totally. Free it of all other thoughts and worries, for you will require all the power your mind can offer. Then, you must do the exact opposite. Focus with every bit of strength and energy you can muster up. Summon to the front of your mind all the little fragments that remain of your Vision, no matter how small or blurry or seemingly inconsequential. Bit by bit it should start to reform and intensify. That's when the machine will start to pick up on the signals you are transmitting. Do you have any children, my dear?'

'Yes, yes I do. A daughter.'

'Good. Now remember back to when you gave birth to her. It was neither a quick nor a painless process. Transmitting your Vision is much the same. Even when it starts to appear on the screen, you must keep focusing, keep straining, until it arrives in full force. Do you understand?'

'I think so.'

'Then begin. We've a little mantra. Silly really, but we always say it - call it superstition, I suppose. *On behalf of the moribund, I wish you luck.*'

Kate closed her eyes and relaxed the muscles in her face. She took a deep breath. She let the thoughts that occupied her mind drift one by one away – the list of jobs she would have to catch up on for missing work today, the list of groceries she needed to make for her husband, the trip to the dentist on Wednesday morning, the dance recital her daughter was appearing in that somehow she needed to fit into her hectic schedule.

Then she squeezed her eyes shut and clasped her teeth together. Tiny droplets of sweat appeared on her forehead. It began. The initial recollection of the old woman took her breath away – her terror-stricken face chilled Kate, as had so many of the victims in her Visions before that. The jet-black Ford Mondeo; the throngs of people surrounding her body - it was all coming back to her. The memory fragments slowly started to crystallise and assemble, like an explosion, but in reverse, in slow motion. The writing in front of her vanished and the screen crackled and flickered. Images appeared; disappeared; reappeared. A bloodshot eyeball...a dinted black bonnet...a sliver of blue sky. And not just images – a tiny snippet of sound jumped from the speakers, high-pitched but muffled. Then another, this one more unmistakable – a screech.

'It's happening. Keep going, my dear.'

He clasped her hand. She clasped his back. A deep moan, of much lower register than anything she could consciously produce, escaped from her body. She writhed in anguish. And then it appeared – an image, as full and clear as anything the naked eye might capture was up on the screen before her. Her body flopped and she gazed at the screen, more exhausted now than apprehensive.

'Is this your Vision?'

She nodded solemnly. A cloudless blue sky, exactly like the one she saw before she entered the building, dominated the scene. It was a high street, but not a particularly busy one. People milled about and cars occasionally sped past. An old lady, walking alone, a shopping bag on each arm, approached the kerb. She took three steps, whereupon a black car sped onto the scene and knocked her high into the air. The shopping from her bags rained back down onto the road and pavement. The car screeched to a halt. The old lady hit the ground with a thud. Blood poured from her totally motionless body. The nearby shoppers ran towards her, screaming and pulling out their mobile phones.

Kate stared at the screen, ashen-faced.

'I think we've seen enough,' the old man told her, patting her on the shoulder. 'Now for the fun part!'

He picked up a credit card-sized remote control and pushed one of its on-screen buttons. The scene rewound at the same speed it had played. She watched with morbid fascination as the people ran backwards to the pavement, as the groceries flew upwards from the ground and as the old lady dropped down onto the dented bonnet. Gordon pushed another button and the scene paused.

'Watch this...'

He pressed one more button and the camera zoomed right in on the old woman's face, which now filled most of the screen. Words flashed by horizontally at great speed. The blur of words gradually slowed down and stopped at 'Ruby Watson'.

'You don't necessarily need to know that, but it can sometimes come in handy. This, though – this is the important part.'

He pressed yet another button and the camera zoomed back out; back towards the original scene, then back further still until the people were no longer visible and the two of them were looking at an aerial view of the street and the area surrounding it. Words once again flashed past. When they slowed down this time, the screen read: 'Queens Road, Partington. Distance: 8.6 miles'.

'Ah! Quite a close one! Must be beginner's luck. Just one more thing to find out, and you're ready to do your heroic deed.'

He pressed one final button. An egg-timer appeared on the screen, underneath which flashed the words 'Calculating'. A couple of seconds later, the egg-timer was replaced with 'T-1h02m'.

'Ah, splendid. We've plenty of time'.

He pulled off the metal plates, linked arms with Kate and led her back out through the double doors. Her heart was pounding, and she had begun to feel a tremendous surge of excitement and adrenalin. She looked around at the men in the living room to see if they shared her excitement. This time they did not acknowledge her presence at all, but merely continued with their recreational activities. Their faces seemed oddly vacant and expressionless to Kate.

The old man led her outside and to the side of the house Kate had not yet seen. She surveyed the fleet of cars awaiting there, each of them gleaming in the bright midday sun.

'Oh, I know, it probably all seems a trifle lavish and unnecessary, but you have to ask yourself – what else have we got to spend our earnings on? Plus, we invest such a large part of our working day on commuting – why not do it in style? Now, have you any objections to having the wind in your hair on this glorious afternoon? Because I think the Jaguar F-Type is calling my name!'

As Gordon got in the car, the doors of which opened at the scan of his thumbprint, he placed his face close to the dashboard.

'Queens Road, Partington, old boy, and don't spare the horses!'

The dashboard repeated the address.

'Splendid. The car will guide me step by step to the destination. I'll be perfectly honest with you – I know full well where Queens Road is. It's an Intervention hotspot. But I couldn't resist showing off my toy.'

They set off down the gravel road to which Kate felt already strangely accustomed.

'So when did you start seeing your Visions, my dear?'

'Hmm? My Visions? Well, I suppose it must have been in my early teens. Course, back then I didn't know they were Visions. I didn't know what they were. I couldn't understand why I was getting what seemed like nightmares while I was awake. In fact, I nicknamed them 'Daymares'. That's what I'd write in my diary – 'today I had another Daymare'.'

Gordon chuckled. 'Daymare! I like that! Just about sums it up.'

Kate felt comfortable. Comfortable in the old man's Jag. Comfortable confiding in him these dark secrets she had told no one before, even her husband. And comfortable in the long silences that lay in between their exchanges, as she gazed out into the countryside. She'd imagined, in the weeks between receiving the letter and her first visit to the Mansion that the work the Interveners did – and the Interveners themselves, for that matter - would be dark and mysterious and perhaps even threatening. On this gentle, sun-drenched summer's afternoon, nothing could have seemed further from the truth.

'I thought about going to the doctors – it was the headaches and the blurry vision I hated most. I felt like I was going to pass out – still do. But I was scared of going. I was sure they'd think I was crazy or unstable, having these vivid fantasies of people dying. I was convinced they'd take me away. And, of course, the Visions would happen at the most inopportune times – in the middle of a lesson at school, or on a date. That sort of thing. I hoped they'd go away over time. That it was just a phase. Maybe it happened to all teenagers at some point! They didn't go away, obviously – I just learned to deal with them more discretely. I'm an expert now – I can be sat right next to my husband on the sofa and have a full-blown Vision. A strategically-placed magazine or a well-timed trip to the loo, and he's none the wiser.'

'I suppose I'm lucky,' said the old man. 'I can't remember the last time I had to hide my Visions – I'm always either on the road travelling to and from my Interventions, or else I'm at the Mansion with the others. I never married. I was barely out of boyhood when I joined the Interveners, though it was all so very different back then. Technology has really simplified the process. Anyway, it seemed like my calling, and I haven't had what one might call a normal life since.'

The two travelled in silence for the next couple of miles, during which time the traffic became heavier, the buildings more plentiful and the trees less so.

Kate finally broke the silence.

'Then one day – think I was maybe 27 – it actually happened. I was on holiday, in the Greek Islands. Earlier that day, I'd had a Vision. It was of a young boy in a stripy blue T-shirt, slipping off the edge of a cliff on a windy day. He fell to his death on the rocks below. Then, when I was driving along on the moped I'd rented, I saw the exact same boy, same stripy T-shirt, playing near the edge of a cliff. Exactly like my Vision. *Everything* was like I'd envisaged it. So I stopped the moped and started walking towards him. I don't know what my intentions were – I just felt compelled to approach him. Before I'd got that close, my Vision turned real. He slipped and fell. I ran over to the edge of the cliff, along with the other people who were nearby at the time, and peered over – and, sure enough, the boy had fallen onto the rocks below. There was a pool of blood around him and his arms and legs all seemed to be facing the wrong way. Even from where I was, I could see he was dead. I told no one about it – about the Vision, I mean. In fact, all these years later, and you're the first person I've ever mentioned this to.'

'What happened there on that Greek Island, my dear, was a stroke of good fortune. You may not think it, but it's true. Realising your Visions were something more real than mere hallucinations or fantasies was a difficult but necessary step, and one which all Interveners have to go through. It's like a rite of passage. And it eventually brought you to us. The boy lost his life, and chances are so did all of the many other people who have inhabited your Visions since your teenage years. But as an Intervener, you could potentially save hundreds more.'

'I suppose. If it's really true. There's just one thing I don't understand – where does the money you earn actually come from? Who pays your wages? I mean, it's not like you're providing a paid service to the people you save. They don't even know they've been saved. And surely it's not something the tax payers are funding? The Government surely can't know about it. Can they? So who is it?'

The old man smiled slyly. 'I can't possibly tell you that. Not yet. You're not officially an Intervener. If and when you decide that this is your calling and that you'd like to join us, I'll tell you our little secret.'

Kate suddenly felt a little uneasy. It was the first time Gordon had been anything other than totally candid with her. Her mind raced with possibilities, with speculation. Were they a kind of psychic version of the mafia? Did they steal the money? It was hard to picture this gentle old man holding up a bank at gun point, but she could think of no scenario that made more sense. It was at that moment that reality kicked in – *what the Hell was she doing?* Here she was, in the passenger seat of a complete stranger's car. He could be a kidnapper, a rapist, a murderer, or even all three. She gently patted the pocket of her trouser suit jacket to check for her mobile phone, just in case.

'Mr Waddington, I'd like you to stop the car. Please. Please stop the car.'

'Stop the car? But – why? Was it something I said?'

'No, I just...it's just...well, this whole thing's *weird*.'

Gordon indicated and carefully pulled over.

'I don't know what I'm doing here. I'm not an Intervener. I'm not like you. I've got a husband. And a daughter. And a mortgage and a job in the city. It just...it doesn't feel right. I'm sorry. Can you take me back to the Mansion, please? I want to get in my car and go home. In fact, just let me out here. I'll get a taxi'

The old man sighed and shook his head. 'I'm so dreadfully sorry, my dear. I don't want you to be unhappy. Our mission as Interveners is to bring good into the world, not unhappiness. You can, of course, get out of the car now.'

She reached over to unbuckle her seat belt. He placed his hand on top of hers. It felt comforting rather than threatening or unwelcome.

'But I ask you first to consider this. You've been given an extraordinary gift. With the technology at our disposal, the Interveners can help you to channel that gift into something truly, truly good. Without us, it's just Visions. Just headaches and sweats and – what was it you called it? – Daymares. I implore you – please. Just come with me and in,' he glanced at his watch, '47 minutes, you will witness something amazing. You will save someone's life. If you still don't want to join us, that's fair enough. You gave it a shot, and that's all I'm asking. Oh, and you saved someone's mother or grandmother or sister in the process. Please.'

Kate stared into the middle distance. 'Keep driving.'

Chapter Four

Kate wasn't really sure she wanted the ice cream Gordon had bought for her after they had parked up. Or rather, she wanted it – either the afternoon heat, her nervous apprehension or perhaps both had left her feeling in desperate need of refreshment – but it just didn't seem very appropriate. She was about to witness an old lady nearing the brink of death. Ice cream hardly seemed the right choice to accompany that kind of experience. It wasn't like she was watching a show at the theatre. Gordon glanced at his watch.

'5 minutes and 38 seconds. Are you excited?'

Kate smiled nervously but did not respond. They continued their stroll towards the high street, which at this point was just around the corner.

'You know it's funny. After all these years and hundreds upon hundreds - thousands - of Interventions, for some reason I've got a wonderful fluttery feeling inside of me. I feel excited *for* you, my dear.'

'I feel a bit weird. Besides, what will I actually *do*? When I see the old lady, I mean? How do I Intervene?'

'The simple answer? Any way you jolly well like. Whatever takes your fancy. You've done the hard part now – you've had the Vision, located the potential victim and travelled to their would-be point of death. Now the easy part – you just have to alter the course of the old lady's day by a couple of seconds.'

'But *how?*'

'Well, don't overthink it. You could approach her and ask her for directions. Step in her way and pretend it was an accident. Give the old dear a little shove if you like, as long as you're discrete! You'll learn lots of creative ways to Intervene if you decide to join our team, but for now let's just keep it simple, shall we?'

Kate nodded and took a deep breath. She stopped in her footsteps – *this was it*. This was the exact scene from her Vision. Every shop was how it was in the Vision. The sun was in exactly the same point in the sky, with the same wispy clouds surrounding it. There was a white van parked up obscuring half of the baker's shop and a moustached man sat reading a broadsheet newspaper on the bench a few yards to her right. A chill ran down her spine.

A sharp, nauseous feeling jabbed her stomach. Suddenly, images of the boy falling to his death from the cliff resurfaced at the front of her mind. *Was it going to happen again? Was she going to witness another death?* Where the scene differed from the one in her Vision the day before was that most of the people were different, but she knew all of that was about to change. She chewed her bottom lip, looked up at the old man and then began to scan the area around her. More and more familiar faces were starting to trickle onto the scene. Gordon tapped her on the shoulder and pointed behind her to her right.

It was her.

Ruby Watson.

She took another deep breath. Her ankles had begun to shake.

'Now's your chance to shine, Kate Jenson. Go and save a life!'

He pushed her gently at the small of her back. The old lady waddled towards the roadside. Kate was getting closer and closer to the scene of what would be - could be - the future fatality. Kate knew it was now or never. She quickened her pace and approached the old lady.

'Erm, excuse me. Hi...'

'Yes?'

'Well, the thing is, I'm lost and I need to find my way to...' Kate paused. Her mind had gone blank. 'San Jose!'

She winced.

'I'm afraid I don't know what you're talking about, young lady. I really don't have time for anyone's nonsense. Now if you'll excuse me...'

Kate looked towards Gordon. He gave her a thumbs up and smiled. She shrugged her shoulders and shook her head, then turned back towards Ruby, who by now was right at the edge of the kerb. A black Ford Mondeo, exactly like that of her Vision, whizzed by and then off into the distance. The old lady continued on her journey without breaking her sluggish pace, and within moments she was safely on the other side of the road, heading into the department store.

Kate laughed out loud and ran back towards Gordon. Instinctively, she hugged him.

'Congratulations, my dear! You have saved your first life! You are now officially an Intervener!'

She was jumping up and down like a small child. 'Oh my God, that was...well, it was just...incredible! Thank you! Thank you so much!'

'Oh no need to thank me! It was your Vision that brought us here. Now – let's take you back to the Mansion so you can get home to your family. You've decisions to make.'

Chapter Five

Kate and Pete lay side by side in bed. He was holding a book, but she simply lay with her arms across her chest, gazing with wide eyes towards the ceiling, the edges of her mouth turned upwards ever so slightly.

'How was your day, babe?'

'My day? It was...pretty good, actually! Yeah, not bad at all!'

'Really? Oh, that's good to hear. So the old dragon's not been breathing quite as much fire down your neck today, then?'

'Ha ha! No. She's all right really. We closed the Watkins and Sons deal today, which is a bit of a coup for us, so everyone's been in a really good mood. Oh, and it was Matt's thirtieth birthday at the weekend, so he bought in a cake to celebrate.'

'So what about that other job? Are you going to ditch that?'

'Oh, I don't know – I still need more time to think. The person who interviewed me said I could have as long as I liked to decide. Anyway, enough about me – tell me about your day!'

Pete smirked.

'Me? Well, after I dropped Lola off at school this morning, I popped into the bank where – whaddya know? – an armed robbery was taking place. Anyway, using my best Bruce Lee ninja moves, I disposed of the robbers and within minutes, the film crews arrived, and there I was on the National News being branded a hero. Surprised you didn't see it. Then, on my way to Tesco a couple of hours later, *Calvin Klein* of all people stopped me and asked if I had ever done any modelling. You might be wondering what a top international fashion designer was doing in the middle of Woodborough – but there he was! Anyway, long story short, if you buy this month's Vogue magazine, there's a double-spread of me posing in my underwear. Very tastefully done. Oh, and I got a call from NASA about half an hour before you came in telling me they had astronaut vacancies, but I told them I was just too busy raising my daughter and carrying out the daily chores. Ah, the glamorous life of the househusband – I tell you, the excitement just never ends!'

Kate stroked his cheek. 'Oh you! What are you like?'

'You don't believe me do you? Ah, I can't get anything past you, can I?'

'No way, Jose.' Kate grinned to herself - it was the second time she had used that word today, in two very different contexts. 'Anyway, whatever NASA wanted to pay you, I'll pay you double. Or at least I'll pay you back in some other way, if you know what I mean. There's no way I'm letting the world's greatest daddy and husband slip away!'

'Pay me in kind? Why, Mrs Jenson, what DO you mean?'

'Well – I'm not really all that tired and Lola is asleep! Maybe I'll give you a little sneak preview!' She shuffled up to him and started to nuzzle his neck. 'How about we fool around for a little while and see what happens?'

Pete clapped his hands to turn out the lights and pulled the covers over himself and his wife.

Chapter Six

'Morning everyone!'

The gang – all present on this occasion – reciprocated Kate's cheerful entrance with a chorus of pleasantries, apart from Chris, although he smiled weakly. She moved towards them and jumped into the recliner.

'Well, if it isn't the world's newest Intervener!' said Sally, smiling warmly. 'To what do we owe this pleasure?'

'Well, I've been giving it lots of thought. In fact I literally did not get a wink of sleep all night. Anyway, what I've come to tell you is that if you would have me,' she smiled, squeezed her eyes shut and took a deep gulp of air, 'I would very much like to join the Interveners on a full-time basis.'

The gang applauded spontaneously. Sally hugged her and the old man clasped her shoulder. Only Chris showed no emotion.

'Well now, that is wonderful news!' beamed Gordon. 'We should have a glass of champagne to celebrate! I've been hiding a bottle of vintage '92 for just such an occasion.'

'Champagne? But it's 9.30 in the morning!'

Zak winked at her. 'Welcome to the wonderful world of the Interveners! If you haven't already noticed, we're a bit of a maverick bunch, and we play by different rules to most folks. Champagne before lunch? Why the Hell not, we're not doing anything else right now!'

'Well, thanks all the same, but I actually can't stay too long. I've got to get back to work and hand my week's notice in. They think I'm at the doctor's at the moment.'

'Ah well, it'll be on ice, then! We must get you to sign on the dotted line and hammer out your contract before you pop off.'

Nigel put the book he was reading back on its shelf, folded his glasses up and put them in his shirt pocket. 'So then. When you said you were joining us full time, did you mean full time? Or *full* time?'

Kate looked at him confused. 'I'm sorry?'

'Well, I mean – there's full time like your current job's full time. And then there's full time like myself and Gordon and Chris do it. For us, it's a 24-7 job. We never leave. We live here. We're permanently on call. We're here forever.'

'The choice really is yours, my dear.'

'Forever? Like a cult? Oh God, is that what this is?' A chill ran down Kate's spine. The naivety of the situation hit her suddenly. She was going to leave her well-paid, comfortable job to come and be with a bunch of people she knew next-to-nothing about, doing a job that seemed more than a little vague, even murky. The gang broke the silence with a hearty, spontaneous but synchronised laugh.

Zak interjected. 'It's not a cult, don't worry! I don't live here. I live with my brother on the other side of town. You can come and go as you please here – in fact, that's one of the best parts of the job. The hours are flexible, so it's a pretty sweet deal.'

'He's right,' said Sally. 'In fact, just the other week, I had a stinking hangover, so I didn't come in at all that day. Stayed a bit longer the next couple of days to make up for it. Couple of months ago, my boyfriend and I had a spur-of-the-moment long weekend in Paris.' She looked in Gordon's direction. 'I texted the boss over there that morning to let him know I wouldn't be coming in – job done! They're good to you here. You'll like it.'

'I see. Well, to be honest, I couldn't live here even if I wanted to. I've got a husband and a young daughter. So,' she pointed her finger towards Nigel, Gordon and Chris, 'do you guys get paid more or something? I mean, why else would you live here?' She scrunched her nose up. 'Sorry, all of that sounded really rude, didn't it?'

'Not at all, my dear!' Gordon assured her. 'We are an open bunch, within reason. To answer your question, Nigel and I do get paid more, but that's because we're Senior Interveners, not because we do more hours.'

'O-kay. Not really getting why...'

'Why we do it?' interrupted Nigel. 'Why we never leave? Why we don't have any other kind of life? Well, consider this. You'll come in here, eight, nine, ten o clock, whenever, and you'll clock out maybe seven hours later. Do your Visions follow that same shift pattern?'

His tone seemed cold and a little unsettling.

'Well, no, obviously. I mean, I get my Visions at all different times of the day and night. I'm sure you all do.'

'Precisely. So what's gonna happen when you get a Vision at two in the morning? You gonna come over and plug yourself in?'

'Well, no – it's a ninety minute round trip for me!' she laughed.

'Meanwhile, the poor sod in your Vision is off to meet his destiny. And that's one of the reasons why I live here. I can be saving lives morning, noon and night.'

Gordon frowned at his second-in-command. 'Now, Nigel! For goodness sakes, man! We don't want to be scaring the poor girl off before she's even started!'

'I just think she should know what she's letting herself in for, that's all. Just be warned – I had a young family too, just like you. And in the end I had to make a decision. This is what I chose.' He picked his glasses back out and went back to his reading, turning his back on the rest of the gang in the process.

Zak shook his head and pointed his thumb in Nigel's direction, smiling sympathetically at Kate. 'It doesn't always have to be that way, though. I've been here for several years now and I still have my family. By which I mean my brother.'

'What does he know about what you do here?'

More laughter.

'He doesn't know! He can't know. No non-Intervener is allowed to know about the work we do here.'

'It's true. My fella doesn't know either. So you can't tell your husband, no matter what happens. If you're gonna work here, you're gonna have to get used to living a lie.'

'If your boyfriend doesn't know what you do, what does he think you do?'

'He thinks I'm studying at uni. I'm halfway through a four year degree in Psychology. It's the perfect cover-up, because luckily for me, he's not one bit interested in Psychology so he doesn't ask me much about it, and if ever I fancy doing a night shift here, I just tell him I'm staying in the Halls of Residence in my friend's dorm. My friend's called Rachel Pointer. She's just over there, look.' She waved into thin air. 'Say hello, Rachel! Oh, she can be a right stuck up cow sometimes.'

Kate giggled. 'So what are you going to do in two years' time, then?'

'I don't know. Maybe an imaginary Post Graduate course. Maybe I'll do some imaginary backpacking around Europe. So many options! I've got plenty of time to decide. And that's the thing, you see. There's a great many things we're not short of here at the Mansion, and one of them's time. We've got all day to cook up the most elaborate lies. We've even got time to rehearse them with each other before we go back to our loved ones. In my case, I read lots of Psychology textbooks anyway – one of those shelves is full of them – so it's not a total lie, and I know enough to keep my stories plausible.'

'Yeah, my bro thinks I'm a cinema usher at the moment. I like to keep changing it up every now and again, just to keep it interesting. I'm thinking of being a school caretaker next. The beauty of me flitting between imaginary jobs is that I can choose ones that have different shift patterns attached to them. So if I decide I want to be a security guard for a while, for example, that means I've got an excuse for not being around at night. And that means I can come and help the guys here with any night-time Visions that come along.'

'And we're very grateful for that indeed! Just as many deaths occur at night as the day, sometimes more so - only we find ourselves down to a bit of a skeleton staff in the evening and through the night. So if ever you find yourself in the position to swing by the Mansion later on, or stay late, or stay over - well, not to put any pressure on you, but please do!'

'What will you tell your husband? Peter, is it?'

'Yeah, that's right. Pete. Well, when I came to visit the other day, I told him I had an interview for another accounting job. I already know plenty about that, so making up stories shouldn't be a problem! I better tell him I've decided to take it!'

'Good choice!' said Gordon. 'Now, let's get you into my office before you change your mind!'

*****

Gordon's office turned out to be no more than an antique desk and two brown leather chairs in the conservatory. He had a panoramic view of the garden from there, which, on this particular morning, was being soaked by a light but persistent drizzle. The desk was totally empty apart from the contract Kate was reading and the Biro next to it. She scrutinised the words with great care, partly so that she didn't get cajoled into anything she wasn't expecting and partly to learn more about the organisation and what her job was to entail. She came across a section entitled 'Golden Rules'.

1. *All reasonable attempts must be made to attend an Intervention. Possible reasons for not attempting an Intervention may include: (a) The Intervention Scene is too far away to be reached in the time remaining; (b) Location data is insufficient / vague; (c) Carrying out the Intervention puts the organisation's secret identity at risk;*
2. *You may not Intervene in suicide attempts;*

3. You may not Intervene in murder scenes;
4. Beyond the stipulations in points 2 and 3, you must carry out your Interventions indiscriminately;
5. Should a Vision appear whilst in the middle of an Intervention attempt, you may not abandon said Intervention attempt, but must first complete it before attending to the subsequent Vision.
6. You must, under no circumstances, speak of the work you do to any other person or persons. Should you decide to leave The Interveners, it must be with the express understanding that you shall maintain the secrecy of the organisation at all costs.

'Just sign on the dotted line, and you're an Intervener!'

'Hang on, I have a few questions first.'

'Ah...'

'Why can't we Intervene in suicide attempts?'

'Because the person who is attempting suicide has *chosen* their destiny. The old lady you saved didn't decide she was going to step out in front of the car. The person who finds him or herself with a razor blade or bottle of pills in their hand does so with forethought and intention. What happens if you are busy trying to save their soul when a Vision of an accidental death comes to you and you have no time to reach it? Besides, chances are that person will make an attempt on their own life again at some point. It's extremely unlikely they'll appear on your Radar the second time around. Just leave them to it, I say. I know it sounds heartless.'

'Well, that sort of makes sense, I suppose. But what about Number Three here?'

'The murder one? Too dangerous. Too dangerous by far. You are putting yourself in the firing line, quite literally in some cases. You have been bestowed with an exceptionally rare gift. There are precious few of us in the world. You die on the job, all those people – possibly hundreds of them – who you would have saved in the future will all meet their premature ends. One life isn't worth hundreds of other lives. It's just simple Maths. We estimate that only one in three million people are born with your gift, and it's hard enough to track them down. We can't afford to lose any of our kind.'

Kate felt uneasy about this. She could see the logic in not saving the lives of people who choose to die – but murder victims were just that. Victims.

She had not anticipated the moral complexities of the role.

'Listen, my dear. You have a choice. You don't have to sign. You can just walk away, go back to your family and pretend none of this ever happened. In fact, if you do walk away, that's exactly what you must do, for the sake of our entire organisation. The fact is, what we do demands little on our time and physical energy, but it often demands much of our emotional state. It can be tough. You *will* have difficult decisions to make. But the rewards are much greater than anyone could possibly imagine.'

Kate nodded pensively. The two of them sat for a few moments in silence.

'Now, speaking of rewards, may I enquire about your current wage?'

'I get paid £47,000 per annum, with occasional bonuses. I can show you my wage slips if you like.'

'No need. We'll pay you £57,000 per annum. Tax free, of course.'

Kate's eyes widened. 'Oh. That's – that's very generous, actually!'

'Indeed. We often wonder if there are any other jobs that pay so much for so little work.' He smiled and began to speak in a hushed tone. 'Maybe being part of the Royal Family.'

What else is there to think about? Kate wondered. *The money's fantastic, I like most of the people here – don't know about Nigel yet – the hours are flexible and I get to be hero. That"s what my job will be. Being a hero. An unsung hero, but a hero nonetheless.*

She picked up the pen, signed her name with a flourish and pushed the paper back towards the old man, who leaned back in his chair and nodded.

And then there were six.

Chapter Seven

Kate sat at her desk, gazing distractedly at the clock. Two more days to go. Though she had had no Visions since the one of the old lady being knocked over, she was itching for her time as an ordinary accountant to end and to begin her new life as a full-time Intervener. She tapped numbers into her computer, her mind by now on auto-pilot. It all seemed so *humdrum.* She yearned for the adrenalin rush she had felt as she watched the Mondeo speed away and the old lady walking to safety.

'Kate Jenson! What the Hell?'

'Hi Susie.'

'Don't you 'Hi Susie' me. Is it true what they're saying? Did you hand your notice in this week?'

Kate nodded. Susie threw her arms around her. 'Oh babe. It won't be the same without you here. Who's gonna stick up for me when Johnson is on my back? Whose shoulder am I gonna cry on the next time I get dumped? Who's gonna hold my hair back when I'm being sick in the loo on our next work do?'

'Ah, it's good to see my skills as a hotshot big city accountant are being fully appreciated!'

'Oh you know I think you're the dog's wotsits. You taught me everything I know.'

'Woah! You be careful before you start throwing around those sorts of accusations!'

They both laughed. Susie gazed at her fondly. 'So what next? I presume you've got a job lined up.'

'Yeah it's at that new place, Roberts, Roberts and Gladstone. You heard of it?'

'Erm, I think I have, yeah.'

Lying cow, thought Kate. *I just made it up on the spot.*

'Anyway, one of their people headhunted me, but let's keep that between you and me. I get paid an extra ten grand a year, and I've got a smaller team to supervise. It was a total no-brainer actually. Sounds like I'll get to see a bit more of Pete and Lola, so I just couldn't turn it down. Don't you worry. I'll stay in touch.'

'You better. Eh, if they have any other decent jobs there – or any decent men for that matter – give me a ring! Promise me you will.'

'I promise,' replied Kate. She was getting good at this lying business.

Chapter Eight

Kate lay on a sun lounger in the Mansion garden, Sally by her side. They were both wearing dark glasses and flicking through gossip magazines. Tall, elaborately-decorated glasses of fruit punch flanked them.

'This is the life, eh, missus?' said Sally, nudging her new friend gently with her elbow.

'I'll say. I can't believe this is classed as work. They're actually paying me to lie around topping up my tan and looking at pictures of celebs without their make-up on! Some mistake, surely?'

'I know!'

'I don't think I'm ever going to get tired of this.'

Sally put down her magazine and turned towards Kate.

'I'm not going to sit here and lie to you. Our job isn't without challenges, as you'll soon come to find out. And one of the biggest challenges is definitely staving off the boredom. You and I – we're both intelligent ladies.'

Kate looked down at her trashy magazine and wondered if she was joking.

'So sunbathing is definitely a nice treat, but it can't be all you do. This is only your second day, so the novelty factor is still there. You're in holiday mode. Sooner or later, you'll have to find ways of stimulating your mind as well. For me it's the Psychology textbooks. And you're lying right in the middle of one of my other great projects. Gardening keeps me occupied – keeps me sane, really. We've all got our hobbies and projects – except Zak. That boy's dumb as a brush. Not too hard to look at though, wouldn't you say?'

Kate peered over her sunglasses and gazed indoors, where Zak was, once again, playing pool.

'Yeah, he's pretty cute, actually. I suppose. But then, I'm married, so I couldn't possibly comment.'

'Maybe you should stop looking at his arse before you get all judgemental, Mrs Jenson!'

Kate blushed, coughed for dramatic effect and returned to her magazine.

'Speaking of Him Indoors, what did you end up telling him?'

'Well, I thought long and hard about it, but in the end I decided it would be easiest if I pretending I was still working at my old place. Save me having to invent a new set of co-workers and issues to bitch about. I told him I turned down the offer. Do you think I did the right thing? Sal?'

Kate turned to look at Sally, who was sat bolt upright. The colour had drained from her face and sweat was dripping from her forehead. Kate could see through the sides of Sally's glasses that her eyes were closed tightly. She knew exactly what was happening and watched her, knowing that interrupting at this point would be the worst course of action. The whole thing lasted for less than a minute, but it seemed much longer to Kate. Sally eventually relaxed back onto her lounger and took off her glasses.

'Vision?'

Sally nodded. 'Give me a second to catch my breath, then get ready to be my partner-in-crime for the day.'

The two of them wandered back indoors and to the darkened Vision Room. Sally placed the plates on her head and the two of them watched as Sally's Vision flickered into life. The whole process was much quicker than Kate's had been the week before.

This time it was a middle-aged man, with wisps of grey in his hair. He was sat with another woman in a restaurant. She was ten or fifteen years his junior. He was eating fish. Suddenly, he dropped his cutlery and began clutching his throat. The woman shouted for help and people started crowding round him. One of the waiters picked him up and attempted the Heimlich Manoeuvre. It didn't work – the purple hue in his face continued to darken and intensify. The woman was screaming and crying, shaking the man violently. Eventually, he dropped to the floor. The Vision ended at that point.

Just as Gordon had done, Sally picked up the remote and rewound the scene. The computer located the scene as Hatherford, just shy of twenty miles away, and the potential victim in question as Roger Mansard.

'Ah perfect! Looks like you and I will be nipping out for a spot of lunch today! And I reckon we can cram another couple of hours' worth of ray-catching in before we have to set off.'

Chapter Nine

Sally's eyes turned to little moon crescents as they wandered around the restaurant.

'Ooh, pretty swanky! Think I'll let Interveners Incorporated pick up the bill on this one.'

A smartly-dressed waiter approached.

'Can I help you, ladies?'

'You certainly can, kind sir. Table for two, please. And,' she gazed around in the hope of locating the greying man and his younger dining partner from her Vision. She spotted them next to the window. 'I don't suppose you have any seats near the window, do you?'

'Certainly, madame. Follow me please.'

The waiter led them to a table which was within earshot of Mansard and his female companion.

'Perfect!' Sally whispered.

'Would you like to see the wine list?'

'Oh, why not? A cheeky Chardonnay spritzer couldn't hurt, could it? Your finest, no less. And bring the rest of the bottle for my new friend, if you please.'

'Very good, madame.'

'I've been accused of being some things in my time, young man, but 'very good' certainly isn't one of them!' She winked at the waiter, who remained stoic as he walked away.

'Sal! It's lunchtime! And I'm supposed to be working! I can't have wine!'

Sally laughed and put her hand on Kate's knee. 'You ARE at work, darling! This is what you do now!'

Kate couldn't help but feel a warm glow. Nothing about this strange new life actually *seemed* strange. She felt totally at ease with Sally, like they were friends from way back when, and though she had yet to get a Vision as an official, paid member of The Interveners, she was relishing her role as a secret life saver.

'So have you got a plan?'

'Yeah, I have. This isn't my first restaurant choking – I had to do one of these about eighteen months ago. It's simple, really – when I see the waiter coming, I'll knock the plate out of his hands. He'll have to get a new one, the guy lives on. Easy-peasy.'

Kate looked puzzled. 'But – couldn't he choke on that one, too?'

'Well, in theory, yes, but in reality it's extremely unlikely. It's a different piece of fish, isn't it? And a different moment in time. Accidental death is all about time, place and circumstance. Alter any of these just slightly, and it's crisis averted.'

'I get it. I guess if we'd got here a bit earlier, we could have told the waiter we had a reservation under the name 'Mansard' and taken his place. That would have altered the circumstances.'

'Hey not bad! I can see you're going to be good at this Intervening malarkey. You're quick on your feet. Although you're presuming that guy made a reservation in the first place. He might not have.'

'Oh right, yeah.'

'Don't worry. There's a learning curve when it comes to Intervening. It's actually not as simple as it sounds. You'll learn to play out the consequences of all the different potential methods of Intervention in your head before you decide on one. Usually, most of your scenarios will lead to a successful Intervention, but it's worth checking.'

Sally peered over at Mansard's table. Finished soup plates lay in front of the couple.

'Okay, keep your eyes peeled, Kate. We're looking for a waiter coming this way carrying a plate of fish. I reckon it could be any time in the next ten minutes.' She looked at her watch. 'Possibly five, actually.'

Though Kate didn't feel quite the same dizzying cocktail of nerves and excitement that had so overwhelmed her on her first – and so far only – tentative trip into the world of Intervention, she couldn't help but be fascinated by the process. Sally's head remained still, but her eyes darted back and forth between the kitchen doors and Mansard's table. A couple of minutes later, a waiter came and cleared the table. She was very much at work. Her darting eyes quickened their pace. She eventually nodded and pushed out her chair.

'Right, here goes.'

Sally stood up and put the side of her hand to her mouth as if she was going to be sick. She charged in the direction of the toilets, in the waiter's path. To her great horror, she narrowly missed her target – the waiter's shoulders. Kate watched, her mouth gaped open. Sally mouthed the word 'shit'. Reacting quickly, Kate kicked her handbag out from under the table with the side of her foot. It slid across the laminate floor and into the waiter's path. He stumbled on it – not enough to knock him off his feet, but enough to halt his measured momentum. The plate wobbled on its resting place of his forearm, and quickly dropped to the floor. It smashed into two, causing the peas to roll around in all directions and the fish to drop between the two halves of the plate. The two women exchanged a knowing smile. Sally continued towards the toilet, though she had no intention of actually using it. Mansard stared up at the waiter in mild annoyance.

'I'm so sorry, sir.'

'Well, it's a bloody good job it fell on the floor and not on my...wife. Isn't it?'

'As I say, sir, I'm dreadfully sorry. I shall go and get the chef to cook you a replacement meal. On the house, of course.'

'Oh my God, I feel terrible about this. I think he tripped on my bag. I hadn't realised I had left it in the way like that.'

Mansard scowled and turned away from Kate to resume his conversation.

You ungrateful bastard, thought Kate. *Don't you know I've just saved your life?*

Sally returned to the table and spoke to Kate in hushed but excited tones.

Nice work, Mrs Jenson! That was some seriously quick thinking! I reckon you must be, by far, the second best Intervener in this restaurant right now!'

'Oh my God! This is all happening so suddenly! I don't know what to say! I mean, what an honour!'

The two women grinned at each other.

'Why don't we raise a toast to another life saved?' suggested Sally.

'I'll drink to that!'

Both women took a sizeable sip from their glasses.

'This is some seriously good pop, Sal.'

'I know! That Gordon Waddington has exquisite taste, doesn't he? Cheers, G!'

Kate smiled. 'So you don't think he'll mind? You charging this to the company?'

'Honey, believe you me, at this moment in time, we're not short of a bob or two down at the Mansion. A nice bottle of white wine isn't going to break the balance.'

Kate stared at her. The burning question, which Gordon had avoided on her first Intervention mission, came back to her lips, themselves somewhat looser as she neared the bottom of her first glass.

'Yeah, I was meaning to ask you about that. Who actually – you know – I mean, where does...how do we...'

'You want to know about the money situation, don't you? If we're a secret organisation, what's with the fabulous Mansion? Am I right? How can Intervention possibly be profitable?'

Kate nodded.

'I'd love to tell you, but it's not really my place. Gordon will tell you, but he'd kill me if he knew I was the one who told you first.'

Kate found it difficult to hide her disappointment. It wasn't so much the not knowing she didn't mind – it was just that she was enjoying the uninhibited bond she'd developed with Sally. The secrecy reminded her that she had, in fact, only known Sally for a matter of days and there was still much they had to learn about each other.

'What I will ask you is this: what overheads do you reckon we have? The Vision Room is a bit of a juice gobbler, so that pushes our bills up. The house we use for our base isn't small, so you've of course got your heating bills and so forth. And obviously, there's the petrol we use going to and from the Interventions. Insurance on those old beauties ain't cheap. But that's about it. The actual life-saving bit costs nothing. So I say choose something nice from that menu!'

They perused the menus but still couldn't decide. Kate lowered her voice again, this time to a barely audible whisper.

'So what do you think their story is? I heard him say 'wife', but...' Sally shrugged and pointed to her bare ring finger. They both looked down at the tablecloth and focused their attentions on listening in on the couple's conversation.

'Roger, when are you going to leave Helen? You've been promising me for months now and I'm getting fed up of waiting.'

'I know my sweet, I know. I've just got to pick the right moment. I want to wait until the kids are away for the night so it's less distressing for them.'

'Ha! Did you hear that? I think that probably answers our question. Dirty git. Should have let him choke.'

The ladies enjoyed an extended lunch. Kate rounded off her meal with a black coffee in an attempt to sober up a little – the two glasses of Chardonnay had left her feeling quite tipsy. She had allowed herself to get carried away to the extent that she had forgotten her car was parked back at the Mansion. Besides, her husband was sure to tell that she had had a drink – how would she explain that?

As they walked away, Mansard was still very much alive and well – he had long-since left the restaurant, although Kate hadn't even noticed.

Chapter Ten

Kate kicked off her shoes and placed the chewed gum in her mouth back in its wrapper. She slipped the wrapper in her handbag, which she let drop to the floor.

'I'm home!'

Lola bounded into the hallway and clasped herself round her mother's leg. 'Hi mummy!'

'Hi sweetie! Mmm, something smells nice! What have you cooked mummy for dinner tonight? Play-Doh on toast is it?'

Lola screwed her face up and giggled. 'No, silly! Daddy is cooking!'

'Daddy is cooking Play-Doh on toast? Well, I must say his culinary standards have slipped somewhat of late!'

The two of them wandered into the kitchen. Lola jumped onto the nearest chair and started playing with her pink handheld games console.

'Hi honey! Nice day?'

Pete did not turn around to face his face as he spoke. 'Hi. You know, the usual.'

'Right. The usual. Yeah, me too. Do I get a kiss, then?'

Pete wiped his hands on his apron, kissed Kate on the cheek without smiling and returned to his pan.

'Dinner will be ready in a minute.'

Kate went to the fridge and unscrewed a half-empty bottle of wine, keen to regain the fuzzy buzz she had felt earlier that day. She leaned on the washing machine as she drank, gazing at the back of her husband's head, her expression one of mild bemusement. 'Everything okay, hun?'

'Yep.'

He spooned the pasta onto the three plates. Kate's heart sank – this was to be her second pasta meal of the day (a less palatable prospect than the second round of drinks). The thought reminded her that, in fact, she was still rather full from her extended lunch.

The three of them ate in silence until Kate could bear it no longer. 'How was school, sweetheart?'

'School was BRILLIANT! You know that dinosaur model me and Daddy made for my homework? Miss Blackmore said it was her most favourite one in the whole class and I had to show it in assembly and everything! So Mr Harrison gave me a special certificate, look!'

She pointed to the fridge.

'Oh, wow, I didn't even see that! Oh, I'm so proud of my little princess!' Kate leaned over and kissed her beaming daughter on the forehead. 'I hope you've told Daddy thank you. You're very lucky to have a daddy who spends so much time with you, aren't you?'

Pete's head remained fixed on his dinner plate. Kate pushed her food around with her fork, occasionally taking in an unwanted mouthful of pasta, which she chewed for much longer than she usually would. More silence followed, until Lola eventually pushed her still half-full plate away from her.

'Daddy, I'm finished. Can I please go on the back garden to play, please?'

'Yes, off you go.'

Yet more silence.

'Okay, I can't stand this any longer. Just what's the matter with you this evening? You're not yourself. Have I done something I shouldn't have? Or not done something I should have? It's not some kind of anniversary for us or something, is it?'

'No. It's nothing.' He exhaled sharply and loudly through his nostrils. 'Have you got anything you would like to talk to me about?'

Kate's suddenly felt hot. 'No, no. I haven't. No. Like what? You want to know more about my day at work? Well, I had yet another bust-up with Nick this morning. I swear he's got some sort of male version of PMT. Oh, and you'll never guess what? Cause some pig keeps leaving the microwave in a mess, we've had to have a rota, and, oh yes, it was muggin's turn today to kick it all off. Patricia told me to give you a ring to do it for me, cheeky cow!'

Pete wiped his mouth with his napkin and tossed it onto his plate, which, like his daughter's, was still half-full with pasta. He calmly stood up, put his chair back under the table and walked into the hallway, which was adjacent to the kitchen. Kate followed him with her eyes, still pushing the pasta around her plate. He pressed a button on the answer machine and placed his two palms onto the table upon which it rested. He fixed his gaze down at the machine, his shoulders slouched.

'Hi, message for Kate. Kate, it's Susie.' Kate dropped her cutlery onto her plate. Her eyes widened. 'Just to let you know that when the new guy was moving his stuff into your office, he found one of your pens. It's engraved – think it's that one your parents gave you when you graduated. If you want we can post it off to you, or you can swing by and pick it up. Actually, I'd like that – then we can have a girly chat and you can tell me how your new job is going. Anyway, miss you loads, speak to you soon. Mwah. Bye.'

She walked over to her husband, who made his first eye contact with her since she arrived at home – an intense, wounded glare.

'What the Hell is going on? You've got a new job and you didn't even tell me?'

Kate sighed and rubbed her eyes.

'Well...yes. It's true. I've got a new job. I'm working at Roberts, Roberts and Gladstone's, a new place in town. I didn't want to tell you because...well, because, to be perfectly honest with you, it's less money.'

Pete continued to glare at her.

'It's less money but it's less responsibility, too. I've just been getting so sick of the stresses and the pressures. I haven't told you because I feel ashamed of myself. I didn't want to admit to you that I wasn't coping.' She placed her hands around the back of his neck. 'You do such an amazing job around here being a house husband and a superdad. How could I tell you I'd become such a failure?'

Pete walked back into the kitchen, took Kate's wine glass and poured the remainder of the bottle into it. He placed it in her hands.

'Why don't you lie down on the sofa and tell me all about this new job of yours, then?'

He smiled, kissed her on the lips and led her into the living room, where Kate weaved together an elaborate patchwork of lies out of the stories she had concocted during the downtime she had had during her brief time at the Mansion and the thoughts that popped with such ease into her head. A great many of the lies were imbued with elements of truth – she was, indeed, much less stressed at her new place of work. She actually was less tired and more relaxed. She did, indeed, feel like she fitted in. She really did prefer her new colleagues to her old ones. And it was no lie at all to tell her husband that leaving her old job for a fresh challenge felt in every way, shape and form like a fabulous decision.

Chapter Eleven

'Well, never let it be said that Gordon Waddington is not a man of his word! Champagne as promised.'

The old man popped the cork on the champagne, the outside of which still sported a light covering of dust (not something that could ever be said about any of Kate's wine bottles at home). The popping sound was greeted with a gentle cheer from all but Chris, though even he managed the slightest of smiles. The opulent circular table upon which the champagne flutes rested was a veritable banquet of as-yet-untouched Chinese food, far too plentiful for the six of them to finish. Gordon walked around the table half-filling each flute apart from his own, into which he poured orange juice. He held his glass aloft.

'And so, ladies and gentlemen, kindly raise your glasses to our newest Intervener and her first successful Intervention. To Kate!'

'To Kate!'

Kate's cheeks pinkened slightly and she smiled coyly, though in fact she couldn't help but enjoy the attention.

'And now, please tuck in!'

Zak rubbed his hands together gleefully and the gang began to devour the mountains of food. They exchanged nothing but short, polite requests for cartons and cutlery to be passed around for the first few minutes of the meal. The table was a jolly frenzy of activity, and an excited buzz filled the room. It was Kate herself who eventually began the proper conversation.

'Guys, I can't thank you enough for this. For the meal. For the champagne. For everything, really.'

'We do it for everyone when they join,' replied Nigel, matter-of-factly.

'Nige, you're a grumpy old sod!' said Zak. 'What misery guts here really meant to say was that we're delighted to have you here. Here's to what I'm sure will be many happy years as one of the Interveners.' Zak tilted his glass forty-five degrees in Kate's direction. His eyes twinkled and he smiled at her before returning to his meal.

'So,' enquired Sally, 'what did you tell the old ball and chain?'

'Pete? I told him I was on a work do. Shelley's getting married and we're all having Chinese to celebrate before heading off for a drink or five in town.'

'Wow, I'm impressed! And only about 75% fabrication! So who's Shelley?'

Kate chortled. 'I don't bloody know! Pete's never even asked me. She's – ooh – let's say the boss's new PA. She's 23. She's just doing the job for a year while she saves up to pay her tuition fees, because she wants to train to be a teacher.'

'Christ, you're good at this lying business!'

'Maybe if Intervening doesn't work out for you, you could become a politician,' smirked the old man.

'Ha! Good one!' smiled Kate. 'Can we not tempt you to join us with a glass of something a bit stronger, Gordon?'

'No, my dear. I'm afraid tonight I've drawn the short straw. I'm the designated driver for the evening, so if any of us has an Intervention, I can get us there. Alas, death doesn't take a night off!'

'Been a quiet few days, though, eh boss?' said Zak. 'So fingers crossed.'

The gang continued to work their way through the feast, drinking as heartily as they ate. The empty champagne bottle was quickly joined by empty beer bottles and empty red and white wine bottles. The table increasingly became a hive of diffused conversations, some involving the whole group but most taking place between smaller groups and pairs, which would themselves keep swapping over. Much laughter emanated from the two women, the old man and Zak. Even Nigel's grumpiness dissolved more and more as the red wine in his bottle became less and less, and the only constant of the evening was that Chris remained silent. He was much less disengaged than usual, however, and appeared to be actively listening to the conversations, smiling now and again at the jokes being offered.

Eventually, the gorging of food slowed down, the gang instead picking and nibbling from the still sizeable amounts of food in the centre of the table before finally stopping completely. The rate of drinking, however, continued apace and, as such, the hum of conversation became louder and louder and words became increasingly slurred. The atmosphere was one of joyousness, frivolity and affection.

Kate's favourite conversation partner was the only other female at the table. They exchanged banter in the same way two people might play tennis, each jokey remark being followed-up by a jokey reply, itself followed by another jokey response and so on and so forth until eventually one of them had no reply and had to concede.

'Well, I have to say, Sally, you do seem like a nice bunch!'

'Mmm.'

'Gordon has been so helpful to me so far.'

'That's Gordon!'

Kate double-checked that the old man was out of audible range. 'He fascinates me, you know. There's something different about him. How does he look so youthful for such an old man?'

'It's not rocket science, babes! What do we actually do all day? Usually, next to nothing. Sometimes actually nothing. Nothing but waiting. Yes, the Visions are draining and the rescues can be frantic, but these things account for such a tiny fraction of our working day. Most of the time, we're just dossing around. It's hardly stressful, binge-watching box sets or playing cards or reading novels. Those are the sorts of things people do to relax when they're NOT at work! We're relaxed for most of the day. I tell you - you can chuck away those expensive face creams, because stick with us and you're gonna stay looking young for a long time yet!'

Kate seized her opportunity.

'Okay, okay, I've got to ask again. It's been bugging me for like – how long have I been here? Anyway, that long! And you won't tell me! So my question to you is,' she hiccupped, 'how the Hell do you manage to get all this money? I mean, it's not like the people you save or their families pay you, is it? TELL ME!'

The gang's smiles dropped and they looked at each other, each waiting for one of the others to speak. It was, to Kate's great surprise, Nigel who eventually did so.

'Go on, Gordon. Tell her. I think she's with us for the long haul.'

The old man sighed. 'Okay. Tell me, my dear – do you ever get any other premonitions? Other than people dying?'

'Well, kind of, yes. But they're ridiculous things. Like I'll have a premonition of a hot air balloon flying over my house, then pretty soon I'll see it. Same colours and patterns and proximity. Same everything. Pretty useless really. Nothing ever comes of it.'

'Right, well, our physic abilities manifest themselves in many different ways. Zak seems to have in-built weather forecasting abilities, although they come and go. Chris occasionally foresees traffic jams – which can actually be quite a useful gift when we're out and about Intervening. And, at the moment, it's Nigel's premonitions that enable us to stay in business, as it were. We're lucky to have him. See, he has premonitions of...the lottery results.'

'Kate guffawed into her wine glass. 'You're kidding? You are, aren't you? You're winding me up. This is all part of your hazing process. Good one!'

The gang shook their heads.

'What, really? You can predict what numbers are going to come up?'

Nigel gazed at her earnestly. 'I wouldn't say 'predict'. That makes it sound like I try to do it. I don't try to predict the numbers any more than you try to foresee people's deaths. Or any more than you try to breathe in and out. It just happens. It has to happen. The numbers just come to me.'

'So what are you still doing here? How come you're not sunning it up in your luxury villa in the Bahamas?'

'We're humanitarians here at the Mansion. We were put here on this Earth to Intervene.'

'How very noble. Well, okay then, so where are your millions of pounds? Are they here, in this mansion?'

The gang laughed.

'We don't have millions of pounds. Never have. I don't play all of the numbers. I could but I don't. I have to make sure at least one of them is deliberately wrong. Just enough to earn a decent wage. The most I have ever won in one go was £5,000. That sort of money doesn't arouse any attention or suspicion. It won't get you in the papers. But even still, once I've won the money, I'll leave it for a good long while before I play again in the same place. I travel around a lot – have weekends in different parts of the country and play the lottery while I'm there. Sometimes I even go to other countries and play there. Always for modest winnings. Like I say – it's a wage. And it keeps us in the Intervening business. We're not greedy or anything.'

Kate's eyes subconsciously wandered around the fabulous building and she thought about the fleet of brand new and classic cars outside.

'Sometimes,' Zak responded, 'Nige will give the info to one of us, and we'll go out there and play the numbers, just to mix it up a bit. We've GOT to be careful. Soon as someone twigs on to what we're doing, we're screwed. We can't Intervene for free. Got to put food on the table.'

'Nigel is a real boon to our organisation,' said Gordon. 'He's been with us since long before the National Lottery came about, and believe me those were times of relative austerity. Isn't that right, Nigel?'

Nigel shrugged and removed himself from the conversation, picking up a crossword puzzle book.

'Back then we had to operate as I gather so many other centres do – we juggled part-time jobs with our Intervening work. Anything to make ends meet, really, as close to the little old house we used to live in and operate from as possible. I helped out at the local greengrocer's for a while and was a security guard at a large factory. Nigel was quite an adept house painter and quite an inept baker. We lived on the breadline. Excuse the pun. And the harsh reality was that whenever we were at work, that was it. There were only so many times we could feign an illness and ask to go home before questions were asked or before we lost our jobs, as we so often did. While I was carting sacks of potatoes about, people were dying deaths I could have prevented, but what choice did I have? So when we discovered Nigel could foresee the lottery numbers – it was a dream come true. It meant we could devote all our time and energy into saving lives, and live in greater comfort.'

Kate screwed up her nose, still not entirely convinced by what seemed quite a tall story. 'So this life of luxury you lead – you must be the envy of the other Interveners across the country. Presumably no one else has Nigel's gift.'

'I couldn't possibly say. They might have. Either way, I wouldn't presume none of them live in the same favourable conditions as us. One hears stories – rumours, really – about other centres and how they get by.'

'Like?'

'Like drug dealing,' Zak piped in. 'Growing their own stuff and selling it.'

'Drug dealing? Well surely that just goes against everything you – we – stand for? Drugs kill people!'

Gordon shook his head. 'Derailed trains kill people who don't deserve it. House fires kill people who don't deserve it. If a person chooses to take drugs and ends up dying as a result, then I'm afraid to say that in my opinion they deserve it. You remember rule two?'

'How we can't Intervene in suicide attempts?'

'That's right. Well to me an accidental overdose is not so far removed from a suicide attempt – they know full well what they're doing – and the brutal truth is that I do not try to Intervene if I get a Vision of that ilk. So by that same logic, I cannot judge too harshly any Intervener who funds his noble cause in such a seemingly ignoble way. They'll save far more lives than they'll ultimately end.'

This silenced Kate, who racked her brains for a convincing counter-argument to what seemed like spurious logic, but she had to admit that the old man was probably right.

'So really, I should count myself lucky that I live where I do, and not near some drug dealing centre or some little tinpot organisation where I'd still have to do accounting on the side? Well don't you worry. Your secret's safe with me.'

Kate shot the gang an exaggerated wink. The conversations began to scatter and diverge once again, leaving the newcomer and the old man to continue their exchange.

'Ah, thank you kindly,' smiled Gordon. 'You know, Kate, we're grateful to have you too. It's been a good while since we were able to track down a potential Intervener.'

'Yeah, I wanted to ask you about that – how did you track me down, exactly? I mean, I got that pamphlet through the door in the envelope with my name on, which to be honest raised more questions than it answered. It was hand-delivered, wasn't it? I just don't see...'

'You've Sally to thank for that. Or blame, if you will!' Gordon laughed the same subdued, half-laugh with which Kate seemed already highly familiar. 'We all have the power to detect other Interveners when they appear on our inner Radars. Even if you stepped into this room blindfolded for the first time, you would have a vague image of each of us. At the very least, you would know how many Interveners were in the room. Try it some time! Some, with more powerful inner Radars, would be able to detect the gender of those Interveners. Sally has been gifted with an exceptionally strong inner Radar.'

Upon hearing her name, Sally abandoned her conversation and joined in.

'Indeed I have! That and these movie star good looks, of course.'

'Don't forget your exceptional powers of modesty and humility,' deadpanned Gordon. Sally screwed her nose up playfully.

'So, yeah, there I was, in the middle of an Intervention mission on my own one morning, maybe four or five miles away from your house, and I sensed you. I didn't have a clear image of you at that point, or exactly how far away you were or anything like that, but I knew you were out there. I made a mental note of the location, and on the return journey I did my best to track you down. Took me hours. As your face became clearer and sharper in my mind, I knew the net was closing in. As it faded, I knew I was going off the scent, so I'd backtrack.'

'So how did you know exactly where I lived? And the pamphlet had my name on it – did you sense that?'

Sally blushed and looked sheepish. 'Ahem...not exactly, no. As soon as I felt sure I was in the right general location, I did a little bit of, well, stalking.'

Kate giggled, but it was a giggle mixed with a hint of incredulousness. 'What?'

'I hung around your street in my car. It's a good stalking spot, your street! Plenty of big trees. Anyhow, I kept a look out and eventually I saw you coming out of your car in a trouser suit, carrying a laptop bag. Your face matched my Vision. I left, came back the next day with a pamphlet, ferreted around your bins for something with your name on – you really should shred those bills, you know, there are some unscrupulous people out there – and scrawled it on the pamphlet envelope. I'm a good stalker, aren't I? Did a bit of it in my teenage years to catch out cheating boyfriends.'

'Wow. I'm impressed. And a bit violated.'

'Ooh, you lucky thing! And this is only our second date!'

Gordon interjected. 'The point is, welcome; we're glad to have you. Interveners are in short supply. Who knows when the next one will come along? A percentage of a percentage of people are born with varying degrees of your gift, some of them with a very feint ability to foresee people's deaths and some much stronger. And most of those escape our net, to use Sally's metaphor. If only we could track down each of them.'

'Well, how many do get tracked down?'

'What, worldwide?'

Kate nodded.

'Hard to say for sure. But if you think there are about seventy million people living in this country. Only six of them are here right now, which is, give or take, about the same number of people working at the three other Intervention Centres in the United Kingdom – well, you do the Maths. We know very little about other Intervention Centres and how they operate, but we do know that they are scattered across the world. When you consider the technology required to carry out these operations, you'll appreciate that in a great many countries, there is no such thing as Intervention. There are surely would-be *Interveners* – that is a gift bestowed upon you whether or not you have the capability to do anything with your Visions – but they would end up knowing nothing of their potential. It's a tragedy, really.'

'But surely we're talking limits here? You can't have too many Interveners or Interventions, can you? I mean, hypothetically, let's say there were, ooh I don't know, a million Interveners operating in the world – that would mean a massive, massive increase in the number of people cheating death, wouldn't it? So wouldn't the planet start to get a bit overpopulated? I mean, not with a million extra people, but *hypothetically*...'

The old man mustered up a weary smile and nodded. 'And that, dear lady, is the crux of why our organisation can never become public knowledge. That's how people would see us – the nut jobs who were going around stopping the natural order. God's way, whatever you want to call it. I doubt we'd be too welcome during a Sunday morning sermon over at St Mary's.'

Zak chortled. 'Funny, though – the same person who would have us down as some maniacal antichrists would shake us by the hand if they knew we'd saved their Auntie Doreen from a pack of rampaging lions earlier that afternoon.'

'Zak is being flippant, but his point is valid. And so is yours. The principle of Intervention is wonderful in relatively small numbers – but we grow too much and we start to upset the balance. We DO need new blood here, but not too much of it. Quite apart from anything else, we need to remain covert. The more of us there are, the more chance of us being found out and therefore the more chance of the Intervention system imploding.'

'But what I don't get is this: how come you don't all get the same Vision at the same time? Or do you? If someone is about to die and they're in relatively close proximity, how come you don't all pick it up?'

Gordon stroked his bearded chin. 'Well, my dear, it isn't an impossibility that more than one of us could get the same Vision at the same time, but it's an improbability. In fact, in all my years of doing this strange and wonderful job, it's never happened. How many people die accidentally in this country every day, do you think?'

'Well, Jesus, who knows? Loads I guess.'

'Quite. Who knows? Not I. Not anyone here. But how many of those people appear on any of our radars? Loads?'

'No. No, not loads. Some.'

'Correct. A small fraction. A tiny percentage. It is pure good fortune for someone if their demise appears as a premonition of any of the staff here. To appear as a premonition of more than one of us? Well the odds of that happening must be astronomical.'

'Blimey, it's a proper fascinating world I've stepped into, isn't it? I'll bet you've got some amazing stories.'

'Yes, Kate, indeed we have. Why, just in this room alone, you've got some true heroes – we've had broken limbs, concussion and countless brushes with our own mortality, all in the name of being a stranger's secret saviour. We've scaled dizzy heights, hung from window ledges, stepped into traffic – you name it, we've done it. There have been a few funny ones, too. Like one time I had a Vision of a man, strangely dressed he was in these very old-fashioned clothes. I wondered if I was just getting a bad signal, because the room itself was strange - both darkened and brightly lit at the same time. And the man took a drink of something. It must have been poisonous because it killed him almost immediately. I had a call to make - was it suicide or not? One gets lots of Visions of hangings, overdoses, folk jumping off buildings - but never self-poisoning. I decided it had to be an accident - though it might equally have been murder, and you know the rules there. What a quandary! So, as you can well imagine, it was a nervy drive to the city centre address, just Nigel and myself. Neither of us had a clue how we were going to prevent the death - it was at least going to involve some breaking and entering. Beyond that we hadn't a clue. We needn't have worried - the address led us to a theatre. The 'death' was just part of some old play.'

'No way! So what did you do?'

'Forked over forty quid and got comfy! Very good it was too - great acting! No wonder the death scene made its way onto my Radar! It certainly did bring a new meaning to the phrase 'dying on stage'.'

'Boom boom. You made that up just so you could use that punchline.'

'No, it happened! Scout's honour.'

'I don't trust you as far as I can throw you, Gordon Waddington.'

'Probably for the best, my dear.'

Kate knew she should mingle but at that time felt magnetically drawn to Gordon. There was something else she wanted to know.

'So you've been doing this for decades – right?'

He nodded.

'So presumably you've seen lots of people come and go. Staff, I mean.'

He nodded again.

'So what about when someone leaves the organisation? How can you be sure they're not going to blab? Tell their friends? Tell their family? Tell the police? Tell the press?'

'We can't. But we still are. Yes, we've had our fair share of people leave - at times it's been nothing short of a revolving door. Yes, some of them have left with sourer grapes than others. Yes, some of them might have stories to tell that would be of interest to the police.'

'Stories?'

'Stories. Not necessarily about what we do for a living here - why, the machinery in the Vision Room? Just the work of a bunch of wacky, wannabe inventors. That's what we'd tell them. Are they really going to believe we use it to locate people who are about to die? How could such an accusation even be proved, unless by amazing coincidence someone happened to be in there at that exact time having a Vision? Stuff and nonsense - that's all they would see.'

'Then what do you mean by stories?'

'What I mean, dear, is the steps that are sadly sometimes necessary in our nobler pursuit.'

She rolled her eyes. 'Great, thanks. Well that's cleared that one up.'

'Didn't your mother ever tell you that in order to make omelettes one has to break eggs? And at the moment I wish to leave it there.'

'Well okay, fine, but back to my original question - what's stopping anyone from blowing the lid?'

'BECAUSE - like I say, it's a nobler pursuit. Whether a person enjoys being an Intervener or not, whether or not they agree with our - shall we say - policies, and in whatever circumstances they leave, what no one can deny is the good that we do here. Ultimately, we save lives. If someone wants to spoil that, they have to have potentially thousands of deaths on their conscience until their own death comes, which would probably be a sweet relief after carrying such a burden. Our secret's safe, believe me.'

'Right, so go on then. I'm probably putting two and two together here and getting five, but I think I might know what you're skirting around. So let's play Devil's Advocate. What happens if Pete finds out I'm an Intervener? Maybe I feel like I can't hold it in any longer and need to confide in someone. Maybe in spite of all my best efforts, I do or say something that leads him to the realisation that his wife has been leading a double life. Suddenly he knows all about The Interveners. What are the consequences of that?'

Waddington remained silent.

'Gordon, did you hear me?'

'Yes.'

'And?'

Silence. Kate's let out an involuntary gasp.

'Oh shit! You'd kill him, wouldn't you? Gordon, for God's sake, talk to me!'

'We would have a problem on our hands. Our next act would be to convince him not to tell another soul - and convince ourselves, beyond any shadow of a doubt, that he wouldn't.'

'And if there WAS any doubt?'

Gordon's tone suddenly grew uncharacteristically snappy – to the extent that it killed the frivolities of the room and the rest of the Interveners looked in their direction. 'Kate, I told you I didn't want to speak any more on the matter! Now please show me a modicum of respect and change the subject!'

Kate dropped the line of questioning but did not change the subject, instead choosing the third option of a deeply uncomfortable silence. She suddenly felt more than a little afraid of the old man by her side. Clearly, there was still plenty she did not know - about Gordon specifically and the act of Intervening generally. She suddenly felt riddled with doubt and regret, with fear.

Sally banged her palms against the table. 'Right! That's it, you bunch of boring old farts! We'll have no more talk of Interventions, not tonight! Okay? We've got booze to demolish, so less yapping and more drinking, please!'

*****

The evening drew on, and the midnight curfew Kate had placed upon herself to appease her husband drew nearer and nearer. The celebratory buzz had gradually returned, and soon Kate had drunk enough to have put her conversation with Gordon to the back of her mind. The jubilation was disrupted temporarily by a sound Kate had yet to hear during her brief time as an Intervener – that of Chris's voice. Though soft and whispery, its sheer rarity managed to cut through the noise.

'I'm having a Vision.' His face was white and droplets of sweat had appeared on his forehead, but all in all his reaction to the Vision process was much less animated and dramatic than Kate's own experiences, both of her own Vision and of witnessing Sally's. Chris leapt up and into the Vision Room, onto the Electric Chair, with Gordon following suit.

A few minutes later, they returned and headed for the door, whereupon Gordon collected his car keys and the two of them threw on their jackets.

'This one's a bit of a distance away. A drunk falling down a manhole. I hope we make it,' Gordon told the rest of the gang. 'Either way, we'll be gone for a good few hours, so I'll say goodnight to you all now.'

The pair exited.

'Guess that leaves just the four of us party animals!' said Sally.

'Make that three,' Nigel replied. 'It's past my bedtime. And do me a favour. Turn that bloody racket down, or preferably off.'

Nigel stumbled upstairs and into his bedroom without saying goodnight to the remaining three Interveners. Zak stuck his two fingers up and waved them in the direction of Nigel's bedroom before collapsing onto the sofa with laughter.

'Hey listen,' Kate slurred. 'I've had a really great time tonight. Thanks for welcoming me into your little group. You two are really cool. I feel ten years younger all of a sudden. I wish I didn't have to go home.'

'So don't go!' Zak told her. 'Don't forget, one of those bedrooms up there is yours! Why don't you stay over tonight? We are!'

'I can't do that! What would I tell my husband?'

'The same thing you always tell him,' said Sally. 'A pig bile of pork pies! Wait did I just say...ha! You know what I mean. God, I'm PISSED!'

'Okay, okay, you've twisted my arm. Honestly, a few drinks down me and I always get so suggestible.'

'That's worth remembering!' guffawed Zak, and he nudged her with his elbow, much less gently than he had intended. She pushed him back playfully.

'Right, right, I'm going to ring my hubby. Got to make this convincing.'

'I've got just the thing!' said Sally, jumping up. She headed for the sound system in the corner of the room, perused through the CD collection and held one of them aloft in victory before putting it on, removing the soft-rock compilation which had been playing. Lively dance-pop music blared out of the speakers. Kate stuck her thumb up in approval and fished her phone out of her handbag. She dialled home.

'Hi baby, it's me! Yeah, I'm having a great time! The Chinese was delicious. I'm just in O' Hare's now, dancing around my handbag.' She threw her bag down on the floor and danced around it in as ridiculous a fashion as she could manage, which was greeted with howls of laughter from her small audience. Kate stopped dancing and put her finger to her lips to shush them, trying her hardest to suppress her own giggles. 'How's my little angel doing? Is she asleep? Oh, that's good, that's good. Listen honey, hope you don't mind too much if I stay out tonight? One of the girls has got a flat just outside of town and we're gonna get a kebab when we've done, head back to hers and have a few more drinks. Is that okay? Oh, you're the best! Love you! Bye!'

Sally was bent double with laughter. 'Oh my God, give this girl an Oscar! What a performance! What a LIAR!'

Zak fished around for an empty wine bottle, which he held to his chest as he approached Kate. He mimed the opening of an envelope. 'And the award for Lying Cow of the Year goes to...Kate Jenson!'

He presented her with the bottle, embraced her and kissed her on the cheek. As he did so, Kate instinctively turned her face towards his and what followed was a clumsy peck half on Kate's cheek and half on the side of her lips. Sally applauded wildly.

'Oh, wow. I mean, what an honour. Gosh, I haven't prepared a speech or anything. Looking around this room at my peers, I see so many world-class liars, and it's an honour just to be mentioned in the same breath as them. I tell you, I've dreamed of this moment for as long as I can remember. I'd like to thank my fans. I'd like to thank God. And, of course, I'd like to thank my husband, for being such a gullible son of a bitch and believing my whoppers!'

'And now, ladies – it's time for the after show party!' Zak turned the music up and the three of them danced for the next hour or so, swigging from the various bottles available to them as they did so. It was Sally who succumbed first to sleep, eventually collapsing onto a sofa and within minutes closing her eyes, a bottle still in her now limp grasp. Kate turned the music down to half its volume, but continued to dance with Zak. With each song played, the two seemed to be dancing closer and closer. Fewer and fewer words were being exchanged, and the amount of eye contact was increasing; gazes were becoming longer and longer. Physical contact, too, was becoming more frequent. Occasional hands on arms as the two spoke had, by the time the night had neared its end, turned into a full-blown embrace, Kate's arms wrapped around Zak's neck and his around her waist as they danced, stopping momentarily every now and again to guzzle the never-ending wine supplies, then resuming their positions unselfconsciously.

It was to break the spell of a particularly lingering gaze that Kate eventually spoke, her words slurred. 'Oh my God, I'm absolutely trashed!'

'Me too. I suppose it's bedtime. Hey listen, I've really enjoyed tonight. And I'm bladdered, so I'm just gonna come straight out with this. I don't suppose you fancy spending the night with me tonight, do you? I know you're married. That's not what this is about. I just mean, let's have a cuddle and fall asleep together. It's been so long since I've done that with anyone.'

Kate hadn't given Pete a second thought since their telephone conversation. She considered him for a moment. She thought about how much she had enjoyed the attention Zak had bestowed upon her that night; the long, lingering looks. He was younger than her husband and undoubtedly more handsome, so the whole thing had been something of an ego boost, as intoxicating as the alcohol.

Then she thought about Pete. She would be lying to herself, she realised, if she said she was getting no attention from Pete; in the precious time together that her previous professional duties had afforded them, Pete had positively devoured her company. If their sex life had waned a little of late (and it had), it was certainly not for want of Pete trying. She knew – partly because he told her so frequently and partly because she could see it in his eyes – that her husband was still as infatuated by her as when they were newlyweds. But Zak. *Zak.* There was something so new and exciting about that moment in time, about him.

She smiled and slipped her hand into his. He led her to his room.

Chapter Twelve

It was just a few hours later, when the first slivers of sunlight started to slice through the bedroom window, that Kate awoke. She was still in Zak's bed, still in her underwear. Still a little drunk. She stumbled into her jeans, pulled her top on and tiptoed out of the room, looking away from Zak at all times. The house was, for the first time, absolutely silent and still, in stark contrast to the rowdiness of last night, although evidence of the party was everywhere.

Her first port of call was the kitchen, where she poured herself a large glass of water. As she lifted the glass, the sunlight glinted off her wedding band and into her eyes. She took the remainder of the glass to her room, collapsed onto her bed and slept for another few hours.

What awoke Kate next was a vivid nightmare, the culmination of which was a teenage girl lying unconscious at the bottom of a set of stairs, blood gushing from her head, surrounded by shards of glass. Unsure of whether this was an actual nightmare, of the kind any normal human being would have, or whether it was a sleeping manifestation of her 'Daymares', a still groggy Kate dragged herself over to the mirror, winced at the sight of her bloodshot eyes and quickly smoothed her hair down, before going to find Gordon downstairs.

He was sat, with the rest of the crew, in the living room, all of them drinking coffee. The only person missing was Sally, who was making the most of the pleasant weather by busying herself in the garden.

'Well, good morning, sunshine!' beamed Gordon, folding up his newspaper. Nigel looked up and nodded but continued to read his own newspaper. Zak smiled weakly at her, and she reciprocated. He then continued his card game with Chris.

'Morning, all! I hope I don't look as rough as I feel. Gordon, listen, I've just had what could be a Vision, or there again it could simply be a bad dream.'

'Well, my dear, no harm in checking it out, is there? Let's pop you into the Vision Room. Chris, get the kettle boiled for Kate, will you? There's a good lad. Black coffee, please.'

Kate's second experience in the Vision Room seemed, implausibly, even more surreal than the first, doubtless as a result of the alcohol in her bloodstream and her still sleepy state. Gordon uttered once again his strange mantra, 'On behalf of the moribund, I wish you luck', which brought back to Kate's mind the nagging sensation that this was a bit like a cult, or some deranged new religion. The metal plates felt especially cold against her temples, and the whole thing seemed now more like some bizarre Science Fiction film from the 1950s that Pete might force her to watch. It certainly didn't seem like a paying job.

She persisted nonetheless, and went through the same process of first relaxing then focusing her mind. Eventually – after the same ritual of shakes, beads of sweat and low moans – her Vision appeared on the screen. There she was again, the teenage girl of whom she had not long-since dreamed, this time at the top of the stairs, carrying an empty glass and an empty bowl on a tray. In front of her was a small toy car, upon which she trod and slipped, sending her tumbling down the stairs, the glass and bowl flying into the air and smashing on the floor at the bottom of the stairs. As the girl hit the bottom, she gashed her head on the corner of the radiator. Then nothing; the girl did not move (though the blood continued to gush, soon enough forming a large puddle) and nor did anyone rush to the scene.

Gordon zoomed in and the computer recognised the girl as Georgia Tompkins, at a location 71.2 miles away.

'We've got quite a journey ahead of us! Would you like me to accompany you? Or perhaps you would prefer someone else's company this time! I promise I shan't be offended!'

Realising that 'someone else' could turn out to be Zak, Kate chose Gordon without hesitation, which seemed to please the old man.

'How long have we got, Gordon?'

He pressed the final button to complete the Vision process and the screen flashed 'T-8h37m'.

'Oh, a little while yet.'

'Great. Do you think I could pop home and see my family for a bit?'

'Why, of course. This isn't prison, you know! You may leave on one condition – you drink that coffee and have a quick shower. Can't have you getting in any accidents; you're much too valuable, you know. Will you do that for me?'

Kate smiled and obeyed.

Chapter Thirteen

Kate was glad to see her husband, and embraced him for a couple of seconds longer than she normally would have, relinquishing at the point when she realised that if the hug lasted any longer, Pete might get suspicious about exactly what had happened last night. She was glad, too, that her daughter was home from school, though it was plain to see that Lola had nothing more than a simple case of the sniffles and was clearly enjoying a day off with her father. The floor was lined with board games and crayons, and a Disney DVD was playing to no one in the lounge. Kate explained her unexpected visit as a spur-of-the-moment whistle-stop lunch on the way to a client.

She plied her husband with questions about his own evening and the day he was spending with Lola. When he did manage to get a word in edgeways and enquire about her night, she responded with generic phrases about having a 'great time', 'must do it again', 'good to blow off steam' and so forth. Her brain was still too frazzled to come up with her usual web of lies.

After few triangles of brunch-time sandwiches, hastily prepared by her husband, Kate was off once more, driving to the town centre and parking on the street in which she had arranged to meet Gordon, who had taken a slight detour *en route* to Kate's next Intervention. She felt a small twinge of excitement as she stepped into the Jag.

As they set off, Gordon presented her with the paper he had been reading that morning.

'Take a look at page 62. It's the fourth one down.'

Kate did so – she seemed unable to resist doing anything the old man told her to do, a departure from the independent twenty-first century career girl she had worked so hard to become. Page sixty-two was part of the Obituaries section.

'The ones that got away from us!'

The fourth obituary down featured a familiar-looking face. It was that of an eighty-two year old lady, Mrs Ruby Watson. Kate's smile dropped and her forehead creased. Her queasiness returned.

'But – I saved her! This can't be right!'

'Keep reading.'

The bottom of the obituary made mention of donations being made to Cancer Research in lieu of flowers.

'So it was all a waste of time! I saved her, but she died anyway!'

'Not a waste of time, my dear. Please don't see it that way. You bought her a final couple of days on this Earth. Maybe a final cuddle from her grandson. Noah, I think it said his name was. Maybe in that couple of days, she got to experience something she had never experienced; see something she never thought she would live to see. And maybe she just had a really good plate of beef stew and dumplings! Who knows?' Kate gazed at her picture in silence. 'The truth is that we don't stop a person from dying – we just postpone their death. They're still going to die. Could be ten minutes later for all we know. I apologise if I've upset you, but I just thought it was something you needed to see.'

'So what are we saying here? Intervening is just a waste of time? There's some sort of 'Final Destination' shit going on or something?'

'My dear, I'm quite sure I have no idea what you're talking about.'

'It's a film. A bunch of people cheat death, but then they all end up dying soon after anyway. Message - when your time's up, it's up.'

'Well I have no clue what becomes of these people after we save them. None of us have. And nor is it our concern. All I know is that we've extended their lives. We've done our good deed.'

'Right. Well. I see.'

Sensing that Kate was not in a particularly chatty mood, Gordon put the radio on, tuning into a station that he knew Kate would enjoy more than he would. She eventually fell asleep, and Gordon turned the radio off entirely.

When she awoke, they were at the destination. Any lingering traces of a hangover had disappeared and she felt much more like her usual self.

'Ah, welcome back to the land of the living! We've still got a bit of time before she falls down the stairs.'

Kate stretched and yawned. 'Righto. But – I mean, couldn't we Intervene now? Sal said it's a matter of altering the course of their day slightly. We could do that now and be off, couldn't we?'

'Well, yes, theoretically. But the longer the gap between Intervention and the time of the supposed death, the more chance there is of them falling back into the trap, as it were. The best Interventions take place just seconds before the incident or accident. That way, you can get right in fate's way. Besides, if we leave now, you won't get to find out whether our young victim here gets to go to the discotheque tonight, or whatever it is young people do on a Friday night these days.'

'Oh, I see. You're right.'

Gordon shut off the engine and the two off them unbuckled their seatbelts, relaxing in their luxurious seats. They gazed towards the house. Eventually, they caught sight of the young girl walking through the living room, carrying the same wooden tray Kate had Envisioned, the only difference this time being that the glass was filled with a dark liquid and steam was visibly emanating from the bowl. She then disappeared from view, towards what Kate presumed must be the stairs.

'Ah. We may have a small problem here. Should be nothing, but we might need to press on with this one sooner rather than later.'

'Why? What is it?'

'You'll learn to notice little, seemingly inconsequential details like this which could block or alter your Intervention. Did you see the wires?'

Kate shook her head. 'No. What wires?'

'She appeared to be wearing earphones. Which could mean we have trouble getting her attention, if she has the music loud enough. And, you know teenagers, she probably does. See, where this one differs from old Mrs Watson's Intervention is that hers was a public scene. In this case, our young lady is in the privacy of her home. Access is not quite so straightforward.'

'But surely loads of your Interventions take place in someone's house? You must be used to it by now.'

'Oh, indeed I am. As I say, it's the earphones that are the potential problem here. I'm not prepared to risk waiting until the last minute only to discover that she can't hear our knocks. Right, let's do it. Do you fancy being a door-to-door saleswoman? Jehovah's Witness? Visitor to town who needs directions? The choice is yours!'

Kate gazed into the distance, and did an exaggerated chin stroke. Tonight, Matthew, I'm going to be…a saleswoman! But – hang on! I haven't got anything with me to sell.'

'Yes you have!'

Gordon popped open the boot of his car and beckoned Kate towards it. In there were all sorts of props – wigs, changes of clothes, and a random variety of objects of all shapes and sizes. Gordon pulled out a complex-looking mop and a portfolio, the front of which bore a picture of Sally holding the mop and the slogan 'Don't just clean it – Intervene it!'

'Allow me to introduce to you the Intervener 3000, so-called because when your floor's not clean, one simply has to Intervene! It's just a little something we knocked up as a team one uneventful rainy afternoon. Everything you need to know about this mop is inside, should the potential customer actually want to find out more about this piece of rubbish. It hasn't happened yet.'

'Wow, you guys have a LOT of free time on your hands, don't you?'

'Guilty as charged. One of the hardest parts of our job is staving off the boredom. You can be waiting for days for a Vision to appear. And another tough aspect to the job is keeping the Intervention part interesting. It gets repetitive – you know the score. You get the Vision, you bring up the victim's details, you locate them, you stand in their way for a couple of seconds – voila. Life saved. Back to base and do it all again. It's a magical thing we do, I suppose – but it's a routine magic. Like being a midwife or something. But, unlike midwives, we get the chance to get creative in our delivery, so to speak. One day you're playing a traffic warden, the next a charity worker, and so on and so on. It's amateur dramatics, in essence.'

'I suppose, so! Right, in that case, prepare to be bowled over by both my acting skills and my saleswoman skills!'

The two approached the door. Kate knocked and waited; no reply. She tried the doorbell; no reply. She banged the letterbox against the door; no reply. She then opened the letterbox and peered through. She could not see the girl, but what she could see, directly in front of her, was the bottom of the stairs, which looked exactly like the ones in the Vision, only from a different angle. Gordon made a fist and pounded the door with it; no reply.

'Oh dear. I feared this might happen. I'll go round the back and see if we can get her attention from the back door.'

Gordon returned moments later shaking his head. 'Right, back in the car. It's time for Plan B.'

Plan B involved using the internet facilities built into the dashboard of his car to locate the telephone number of the house; a simple enough task when armed with the information they had at their disposal.

'Right, let's hope she picks up. I'll put on my best foreign accent and enquire about her interest in making long-distance call savings. While I'm at it, you go straight to the door and knock loudly as you can.'

Gordon rang but the call eventually went to answerphone. He tried again, several times, but the same thing kept happening.

'Damn. Damn, damn, damn. Right, it's panic stations, I'm afraid. Forget the mop thing. We now need to get her attention any way we can. You go round and bang on any window you can find. I'm going to throw pebbles at the upstairs windows. I'll smash the damn things if I have to. One of them has to be her bedroom window.'

It was to no avail. The two were unable to capture the teenager's attention. They regrouped at the front of the house. Gordon placed his hands on his hips and chewed his bottom lip, looking up towards the top of the house in a desperate bid for inspiration.

'Gordon, listen. I've got an idea. It's probably stupid, and you'll say I haven't thought it through. You'll be right. Thing is, when I was round the side of the house, I noticed one of the windows was open.'

'You're talking about breaking in?'

'Well...yes.'

'You're quite right – it is rather silly. What will you do when you get in there?'

'I'm sorry? What will I do? I actually meant for you to squeeze in there! You're skinnier than me! These, my friend – these are child-bearing hips. I really doubt they'll fit through that little hole.'

Gordon guffawed. 'My dear, I'm seventy-nine years old! I can't go climbing onto window ledges and contorting my body into tight spaces! My old bones simply won't take it!'

Kate narrowed her eyes and gazed at him suspiciously. *You don't look seventy-nine*, she thought, *and you're just as athletic as the next man anyhow.*

'And besides which, you've yet to suggest what you would actually do.'

'Well, you know. Just, I don't know, creep up the stairs and move the toy out of the way. This Intervention doesn't really need to involve physical contact. I don't even need to see the girl.'

'That's true, but I want you to stop for a minute and consider my reservations. What you are doing, though secretly quite noble, is in fact illegal. If the girl sees you – and I'd say there's a more than decent chance of that happening – she will contact the police. Even if we manage to get away, she has your description. You are putting yourself, and thus our entire organisation, in jeopardy. Remember rule 1(c) of the contract – the organisation is worth far more than any individual life.'

Kate smirked and nodded in the direction of the car boot. 'I think you might have just the thing to solve that problem. The person who breaks in will do so in disguise.'

The old man frowned. He admired her gusto, energy and quick-thinking, recognising that she already had the makings of a great Intervener. 'How about we toss a coin? Heads old man Waddington, with his creaky old joints, breaks in. Tails the lithe young newcomer Jenson has to do it.'

Gordon fished out a coin from his pocket and flicked it in the air. He missed the catch and it landed on the floor. They both stooped down to see it was tails up. Kate groaned.

'I forgot to tell you, young lady – one of my psychic powers is the ability to predict coin tosses.' She frowned at him. 'No, I'm just kidding. Now, go and get yourself disguised. And do hurry – our time is growing short.'

Kate returned in a simple disguise of a curly blonde wig, which looked less than natural alongside her brown eyes and brown eyebrows, and a pair of half-rimmed glasses. The two of them made their way to the open window and Gordon did his best to hoist Kate up to the ledge. She scowled at him, 'Oi! Your joints seem just fine to me!'

As she had predicted, Kate was able to squeeze her top half through the gap, but her bottom got lodged. Gordon pushed her upwards using her ankles, but this served only to get her more stuck. It was at that point that she heard the scream and was forced to witness the teenager tumbling down the stairs, ostensibly to her death. Kate yelped. Gordon tugged her ankles this time and was able to release her from the jam, lowering her to safety. He already had his mobile phone out and with his remaining hand had covered a hysterical Kate's mouth. To her great surprise, it served to comfort her rather than panic her.

'All is not lost! We have one last shot at this!' He dialled 999. 'Now watch and learn. Oh my God! Ambulance please! Oh god, oh God, oh God! You hang in there, my princess! My daughter has just fallen down the stairs. She's unconscious and there's blood everywhere. The thing is, I'm locked out but I can see her. We're at 86 Maple Grove. Come quickly. Don't you die! Don't you dare die!'

Gordon ended his call and reverted straight back to the calm, measured presence Kate had known up until this bizarre episode.

'Like I say – amateur dramatics. I reckon with all my years of Intervening experience, I ought to have a pop at Hamlet before I shuffle off this mortal coil.'

Kate, meanwhile, could not shake her own panic at the dying teenager lying just feet away from her.

'What do we do now?'

'It's your choice. Either way, we go back to the car. We can play the waiting game with fingers crossed, or frankly we can just leave. When you've seen as many people slip through the grasp of Intervention as I have, I'm afraid to say you become hard to it. If we drive away now, I'll never give it a second thought, but I know it will torture you. If we stay, you have to face the possibility that you're about to see a dead girl.'

'We have to stay! I have to know!'

'Very well.'

It was only a few minutes later that the ambulance arrived, along with the fire brigade, who quickly gave up their fruitless search for the girl's dad and barged down the back door. It was with much less bustle that they carried the girl away from the house minutes later on a stretcher, a blanket over her head.

Gordon squeezed Kate's hand and gently removed the wig and glasses she was wearing. 'You'll get used to it. Let's get you home.'

Not a single word was exchanged during the long journey back to Kate's car. Images of the boy falling to his death from the cliff top all those years ago had re-entered her cycle of thoughts, intermingled with thoughts about the girl she had just witnessed falling to her own death. She lamented everything the youngster would miss out on. She speculated on how, where and when her parents would learn of her death. As a parent, putting herself in their shoes seemed all too easy. Suddenly, far from feeling like a hero, as she had done when saving the old lady, she felt a failure. She was enveloped not by pride or jubilation but by a strange sense of grief, even guilt, as if somehow it had been partly her fault. A tear rolled down her cheek.

Chapter Fourteen

Kate snuggled up to her sleeping husband in bed that evening, burying her head in his chest. It had been a most peculiar twenty-four hours – indeed, her whole life had been peculiar since joining the Interveners. As unsettling as it was thrilling, full of highs and lows, twists and turns. It felt good to be back at home, in some semblance of normality. Her plan now was to enjoy the weekend with her family and forget all about saving lives. Just listening to Pete's heartbeat was proving enormously therapeutic, and soon enough, guilty thoughts about her night with Zak and helplessly watching a young girl fall to her untimely death faded from her mind. She drifted off to sleep.

She was awoken in the early hours of the morning by the shrill and protracted scream of her daughter. She rushed into her room, swaddled her with her arms and kissed her sweaty forehead. Lola was shaking and sobbing.

'Ahh, my little precious! What's the matter? Did you have a bad dream? You're all right, mummy is here with you.'

'I want Daddy.'

'Daddy is asleep. He's had a long hard day looking after you. Now, why don't you tell mummy all about that dream, hey? I'm sure it was nonsense. I bet it had monsters in it again or something. Monsters aren't real remember, Silly Billy?'

'No, it wasn't monsters this time, mummy. I dreamed about a man and he had a sack on his head. And another man made him kneel down on the floor and,' Lola started to wail again, 'he got a big sword and chopped off his head!'

Kate pulled Lola's head to her chest, partly to comfort her daughter and partly so Lola could not see the worried look on her mother's face.

'Oh, baby! I know dreams can be horrible, but you have to remember, they're just dreams. Nobody has really died, have they? You're here safe with mummy. Now, how would you like to come and sleep in bed with me and Daddy? Will that make you feel better?'

Lola nodded, and within moments, all three of the Jensons were sound asleep.

Chapter Fifteen

It was in the middle of a lavish Saturday morning breakfast, cooked by Pete as per their weekly tradition, that a story on the news drifted through to the kitchen from the living room, where the television was playing once again to an audience of no one. It was announced as a breaking news report and bore the headline caption 'British hostage executed in Iraq'. Kate put down her newspaper and wandered out of her seat, unnoticed by either her husband, who was engrossed in his own broadsheet, or her daughter, who was colouring in a picture with one hand and lifting spoonful after spoonful of frosted cereal into her mouth with the other. Kate watched as the story unfolded, engrossed by the home video footage of the victim's masked captors, toting guns beside a sobbing man and barking demands in broken English into the camera. One of the captors then placed a sack on the bound hostage's head and the footage ended there. The report went on to say that the man was decapitated a number of hours later.

Kate flicked the TV off and returned to the kitchen, doing her best to appear nonchalant and unperturbed, though deep down she was more than aware of the significance – at very least potential significance – of all of this. She turned towards her daughter.

'Darling? You know that bad dream you had last night, about the man dying?'

A saddened expression formed on Lola's face as she nodded.

'Well, do you ever get any other horrid dreams like that? I mean, where people get killed?'

Lola squinted, pursed her lips and gazed skywards, in order to aid the thinking process. 'Yes, mummy, sometimes I do. I can't remember any now, though.'

'Okay, and does it ever happen when you're not asleep? Like, in the middle of the day, maybe at school or something like that?'

Lola paused again, contemplating the question deeply. 'No.'

The little girl finished her last few mouthful of cereal and pushed her bowl into the middle the table before going into the living room to watch Saturday morning cartoons.

Pete lowered his newspaper, which he continued to read as he addressed his wife. 'What was all that about?'

'Oh, nothing. I was reading this article the other day about how children who have recurring nightmares or fantasies about death are often feeling under particular amounts of stress or anxiety, usually at school.'

Pete put down his paper altogether. 'Right. I see. Stress, eh? Maybe she's being bullied. Or maybe I'm putting too much pressure and expectation on her when I help her with her homework. Sounds like something we should be monitoring. Maybe I should pop into school first thing on Monday morning.'

Kate waved the air as if to brush off the notion. 'Nah! Let's not worry them unnecessarily. How about we see how things develop? It may just be a phase. Maybe she saw something scary on the TV or something. Who knows? I mean, have you been checking everything she watches when you're at home together?'

'Well, no. No, I suppose I haven't. I'd better be a bit more careful.'

'I mean, I'm sure it happens to most kids – most adults, even.' Kate sensed an opportunity. 'Don't you ever have strange dreams about people you've never met dying? I'm sure I do sometimes. It doesn't mean anything.'

'Nope! Can't say I do. At least, not that I can remember, but I don't really remember many of my dreams.'

'Yeah right. Unless they involve Angelina Jolie writhing around naked on a unicorn I'll bet.'

'Sweetheart, YOU'RE the woman of my dreams! I keep telling you that.'

'Woo woo woo! Top answer. You big smoothie. Now get back to your paper, you.'

Kate knew then that her husband could not possibly be a potential Intervener. Getting a Vision was such an intense experience, such a *physical* as well as mental drain, that a person could not simply forget about it or be unaware it had happened. Her daughter, she was not so sure about.

'By the way Kate, did you ask Lola when you went into the room who it was she was dreaming about?'

'Yeah. She said it was some girl, falling down the stairs or something.'

Chapter Sixteen

Kate returned to work on Monday refreshed and more positive about her role, resolving to focus not on the potential sadness her job involved but on the potential happiness and satisfaction it could bring to her. A lifesaver. Like a doctor, saving people from the brink of death. She had coined for herself a new phrase to describe her job – 'fatefighter'. Like a firefighter, except she was stepping in to save people from a perilous fate rather than a blazing inferno. Of course, there was none of the public heroism afforded to doctors and firefighters – it was a frustratingly thankless calling – but it still beat being an accountant.

Alas, despite her renewed excitement, there was to be no Intervention that day – not for her or for any of her colleagues. It was a day of lazing around and generally doing her best to avoid being in close proximity to Zak. She still felt somewhat awkward and embarrassed about Thursday night's drunken proceedings, and neither of them had brought up the topic.

There was, of course, much to do at the Mansion during down time. The Games Room was a particular favourite congregation point for Zak and Chris, who wiled away the hours in what was in essence a souped-up youth club. The pool table was used daily, and more often than not several times daily - the clonking of one ball into another soon became such a familiar and regular sound audible from the main living room that Kate no longer registered it. The muffled thud of dart into dartboard was not far behind in terms of frequency, and nor was the pat-pat of table tennis. These were noises easily filtered out by Kate as she indulged in her own, usually quieter, pastimes - the same could not be said of the incessant beeps emitted as Pacman popped pills in the authentic full-size arcade machine from the early eighties, bought by Gordon as a present for the boys the Christmas before. One corner of the room was, effectively, a video games museum, decked out with numerous consoles ranging from one of the primitive Pong machines from the seventies to the latest cutting-edge kits from the present day, and everything in between. The speakers of the huge television vibrated and boomed with gunfire and explosions when they were in use - Kate often found the noise unbearable and the fact that this pair of professional lifesavers took such pleasure in digital bloodshed more than a little ironic. Equally irritating were the clunks, whooshes and whizzes as they racked up ever-higher scores on the pinball machine - again retro, again full size, again ludicrously expensive. When either of those activities was in full flow, Kate made a beeline for her bedroom or the garden. Not all the activities in the Games Room were noisy ones, however - the poker table was in semi-frequent use, and even Gordon, Nigel and Sally would often join in. Kate would decline Sally's offer of tuition, but instead sat and watched in the hope of picking up the intricacies of the game and one day surprising everybody by taking a seat at the table.

While they certainly enjoyed their indoor contests and competitions, the boys also loved the outdoor pursuits on offer to them. Basketball was a favourite way of keeping fit, with Zak always insisted on playing shirtless, something Kate fought many losing battles trying to ignore. The vast garden had ample room for a putting green, for when less energetic pursuits were craved - Nigel and Gordon could be found there just as often as could Zak and Chris. The Interveners also had the space - and the money - for a full-size tennis court. Kate had played lots of tennis in her youth, and enjoyed going up against Sally - not least of which because she more often than not beat her. A giant chess board was popular with all the Interveners in fine weather (and the regular-sized version popular when it was not fine).

It was nobody's idea of a place of work - and, save for a relatively tiny room used for relatively tiny portions of the day (if that), it really wasn't. It was a place of leisure and pleasure. Practically a holiday camp. It just so happened that Kate got paid for idling around in it, and the buzz she got whenever she stepped back to consider that fact was evidently still very much there.

*****

It was three days later that Kate got her next Intervention experience. In contrast to the slow start to the week, it had been a fairly hectic day. By lunchtime, Gordon had had a Vision and had yet to return, accompanied by Zak. Nigel had also had a Vision, choosing Sally to be his partner for the journey. They, too, had yet to return to the Mansion. That had left Kate and Chris. As was the usual case, Chris had not engaged in conversation with Kate, and by this point Kate had given up trying to coax conversation of any description out of him. Rather, he had busied himself playing Solitaire and she had engrossed herself with a book of number puzzles in an effort to stop her previously highly active brain from becoming rusty.

It was just midway through lunch – which the two had eaten at the table together in silence but for the radio Kate had turned on – that Chris threw down his cutlery, his body seizing up and sweat appearing at his brow. Kate followed him to the Vision Room and uttered the phrase she had heard so many times but not yet said: *'On behalf of the moribund, I wish you luck'* (though she still did not understand the necessity of it, if indeed it was a necessity). She helped to operate the high-tech machinery surrounding the Electric Chair as best she could, but it was clear that the more seasoned Chris had the situation well under control. The Vision this time was that of a middle-aged man being electrocuted as he mowed his lawn, 36.9 miles away. Kate had still yet to harden to the spectacle of death in the way her colleagues had, and the image turned her stomach.

Chris and Kate walked in silence to what was left of the fleet of cars. Chris drove, much to Kate's dismay – she was itching to get behind the wheel of one of these magnificent vehicles. Itching, also, to regain some semblance of control; everything she had done so far during her time as an Intervener had been passive, subordinate, second fiddle. The new girl. The student. It was a far cry from her days as a high-powered big city accountant, where *she* had all the experience, where *she* so often called the shots. Even choosing the kind of car to drive would have been a step in the right direction.

Chris spoke the location into the car's computer, so softly that he was asked to repeat it, but apart from that retained his selective silence. Kate tried several times to break that silence, which seemed to be prolonging the journey to the point of it being an agonizing experience for her. Kate loved people, loved interaction, loved conversation, be it feather light chit-chat with a friend or heated intellectual debate with people whose views she did not share; she was equally adept at either. From Chris, she was getting nothing, and it was starting to prove frustrating. Each time she made an enquiry – for instance about his life before the Interveners or how he had discovered his gift or his experiences since meeting the gang – it was rebuffed by his staunch silence.

It was about three quarters of the way into the journey that it happened. Chris's body seized up, causing the car to swerve, which led a chorus of beeping horns. Kate quickly, instinctively and with a coolness that surprised even herself grabbed the wheel. She swung her leg over to the driver's side, kicked Chris's out of the way and squeezed the brakes, pulling over to the side of the road and shutting off the engine.

She knew full-well what was happening – Chris was having a second Vision. This time something was different, however. Chris appeared to be in a much deeper state of anguish; more so than during his previous Visions. More so than during *any* Vision Kate had witnessed in her admittedly still short tenure as an Intervener. All the blood seemed to have drained from his face. His eyes – usually so vacant during the Vision process – were squeezed shut, and Kate thought she was able to make out a teardrop rolling down his cheek, though it could so easily have been a stray bead of sweat. No sooner had his body finally relaxed itself once than he had restarted the engine and, without checking for oncoming traffic, he had performed a U-turn.

Kate looked at him, aghast. 'What the Hell are you doing? You're not going to Intervene in the Vision you have just had, surely? You know the rules. Number Five. You're not allowed to abandon an Intervention attempt to attend another one. You have to finish this one first. We're nearly there!'

Chris glared at her. 'Fuck you! Fuck the rules!'

It was Kate this time who fell silent, dumbstruck (if not slightly intimidated) by the sudden ferocity being displayed by her colleague. He had been nothing other than consistently placid during the short time she had known him. This sea change had sprung from Chris's most recent Vision, which Kate knew must have been no ordinary premonition. She dared not offer any more questions or suggestions, however; nor did she dare attempt to persuade him to reduce his speed, though he was going well above the limit and it scared her.

Despite the unlawful and dangerous speeds being travelled, it was a long and intense ride back to the Mansion. When they arrived, Chris made a beeline straight for the Vision Room, Kate dutifully following in his wake. Before she had reached the room, however, Chris had locked the door.

It was with a pleading and panic-stricken stare and shaking hands that Chris eventually returned. In a hushed tone more akin to the one Kate was used to, albeit one cut with urgency, Chris asked his new colleague if she would drive. A hurried walk back to the fleet of cars followed. Kate – trying her best not to enjoy the process of choosing between the luxury vehicles – opted not to return to the Rolls Royce, instead choosing the Porsche.

Chris spoke the address into the computer – a beach twenty-six miles away.

Kate instinctively knew by her partner's hand-wringing and jolty head movements that she needed to put her foot down, though it was never more than around fifteen miles an hour above the limit. The two had travelled for a number of miles before Kate dared to venture forth the question she had longed to ask ever since Chris's most recent Vision.

'Are you okay, Chris? I mean, you don't have to talk to me if you don't want, but you seem really upset about this one. I'm all ears if that's what you want.'

Kate placed her left hand on Chris's knee and squeezed it gently. A trace of a smile formed on either side of Chris's lips. Her touch seemed to calm him.

It was at least a minute before he replied and when he did so, it was with both a softness and a sadness. Kate let him talk without interjection but listened to what he had to say intently and with great fascination. His sentences were punctuated by long pauses, as if he was building up the courage to continue speaking.

'The Vision I had...it was of an older couple swimming in the sea. A big tide came and swept them away. The thing is, I know the people in it. They're my parents.' Kate's stomach sank. She suddenly appreciated the urgency of the Intervention. 'I haven't seen them since I joined the Interveners. Well, since I moved out, really, when I was seventeen. I'd fallen on some hard times. Started hanging around with some bad kids in my last couple of years at school. My grades started to fall and I got into drugs in a big way. Well, started off small, cannabis and what have you, but worked my way up. I even did heroine once. I did a lot of acid, too. So when the Visions came, I just thought they were some horrible side-effect of the drugs, like a sort of flashback to something that never actually happened or a bad trip emerging out of nowhere. I had no idea I was psychic. Anyhow, things went from bad to worse. I finished school without even sitting my final exams and I became unbearable at home. My folks knew what I was up to. They tried to help me, but when I kept going back to the drugs, they eventually kicked me out. I moved into a right shit-hole and tried my hand at all sorts of crappy part-time jobs in an attempt to pay the rent, all the while feeding my filthy habits. Of course, it was those same habits that kept costing me the jobs, and before I knew it, I was out on the street, begging for change. What little I did get, I spent on scraps of food and drugs. I ate *dog* food once. Fucking dog food, just so I had enough money to buy my next fix. All the while, I was angry. Man, I was just so angry. I hated my parents for abandoning me like that. I vowed they'd die without me seeing them again. Or, probably more likely, that I would. Anyway, that's when the Interveners came in.' He smiled, gazing out into the middle distance. 'They saved my life, really. I mean, I know that's what they do anyway, but you see what I mean. One day I was out there on the street, stick-thin and half-frozen, when this old fella came along. His name was Lars. He's dead now. He told me all about the Interveners, explained about the Visions I was having. He can't have been talking to me for more than two minutes before I found myself in the back of his car, gobbling up the sandwiches he'd brought for me. Those guys became my family. They worked with me night and day to help me kick my habits. They cared about me. I loved them. Hell, I still do. Even Nigel. In fact, he was the one who gave me the most support to kick my addictions, never giving up on me even when I stole some of his lottery money and fell back into my bad habits. They didn't pay me at first, you see. I was the only one who didn't get a wage, cause they knew full well what I would spend it on. They gave me what I needed most – love, support, a roof over my head and food in my belly.'

Chris fell silent for a good few minutes. Kate eventually decided it was appropriate for her to start talking again.

'Wow. What a story. You poor thing. I mean, I had no idea – none of the others has ever mentioned any of this. But, there's one thing I just don't understand – why don't you talk?'

'I hate it, Kate. I hate all of this. I hate the job I do. Death is our daily bread – like an undertaker or something. I can't stand getting the Visions and the pain they bring. Yes, I've saved lives – but I've seen people die, too. Loads of them. People I just haven't been able to reach in time – you know what I'm talking about. Think of how you felt when you couldn't rescue that girl – well that's happened to me probably a hundred times now. And I keep seeing their faces. When I'm asleep. When I'm awake, too, in those long, god-forsaken days we spend in that house waiting for the Visions; they just appear. They haunt me. I tell you, this is no way to lead a life. So I think I just got a bit shell-shocked one day, and found it hard to join in with conversations. It soon started to snowball, just like my drug addictions all those years ago. The rest of them, they seem to handle it all so well. Not me. I don't talk because I just don't want to talk. Don't want to engage in this weird and horrid little world I've found myself in. I know I could have left many times, but where to? What to?'

Chris continued to pour his heart out to Kate and she continued to listen. The conversation only ceased towards the end of the journey when Chris could see it was to be a matter of just minutes until his parents' potential death. He glanced at his watch every few seconds, then immediately at the navigation system to see that they were still on track. They were, but only just. Even a small traffic jam and it would be game over (though Kate hoped if there was such a thing ahead, Chris would be the one to pick it up in advance and take a detour). A string of red traffic lights and they would be too late to Intervene.

Kate applied a little extra pressure on the accelerator as the last few miles were upon them.

As they arrived at the beach, Chris darted from the car and ran until his parents were in view. He could see they were getting changed in preparation for their swim. He had done it.

Preventing his victims' deaths by altering the course of their day was an easy act in this case; all Chris needed to do was hug his parents. It was a long and tearful embrace, full of sobbed apologies. Chris did not even notice the giant wave which was supposed to engulf his parents crashing down on the shore before returning empty-handed to the sea.

He eventually returned to the car but did not get in.

'Kate, I need to leave you now. I'm not coming back to the Interveners. Although we make it our life's work to get in the way of fate, I believe it was fate itself that brought me here today, to be reunited with my family. I'm going home, Kate. Say goodbye to the gang for me, please, because there's no way I can go back and face them. Tell them I said thanks. For everything.'

Chris leaned through the open window and hugged Kate briefly before walking back to his still emotional parents.

And so the staffing at the Mansion changed once again, Kate's entrance being followed relatively closely by Chris's exit.

When Kate returned to the house later that day and told the gang the news, they were inevitably upset; they had lost a friend and, perhaps even more significantly, had lost an Intervener. Kate's reward for her part in the day's proceedings was to be docked a day's wages by an angry Gordon as punishment for her assistance in breaking rule Number Five. She was warned that under no circumstances were any more rules to be broken, and if they were that much tougher sanctions would be imposed.

None of the Interveners ever heard from Chris again, and nor was any contact attempted.

And then there were five.

Chapter Seventeen

Kate and Pete were lying in bed, on the surface of it just as normal couple. Of course, they were anything but. Neither of them knew of any other families whose numbers included a househusband – a situation that had arisen when Pete's time as a builder had ended due to a workplace injury which had yet to heal. Not that he was in any great rush to get back to work – he had come to enjoy his role as a home-maker. Kate liked it that way too – she felt a warm glow when she returned home to see him attaching adhesive clothes to princesses in Lola's sticker books, or plaiting her hair ready for her classmate's party (a skill she had yet to master). She knew her daughter was getting a good deal. Of course, it was also nice to return to an immaculately clean and tidy home, and walk into the smell of a freshly-cooked dinner. Besides, she earned much more than Pete (much, much more now, though not all of the money was making its way into their joint bank account). And Pete himself seemed happier – less stressed. This in turn made him more thoughtful, more considerate, more attentive. She appreciated that it couldn't busy easy for Pete on those rare occasions when he went to the pub with 'the lads', but she doubted anyone in her world had a better husband than she.

This was not what stopped them being a normal couple, though. Surely none of Kate's friends, and none of Pete's, were leading any kind of double-life (let alone one so unbelievable). Every minute she spent with her husband was a lie.

She flicked through a magazine. He put down his iPad.

'Sweetie, I had a thought earlier on.'

Kate removed her reading glasses and put them on the bedside table. She doubted she was going to like what Pete had to say.

'O-kay...'

'I don't actually know your new work address! I probably should.'

Her instincts were right. It wasn't that his tone was accusing or suspicious or anything, but this sort of prying could only possibly be a bad thing for Kate.

'Should you? Why?'

Pete chortled. 'Why? Well, why not? I mean, what if, God forbid, Lola has an accident or something and I can't reach you on your mobile?'

That wasn't the reason for his asking and Kate knew it. Pete was exactly the type to put together a showy romantic gesture - have a bouquet of overpriced flowers delivered to her workplace or swing by with a picnic hamper or something. He'd done it before, at her old place, and she'd hated it, though of course her female colleagues had gushed and fawned (and the male ones had looked vaguely pissed off that other husbands were setting this kind of bar). She needed to mull over her options, and fast.

Option one - she could tell him the actual address of her actual new workplace. Then hope to God he never actually visited it. The stately old Mansion looked nothing like the small business she had told him about. The game would be up, instantly.

Option two - she could give him a fake address. It would be easy enough to make something up on the spot. Any of the city centre streets with which she was so familiar would do. All she had to do was stick a number in front of it - 8 Market Square or 22b Chaucer Street or some such. Of course, as soon as he actually swung by - for he inevitably would at some point - he would find out she did not work there. If that happened, all she would do would be pile on another layer of lies when questioned that evening. *Oh God, did I tell you 8 Market Square? It's 18!* Or *Did I really say 22b? I am a silly moo! It's 22a.* A further round of lies would then be required, but she would cross that bridge when she came to it - it would at least give her a bit of breathing space and get her out of her current predicament.

She went with option three. She unbuttoned her pyjama top - itself not remotely sexy, but she knew that what was underneath it would totally derail her husband.

He grinned sheepishly. 'And what do you think you're doing, Madame?'

She adopted a low, husky tone. 'It's what you're doing that counts. Or rather, who you're doing. I really, really don't want to talk about work right now.' She slid off her pyjama bottoms and positioned her naked body on top of Pete's groin. She peeled off his T-shirt. She wasn't in the mood for sex one tiny bit - getting back to her magazine or drifting off to sleep were both more appealing options - but she was an adequate enough actress to pull it off. Pull it off was exactly what she did next, walking her hand down to Pete's already erect penis and bashing away. The more vigour at this point, she reasoned, the speedier the actual act would be. His eyes rolled back and his toes curled - she knew full well he wasn't thinking about her work address any more.

Eventually he pushed her off and they switched around. Pete made his way inside her and began his process. He was, as Kate had to admit he always was, an attentive and considerate lover, just as interested in getting his wife to her climax as he was in getting himself there. He kissed her neck and first stroked then tugged at her hair - all the things he knew she loved. He ran his fingertips the length and breadth of her body. Almost begrudgingly, Kate was beginning to enjoy it, and when the end came relatively quickly, she knew she only had herself to blame for her own sense of disappointment. He cuddled and nuzzled her afterwards, and, as per their usual post-coital routine, was snoring soundly within a couple of minutes. Kate mulled over options one and two once more, in preparation for the next time he asked (though she did feel that option three still had a bit of life left in it yet and would buy her more time if need be).

Chapter Eighteen

Fortunately for Kate, the usual Morning Ballet distracted Pete just as much as had the previous night's intercourse. The three of them danced and skirted around each other in the kitchen as they frantically got ready for the day ahead. Bread was pushed into the toaster and popped back out of it. Pete waltzed back and forth between the fridge and the worktop, carrying many and various food items from one to the other as he prepared lunch, twirling and dodging to avoid his wife and daughter as they wove in and out of his path, all the while attempting to grab mouthfuls of toast. Lola stretched and ducked, looking high and low for her lost book bag, ignoring her mother's gentle scolds for yet again misplacing her valuable items - scolds which subsided as Kate realised that, as was seemingly the case every other day, she did not know where she had put her car keys - cue a sequence of pocket patting, cushion flipping and exasperated sighs. Coats were zipped up, kisses planted on cheeks and with a final flourish of keystrokes, the alarm code was set. It was the usual start of the day chaos and it was never unwelcome - it was simply part of the fabric of family life for the Jensons. For Kate today, it was even more welcome than usual.

  Of course, for her this was all a charade - whilst she had indeed lost (and found) her car keys, it wouldn't have mattered one iota if she had been late for work, as such a concept did not exist at Interveners Incorporated. There was no clocking in and no clocking out, and she had only kept to the same strict start time as her old job to avoid arousing suspicion.

  The start of her working day was in stark contrast to her manic breakfast - it was snail-paced and uneventful, Vision-free for all five of the staff. There were many days like this at the Mansion, and on some of them Kate resolved to exert herself in some way, so that it at least felt SOMETHING akin to a day at work and she could exit the day with some semblance of satisfaction - helping Sally in the garden, cleaning out the guttering, or even something to stretch her brain like attempting to learn a few basic chords on the acoustic guitar lying around in the living room. She had purchased a book and DVD especially. She was nothing short of terrible at it, but she enjoyed the sense of challenge and endeavour.

On those days, the feeling of trying, struggling and ultimately failing at something was preferable to the feeling of coasting through the day.

On other such days, however, coasting was all she wanted to do. Today, she just felt like dossing - and doss she did. She idled away the entire morning scrolling through endless updates on various social media sites, learning nothing of value from anyone - none of her friends, school friends, family or former colleagues were offering up anything remotely juicy or titillating, and nor were the celebrities she followed. She found the process increasingly tedious and frustrating.

So you've rustled up a chicken curry which you apparently find camera-worthy? Well, guess what world? I'm psychic!

Your kid has just swum a hundred metres? Bravo. I've saved three lives this week. Where's my recognition?

Suddenly she itched and yearned to brag about her current life - hated more than ever being surreptitious. She amused herself by typing status updates then deleting them at the last moment, all of which informed the world about her new vocation.

FFS, will SOMEONE die out there so I can save the day? #bored

Lovin' my new job peeps - I get to sit on my arse all day then swan around in fancy cars! lol #charmedlife

Not to mention my 10k pay rise #justsayin

This ate away the time nicely until her favourite part of the day. Kate found she felt a particular twinge of joy over her new employment come lunchtime. Daily, she found herself recalling lunches at her old job, which, nine times out of ten, were little more than an exercise in putting food into her body as quickly as she could so that she could get back to work. More often than not, she would find herself with a sandwich in her left hand and a mouse in the right, still ploughing through her to-do list or emailing a client. She didn't even have the time to chew her food properly and most days she could be done and dusted within five minutes. No human conversation; no respite from the madness of the day; no semblance of enjoyment. Lunch was just another duty.

Lunchtimes in the Mansion were a different entity altogether. They were long and leisurely, lax and languid. Pete still made Kate's sandwiches every day, and these were certainly an option should she find herself alone at the Mansion for whatever reason (something that had yet to happen), or should she feel peckish by mid-morning. Usually, though, one of the crew rustled up a hot lunch for the others (often three courses), and Pete's lovingly crafted sandwiches made their way to the bin.

Each and every one of her colleagues was quite the chef - and why wouldn't they be? They had the time to develop and refine their culinary skills. Conversely, Kate - who was still new to the organisation and who hardly ever needed to cook for her family - was inevitably not up to her workmates' high standards and much preferred being cooked for than cooking, though she vowed that if she was in the Intervening business for the long haul, she too would learn to serve up such delightful and ambitious cuisine.

It wasn't the food she enjoyed most - though she enjoyed that thoroughly, eating at such a slow pace that she was able to savour every forkful. It was the company and the camaraderie. Engaging in solitary pursuits for parts of the day was a necessary strategy for the Interveners, who otherwise ran the risk of becoming sick of each other. But come lunchtime - half past twelve until half past one every day - everyone came together. Dined together and chatted together. Talking shop was strictly forbidden and the only way anyone was exempt from this wonderful routine was if they were having a Vision or attending an Intervention. It was here that Kate found she really got to know her peers, as they regaled each other with long and candid stories about their lives and former lives in a relaxed and unguarded manner - the loves lost, the glittering successes and crushing failures of their former careers, their personal triumphs, their personal tragedies. The stories she enjoyed most were those of Gordon, whose stock was seemingly boundless. Whether this was because he had lived such a long and rich life, or whether he was a skilled fantasist, Kate cared not a jot. She listened to him weave his yarns as a small child would listen to a parent reading stories at bedtime - chin resting on two hands, eyes unblinking and transfixed, and mouth closed. She enjoyed Sally's stories in a very different way - where Gordon's were warm and bittersweet, Sally's were raucous and rude, usually tales of mismatched ex-boyfriends or debauched weekends with her girlfriends. She made Kate belly laugh. Zak, too, told of romantic conquests, though she found his stories to be brim-full with bravado and not nearly as charming. Nigel's stories were never funny ones, and nor were they embellished or padded out - rather, they were laconic and slightly sad accounts of his former life, and the wife and children he had left behind.

Kate often found herself arriving at the table early, eager for the hum of conversation to kick in - and likewise, she often left it at a time much closer to two, mostly at the same time as Sally. She would leave the table not feeling frantic or stressed or frustrated as she would at the end of her lunch in her accounting days, but rather totally chilled and relaxed. At times like those, the prospect of returning to her old line of work was simply unthinkable. She had, in so many ways, lucked out.

Chapter Nineteen

Kate jumped as she walked through the Mansion doors. There was a stranger in the room. A very strange-looking stranger at that - squat and hunched, his thick-lensed glasses enlarging his pupils to huge proportions, his thinning hair worn in a mullet. He was in the sofa, typing frantically into a small laptop computer. Her blood froze and she found herself rooted to the spot. He looked up. He said nothing to Kate, instead returning to his work.

'Erm...hello? Who are you?'

He shook his head and continued typing.

She spoke in a volume not loud enough to be shouting but more urgent than her normal register. 'Gordon?'

The strange man shook his head once again.

'Sal? Sally?'

No response.

'Nigel? Zak? Someone?"

Still the man continued to hammer away at his laptop keys. Still no one seemed to be coming to her rescue. It was a peculiar and unsettling sight to behold, a different face in the Mansion. An alien. Kate had only ever seen her colleagues in the building, for good and obvious reasons. Who on Earth was this man? A new Intervener? Or something much more sinister - had their secret identity been uncovered?

Gordon walked down the stairs, towelling his long, grey hair. She had never felt quite so glad to see him. 'Ah, good morning, Kate! I see you've met Marco!'

'Well, not really Gordon! He hasn't introduced himself!'

Waddington chuckled. 'And indeed he won't, my dear! Marco is a mute. Or at least as far as we can gather. I've known him for many years now and he's never said a word.'

'Is he...one of us? What's the deal here? What's he doing?'

'He's one of us in the sense that he knows about what we do, but he doesn't possess our psychic abilities. And he's one of us insofar as he works periodically at the Mansion - but he's also one us in the wider sense. He works for all of the Intervention

Centres across the land. He is, I don't think it overblown to say, a technical genius. What he doesn't know about computers - and more to the point the computers we use in the Vision Room - isn't worth knowing. The technology at each centre varies enormously, but nothing is ever too much of a challenge for Marco. At present he's doing his annual diagnostics test, wirelessly transmitting data back and forth to the computers in the Vision Room, seeing if the old girl is operating at her fullest capabilities. If not, he'll go in there, take her apart, clean her up, work his magic and get her back up to speed. In a way - in a very real way - he's a lifesaver too. If the machinery here wasn't fully tuned, we wouldn't be able to pick up in the signals in our brains when we get Visions. If the whole thing went belly up, lives would be lost. We've each of us developed enough in terms of rudimentary maintenance skills to solve minor technological issues. But if something goes really wrong, we ring him, and he comes. Not always straight away, but never too long after.'

'You ring him? I thought you said he was a mute?'

'We ring him. He picks up. We talk. We tell him what's wrong. He listens. We finish speaking and thank him. He puts the phone down and gets here pronto.'

'Where is he based?' His foreign name and olive skin were throwing her.

'I don't know!'

'Who trained him?'

'I don't know!'

'How old is he? It's really hard to tell by looking at him.'

'I don't know, but as I say, he's been with us for a very long while.'

'Who pays his wages?'

'Ah, that one I do know. I pay him every time he visits. Cash in hand. And I pay him handsomely - he's worth every penny. I have no idea whether the money I give him is in line with what the other centres pay him. All I know is he doesn't complain.'

'How did he become involved with the Interveners?'

'I have absolutely no idea how he stumbled into our fold. If he would only talk I suppose we would know. He's a true enigma. Mystery Marco. A secret weapon in our already secret organisation.'

Marco closed the lid of his laptop, nodded at Gordon and ignored Kate. Gordon made his way to the Mansion safe, took out an envelope thick with what must have been cash and handed it to Marco. He nodded once more and exited the Mansion.

'He makes Chris seem like a right old chatterbox, doesn't he Gord?'

'That he does, dear. God forbid he goes the same way as Chris, though - Chris was replaceable. We haven't replaced him yet, admittedly, but he IS replaceable. There ARE other people out there who share his abilities - as you have proved more than adequately. If anything happens to Marco, we are in deep, deep trouble.'

Chapter Twenty

The days and weeks rolled by – or, more precisely, dragged on. As the novelty of her role wore off, Kate found her time at the Mansion more and more tedious and uneventful. She was, however, becoming increasingly successful in her role as an Intervener, desensitising herself to the horrors she was witnessing, both in her Visions and, from time to time, in her failed Intervention attempts.

If the adrenalin-fuelled highs of her rescue missions had dwindled, then it was also true that the grief she felt as part of the Intervention process was disappearing too. She continued to get Visions, the frequency of which varied – on one day she managed two successful Interventions but it was to be the best part of a week before her next Vision. She was making an average of four rescue missions per week, itself about the average number made by any Intervener.

She had found that road accidents in their variety of forms were the stock-in-trade of the Intervener, accounting for almost half of her Visions. Most of the time these required nothing more than a well-timed press of the button on a nearby Pelican crossing and - voila - the pedestrian / motorcyclist / truck driver who should have been killed was afforded a narrow escape. As per usual nobody was any the wiser - it was as simple and routine as that. Often Kate's pulse rate remained unchanged throughout this increasingly mundane procedure and the sense of gratification was, she found, diminishing.

Again to try to maintain some of the giddy thrill and magic of her Interventions, she occasionally found herself deliberately procrastinating when she located her victims, leaving increasingly precious little time before their would-be deaths.

One of the hardest parts of her job was maintaining its secrecy and leading this double life. She also struggled with the 9-to-5 aspect of it, never quite sure whether it was the potential victims or her family who should take precedent and thus performing an act akin to plate spinning. Hence, there were a number of occasions on which she 'worked late', and even the odd Saturday when Kate visited the Mansion to tend to a Vision, telling Pete she was shopping with old friends.

On the other hand, there were weeks when she resolved to treat the job as just that – a job – and so refused to be an Intervener even one minute before or one minute after her working day (though no document had ever been drawn up stating her official hours and nor, indeed, had Gordon even suggested what those hours should be. It was Kate who had allocated herself the hours that would constitute a working day – in essence the same as they were during her days as an accountant).

It was during a particularly eventful week in early December that Kate discovered she had the capability both to prioritise her job over her family as well as vice-versa. Early in the week, she had awoken dripping in sweat after a dream which could just as easily have been a Vision as a horrible nightmare. In it, a young cyclist, perhaps in his late teens or early twenties, had been travelling in darkness without protective or reflective gear and was hit by a lorry, flying high into the air and dying upon impact with the concrete. Unable to return to sleep, her curiosity got the better of her and she found herself powerless to resist visiting the Mansion to check. It was, indeed, a Vision, and she and Nigel were able to successfully Intervene. Kate was back in bed in time to catch an hour's sleep and, though she had a story prepared about going for a drive as she couldn't drift off, her husband was actually none the wiser.

Later on in the week, much the same thing happened again – once again Kate woke up in a cold sweat after yet another nightmare / Vision. This one involved a shop sign falling onto a passer-by's head. However, Lola was performing as Mary in the infant nativity play in the morning, for which Kate had secured a day off. The prospect of falling asleep during the play, as well as the equally bleak prospect of de-icing her windscreens at two in the morning again, was enough to convince Kate to pull the covers back over her shoulders and drift back to sleep. As Lola strode onto the stage with a tea towel on her head, Kate smiled proudly, clapped wildly and fished around for her camera, taking not even a moment to consider the death she had allowed to happen.

Chapter Twenty-One
Whether it was because she was the only other female Intervener or whether it was the fact that she was the bubbliest, funniest, most fun-loving, most unguarded, chattiest and (in the best way possible) rudest member of the crew, she knew not, but Kate found herself naturally and instinctively drawn towards Sally. If she arrived at work last and her four colleagues were scattered around the Mansion, then it was to Sally that she

gravitated. If Sally was in the throes of a Vision, Kate always hoped it would be her that she chose to accompany her when she came round - and more often than not it was. Likewise, if Kate herself felt those familiar pre-Vision twinges, she was glad if Sally was closest in proximity. Time with her was never awkward, forced or strained - she was never hard work. Gordon, for all his paternal warmth, belonged to another generation. So did Nigel - and he was a world-class grump to boot. Zak's cockiness could be grating, and they had nothing in the way of common ground - at least Nigel had once had a family, so there was that tenuous connection. Zak was interested in video games, workout routines and philandering - and none of these things featured in Kate's world. So journeys to faraway Intervention scenes with him could be protracted, mismatched affairs. But Sally - Sally was different.

They had discovered a great many shared interests in the duration of their blossoming friendship thus far. Some things they both already liked (a sizeable number of handsome male celebrities, certain reality TV shows, Monopoly), and some things they had grown to like upon the other person's suggestion. On this particular occasion, however, it was the afore-mentioned Monopoly that was binding them together. It wasn't that the others were not allowed to play - they'd had several full and fun mornings or afternoons playing as a five. But if the others were unavailable or didn't want to play, Kate and Sally pressed ahead anyway - whereas if either of them was unable to play for whatever reason, it simply didn't happen. This time it was just the two of them - Nigel was in another part of the country on a lottery run, Gordon was shopping and Zak was having a day off, playing Laser Tag with his brother.

Following the usual routine of out-of-body vacantness and then visible agony, Sally found herself in the throes of yet another Vision. As she returned to her normal state, her ashen face quickly turned into a smirking one.

'Well, I'll pop in the Vision Room and get the time of death, but I think I'll skip the address this time - I know exactly where this one is. You'll like it.'

Kate's curiosity was piqued. 'Well go on then, spill the beans!'

'Huntingley Manor.'

'The theme park?'

'The tinpot, shithole theme park, yes, that's right. Used to go there all the time when I was a kid. If my Vision is anything to go by, it doesn't seem to have changed much.'

'So what's the story?'

'Well there's a roller coaster there called - get this - 'Death Wish'. Ah, the irony is going to go so unappreciated! Anyway, it was an old, rusty piece of crap the first time I went on it, so I'm amazed nobody's been killed on it so far. Today, a young lady, late teens or early twenties I'd say, is going to go on it and her safety harness is going to come loose midway through. She's going to cling desperately to the bar as the carriage starts to climb the second loop, but she's going to get flung out as it turns upside down. The good news is that she won't hit the concrete but the bad news is that a spiked railing is going to stop that happening. It will impale her.'

'Ouch. Except it won't of course, because two ace Interveners are going to save the day. So get that skinny little arse in the Vision Room and let's have a fun day out!'

'It's Huntingley Manor - so let's just have a day out.'

Sally returned from the Vision Room with the name Janey Lloyd and a four hour timeframe. The two unanimously chose the Jag and headed to Huntingley, which was just under ninety minutes away from the Mansion. It was a cloudy, slightly chilly day. The journey passed breezily with Sally regaling Kate with tales of misspent summer's days at Huntingley Manor and the various boys she'd either met there or taken there, alongside the various minor sex acts performed with, on or by said boys. The duo's bond was growing with every mile passed. Ninety percent cent of the talking today was being done by Sally, the remainder being short, generic responses to her often saucy anecdotes, but Kate didn't mind one bit.

They arrived at Huntingley Manor a little shy of lunchtime and paid without queuing. Kate surveyed the park. 'Holy Guacamole, this place is a couple of hundred customers short of being a backdrop for a Scooby Doo episode - The Abandoned Old Theme Park.'

'I know. I'd say it was the weather, but I just think it's the general crapness of the place. I just can't believe it's still standing. It's a double good deed we're doing today, saving not only a life but a theme park too. The accident would have been the nail in this old place's coffin. They'd have shut it down for sure.'

'So what's the plan? I actually reckon we've got a fair chance of seeing the girl - are we just going to stall her or something? Hey - we could go and buy a notepad from the gift shop and ask her to take part in a survey or something.'

'Fraid not, honey. Not this time. What you've got to appreciate is that that safety harness is surely going to snap today whatever happens and whoever it happens to. If we delay Janey then someone else will sit in her seat and THEY will be the ones pushing up daisies. We need to think bigger.'

'So what have you got?'

'I said we.'

'Why do I get the feeling you're testing me here?'

'Think of it as coaching.'

Kate was incredulous. 'Oh my God, seriously? You have an idea and you're prepared to let this poor girl die a particularly horrible death by withholding it just to put the pressure on me? Sally, come on!'

Sally giggled, which exacerbated Kate's frustration. 'Babe, I never said I had an idea! I don't as a matter of fact!'

'Oh, for Christ's sake, how can you be so calm? The girl whose life is hanging in the balance is someone's daughter! I know you haven't got any kids, but show some compassion will you?'

'Kate, I wouldn't do the job I do if I didn't have compassion. I'm doing this for you. Just trust me. This could be the making of you. This is a big league Intervention. In the morning, this place is either going to be all over the newspapers, or else it's going to continue its miserable little existence and nobody will be any the wiser. And it's you who's going to decide its fate.'

'Gee thanks, Sal. That's a nice feeling.'

'You'll think of something. Then you really will be thanking me. We've got a few hours yet. I'm off to ride the log flume while you rack your brains. The best thing about this place being so shite is that you don't have to queue. Text me or ring me if you need me. If not I'll be back here in an hour. Kisses.'

Kate stuck two fingers up at her friend, who reciprocated the gesture, and the two of them burst into laughter. Kate made her way to the cafe just opposite 'Death Wish', ordered a pastry and a coffee and gazed at the ride, studying it in the hope that a wave of inspiration would hit her. Again and again she watched the same routine of excited customers stepping into their carriages, letting out little screams as they began their slow backwards ascent up a diagonal slope, bigger ones as the ride clunked to a brief stop at the top, and bigger ones still as it began its rapid descent down the same slope, the ebb and flow of the screams matching the twists, turns and loops of the ride.

She did not know which of the seats was the 'Death Seat', but she conceded that this was irrelevant anyway. She realised that her job was to stop the ride altogether, not simply stop Janey from going on it. And not just stop it temporarily either, though she was sure that must have been possible - there had to be some sort of emergency button somewhere in the vicinity of the ride. No, the ride needed to be closed for the day - and some sort of action needed to be taken to stop it opening in the morning.

All of this seemed a long way removed from holding an old lady back for a few seconds so that she didn't step into traffic. Sally was right - this was big league stuff.

As a light drizzle started to cover the park, Kate wandered over to the gift shop to buy a poncho, which she put on as she queued for her next coffee. She mulled over joining the always short queue and actually going on the ride in the hope that that would inspire her. It wasn't the 1-in-48 chance that she would pick the 'Death Seat' that stopped her - she was prepared to gamble with those odds, and besides which the accident wasn't due to take place yet. It was actually her fear of white knuckle rides that was preventing her from leaving the cafe. She would have done it, she told herself, if it definitely meant a life would have been saved. She ordered her third coffee.

Maybe it was the caffeine, maybe the pressure, most likely both, but she was becoming increasingly jittery, her leg moving up and down and her nails finding their way to her teeth without her realising. Her thoughts were becoming wilder, less practical, more far-fetched. She thought of buying a back pack and placing it somewhere innocuous looking in the hope it would appear to be a bomb and the place would be evacuated. She realised people would probably just see it for what it appeared to be, which was a lost bag, to be taken to Lost Property. She even thought of trying to start a small fire, again to clear the park, but she realised this was far too risky. She couldn't possibly jeopardise the lives of these few hundred people just to save one of them. That was just basic Intervening code of practice.

After an almost two hour absence, Sally returned. It didn't take her long to track her friend down in the cafe.

'That was fun. Just like old times, except minus the love bites. Pretty much did the whole park, except for 'Death Trap' here. Obviously. So is the deed done?'

'Yes, Sally, it is, and I've drunk these four coffees by means of celebration.'

'Okay, I'm sensing by the sarcastic tone and the worried look on your face that the deed is, in fact, not done. Right, come on then, let's get those thinking caps on. Two heads are better than one and all that jazz.'

The two sat there in silence, looking down at the table, up at the ride and seldom at each other.

'Sally, I swear to God, if you've got an idea and you're not telling me, there may be another death at Huntingley Manor today.'

'Honestly, I haven't! This is new ground for me too.'

The minutes ticked away. It was Sally who eventually broke the intense silence.

'Kate, I've got nothing. And I hate to alarm you, but Janey is being strapped into her seat as we speak.'

'Oh God! Oh God, Sally, what are we going to do?'

Kate's panicked tone had finally rubbed off on Sally, whose eyes were darting between the ride and her friend. 'I don't know, babe! I really couldn't think of anything! It wasn't a test! I'm sorry!'

'Right, that's it. I'm ringing Gordon. I'm sure he'll know what to do.'

Kate took out her phone. With great efficiency, she scrolled through her contacts and jabbed her thumb on Gordon's name. It was ringing. And then it wasn't ringing. She looked at the screen - it was blank. The battery had died. And pretty soon Janey was about to follow suit.

'Shit! Shit, shit, shit. You try.'

Sally took out her own phone. She bit her lip as she stared at the screen. 'No signal! Oh, Kate!'

'Now what?'

All the riders were now secured into their seats and were awaiting the ride to be put in motion. Sally had broken into a sob. 'Kate, come on. Let's just go. Let's run as fast as we can in the next minute and get as far away from this as possible. I can't be part of what's about to happen.'

She grabbed Kate's arm. Kate immediately knocked it away. That first familiar clunk, signifying that the carriage was about to start its slow backwards descent, acted as a kind of trigger. Kate sprinted towards the ride's entrance, yelling for the operator to stop as she barged through the small queue awaiting what they assumed would be the next ride. All the while, the ride was crawling steadily backwards, and Janey was gaining elevation. Kate hurdled over the gates, jumping onto and over the tracks to where a particularly gormless young ride operator chewing gum had his hands on the controls of the ride.

'Stop this ride now! Please!'

He gazed at her blankly. It wasn't that he was being deliberately non-compliant: he just seemed perplexed by exactly what was happening. As Kate heard the second clunk, meaning that the coaster had reached the peak of its backwards ascent, she yanked the young man out of the way and pushed the biggest, reddest button she could find. The carriage remained frozen at the top of the tracks.

'Listen to me, I was just on the ride and I'm pretty sure one of the safety harnesses was starting to come loose. I didn't think anything of it at the time, but as I was watching the ride starting up, I noticed that the girl sat in my seat looked like she wasn't strapped in properly. She seemed to be wriggling about. Bring the ride back down and I'll show you which one.'

The operator took his radio out of its holster. 'Mr Archer, can you come to 'Death Wish', please? It's an emergency.' He looked back at Kate. 'I only started on this ride today. I just know how to make it start and stop.'

Kate started shifting around on the spot. A disconcerted rumble of noise started to appear from the carriage. People around the ride had started to congregate. It was a full three minutes between Kate stopping the ride and the park manager appearing, though it seemed longer, and in that time a considerable crowd had gathered, many of them running towards the ride, eager not to miss any of what was clearly an unfolding drama. She could no longer pick Sally out of the crowd. Fingers were pointing up at the carriage, and people were pulling out mobile phones either to film the event or tell friends and family all about it. Sweat dripped from Kate's forehead.

The manager arrived, a large hoop of keys attached to his belt, one of which - after a brief exchange of words with the ride operator - he stuck into the machine, and pressed a button. The carriage crawled back to its destination. The passengers grumbled with a discontent seemingly aimed more at the manager than anyone or anything else.

'Madame, I can assure you our rides are tested rigorously and regularly and I'm sure you're mistaken, but would you mind showing us which of these seats you believe has the faulty safety harness?'

His patronising tone rankled her. She couldn't resist her next move. She walked up to Janey's seat and gave the bar a firm tug, at which point a snapping sound was audible and the bar swung free.

'That one I believe.'

A mixture of sounds came from the different assembled groups - those inside the carriage, those in the queue and the sizeable crowd of spectators. Some gasps were heard, and there was even a light smattering of applause, but the overall sound was an indiscriminate murmuring.

Janey looked up at Kate. 'Oh my God, you just saved my life or something!'

'Who knows? Maybe!' Kate giggled and blushed, drinking in the adulation previously denied her in her role as an Intervener. A familiar face appeared at the front of the queue: Sally's.

'Louise! Louise! Come on, we've got to get going!'

Kate joined her friend and they exited the crowd, several of whom patted Kate on the back as she left.

'Oh my God, Sal! I did it! I actually did it!'

Her friend hugged her, briefly, before continuing to usher her away from the assembled masses. 'Well done, you!'

'Hey, what was all that Louise business about?'

'I'll tell you in the car. Just enjoy your moment for now.'

'Well, let's celebrate my victory by going on some rides. Start with 'Death Wish'? Just kidding, obviously! Although I think the Teacups are calling my name!'

'I don't think anyone's going on any rides for the rest of the day, hun - looks like they're shutting the place down.'

Kate looked around. Not one attraction was in operation, all the lights were disappearing and people were stepping off the rides. Park workers were directing customers towards the exit, some of whom were arguing and questioning but most of whom were obliging.

'Well, that just about seals it, Kate. Nobody's dying here today. Hey, there's Janey again! Ah, just look at her there with all her friends, laughing away. That young life should have ended today, and it didn't, because of your actions. Doesn't that make you feel good?'

Kate smiled. 'Absolutely. Thank you.'

'Now let's bomb it towards the exit, because there's gonna be a big bottleneck of folk wanting their money back. We need to get back to the Mansion really. You never know - there might be another Intervention in store for us today, and I'd hate to be stuck trying to get out of the car park while it's happening.'

Within a matter of minutes, the two were back out on the open road. Kate was still buzzing.

'Woo! That felt go-oo-od! Definitely my favourite Intervention so far. Wait til the gang hears about this one.'

Sally sighed. 'Listen, babe, we're going to be keeping this one a secret. Trust me, it's for the best.'

'What? Why?'

'Look, I don't want to take anything away from you here, because you did great. I mean, wow. Talk about working well under pressure.'

'Just spit it out, Sally.'

'Gordon is going to go bonkers if he finds out HOW you Intervened. It was too public. You saved a life, and boy did everyone know about it. No one is supposed to know an Intervention has taken place, otherwise it puts our whole organisation in jeopardy. Today you're just a random woman - Louise - who might possibly have saved a young woman's life. But what if somebody there recognised you? What if questions start being asked? Let's be honest, you milked it there a bit, and you shouldn't have.'

'What? Sod off!'

'Look, don't be mad with me. Gordon will definitely dock a massive chunk of your pay if he finds out. God, he might even sack you! I'm just trying to protect my friend.'

The journey back to the Mansion continued with hardly any exchange between the two women. It was left to the radio to diffuse what would have been an uncomfortable silence.

Chapter Twenty-Two
There were, in fact, no more Interventions in store for anyone that day, and Kate killed the remaining couple of hours before heading home watching daytime television programmes about houses being renovated. Her inactivity was a glum contrast with her earlier, high adrenalin escapades. Sally put on her wellies and spent the time pulling up weeds in the damp garden. She was still there when Kate left, neither of them exchanging a goodbye.

A large glass of wine was how Kate decided to reward herself for her heroism. It would serve the dual purpose of taking the edge off of her niggles - she couldn't help but feel a little cross with Sally for the dressing down she had received, and it was eating her up. She just wasn't used to being spoken to that way - it would never have happened in her previous job, where Kate was much more used to being the one delivering sternly-worded warnings to subordinates. It was on a day like today that Kate missed being able to vent about her day to her husband, who would undoubtedly have listened intently, compassionately and without interjection, before telling Kate everything she wanted to hear about how much of a cow Sally was being, how she was probably just jealous, how Kate definitely did the right thing, etc, etc, whether he meant it or not.

It was, in fact, Pete's voice she heard next, calling her from the living room.

'Kate! Come in here quickly, darling! You've got to see this on the television!'

Kate knew exactly what it was she had to see. Her heroic endeavours had made the local news: she thought they might. Pete had paused the screen, which was showing grainy mobile phone footage shot at a distance of Janey stepping out of the carriage.

Kate's voice felt tight and high as she feigned curiosity. 'What's this honey?'

'There was almost a terrible accident at Huntingley Manor today.'

'Huntingley Manor? That old theme park?'

'That's right. Apparently this woman stopped a ride because she didn't think it looked safe, and she was right! The seat belt thing broke loose when they tested it. They're shutting the whole park down while all the rides are checked. Apparently they're trying to track her down as they're giving her lifetime VIP entry to the park when it re-opens.'

'Wow! She's a bit of a star, this mystery woman! Why are you telling me this, honey?'

'You'll never believe this.' Pete rewound the live TV feed and pressed play, pausing at the point in which Kate was yanking the safety harness open. 'How much does this woman look like you? I mean, exactly like you? Have you got a long-lost twin you haven't been telling me about?'

Kate squinted at the screen. She was thankful of the light rain that had fallen that afternoon, otherwise she would not have worn the poncho that disguised the clothes she had been (and still was) wearing. Explaining her way out of that one would have been an even taller order. 'Hmm! I suppose she does look a bit like me!'

'A bit? Same colour hair, same build, same everything!'

Kate rubbed the bridge of her nose. 'Pete, I've got something I need to confess. You need to sit down. I've been leading a secret double life. I know you think I've been doing people's accounts, but I've actually been going round saving people's lives. For I -,' she pumped her fist into the air and put on a mock-dramatic voice, 'am a modern-day superhero, and it looks like I've finally been rumbled!'

Pete laughed. 'Well that explains that one! I suppose that makes me Lois Lane or something. Jesus, as if being a house husband wasn't emasculating enough!'

Kate ruffled his hair. 'Aah, don't be silly! You're MY hero!'

Pete smiled. 'Jesus, that really does look like you, though.'

'One of those weird things, I suppose. They say everyone has a double, don't they? Mine just happened to have been visiting a nearby theme park today. Hey, look at it this way - this is the first, last and only time I'm going to let you perve over a woman on the telly. So fill your boots, son.'

'I keep telling you, I only have eyes for you - you know that!'

Kate draped her arms around her husband's neck and kissed him on the lips. 'You say all the right things. Now, how about I take you upstairs and show you some of my superhuman powers?'

Kate turned the TV off and led her grinning husband by the hand out of the room, taking a quick detour *en route* to the bedroom to grab her glass of wine.

Chapter Twenty-Three

Kate's normal commutes to work where chirpy, carefree and relaxed. Often she felt a sense of excitement as she speculated on what adventures might possibly be in store. Not today. Today she felt an inescapable dread, and a very different kind of apprehension - she had made an error yesterday. An error with at least one wonderful outcome, but an error nonetheless. Her stomach was knotted and her forehead crumpled. If and when Waddington found out exactly how she had saved that young woman's life, there would be Hell to pay. She already had one notch against her for allowing Chris to escape the fold - and so soon into her new career! He had warned her then that tougher sanctions lay in store if she broke another rule. She dreaded to think what these could be.

She was clearly terrified of the old man. Of all her remaining colleagues, it was he who seemed most capable of flipping - he who seemed most like he was harbouring a split personality. He was an unknown quantity for sure. It was also he whose respect and affirmation she craved the most: he who she was most scared of disappointing. She was already coming across as a kind of maverick or renegade - giving off the impression that she had no regard for the rules by which the rest of the Interveners abided. It wasn't true - she was just making (possibly) bad decisions in the heat of the moment.

She arrived at work: time to face the music. The only one awaiting her in the living room was Sally, who had an arduous-looking psychology textbook open on her knee.

'Morning.'

'Morning.'

The greetings were delivered more as statements that exclamations, without warmth, affection, smiles or eye contact.

'So...erm...where are the others this morning?'

'Do you mean where's Gordon?'

'Yes. That's obviously what I mean.'

'He's showering.'

'And has he...you know...'

'Mentioned anything? No. Not yet. He's been quite chipper as it happens. So he definitely doesn't know. Yet.'

This eased Kate's anxiety, but only slightly, temporarily. 'Coffee?'

'No. Thank you.'

'Just me then.'

She boiled the kettle. The tension in the air was palpable, and Kate could take it no more.

'Sal, please. Please close that book and talk to me.' She did as she was told. 'Tell me what's going to happen to me.'

'Well if you're lucky, nothing. You might just have got away with it. You were on the news last night - did you know?' Kate nodded. 'I saw it. No idea if the others did. If Zak or Nigel saw it, you'd better hope they let you know before they let Gordon know. If they do, you plead with them, reason with them, bargain with them, beg them, bribe them. Do what you need to do to stop them telling him.'

'And if Gordon already knows? Or if he does find out?'

'You're dead.'

Kate gasped. 'Eh? What, literally?'

'No, not literally. Or at least I hope not. I really can't say for sure what he'll do. I reckon that at very least you'll be losing a month's pay. More likely - you'll be out of here.'

'Sacked?'

'Sacked. You'll more than likely be kissing goodbye to this sweet little life. Back to your old job. I'm just playing Devil's Advocate here, but I think he'll see you as too much of a liability. Yesterday was a pretty big balls-up.'

Kate felt a swelling of indignation. 'Well now, hang on here, Sally. I saved a life yesterday. I prevented a really gruesome and untimely death. And as you said yesterday, I probably saved that theme park and the jobs of everyone in it. When it reopens -'

'If it reopens -'

'Okay, IF it reopens, it will be thanks to me. So why the Hell are you making me out to be the bad guy here? And, no offence here -'

'Ah, that thing people always say right before they offend someone. Brace yourself, Sal.'

'- but what were YOU planning on doing? Sweet F.A., that's what. You had nothing. And you're supposed to be more experienced than me.' Sally pursed her lips and shook her head. 'No, no, go on. Please do tell. What exactly should I have done yesterday other than what I actually did?'

'You just said it, Kate. Sweet F.A..'

'Let her die?'

'If it was a choice between letting her die and saving her in that very public way you did, then yes. Yes, you should have let her die. If there had been a third option of saving her covertly - the way that Interveners are supposed to go about their business - then clearly that would have been the one to go for.'

The two women glared at each other, neither of them blinking or conceding eye contact. The uncomfortable stand-off was broken by the rattling of the letterbox as the local and national newspapers were squeezed through it. The Interveners were all thoroughly abreast with current affairs, often reading the papers front to back as a way of passing the time - potentially bad news for Kate.

'You'd better go and see if you're still a media darling.'

Kate hurried over and grabbed the papers, bringing them back to the giant recliner. She started with the national newspaper. Her eyes darted and scanned around the pages as she looked for any reference to what had happened yesterday. Front page - nothing. Of bigger interest to the media was the Royal infidelity scandal, which spilled over to the second and third pages. Fourth and fifth pages - nothing. Sixth and seventh pages - nothing. But there it was, on the eight page. A tiny article, filling about a sixteenth of the page. The headline read: 'Theme Park Closure Over Safety Fears'. So far so innocuous. She continued reading. The article went on to explain how Huntingley Manor would be 'closed indefinitely' - that didn't sound good - until the park met strict safety regulations. The park's owner was quoted as saying that at present the funds were not available to bring the park up-to-speed. He was thankful that no one was hurt yesterday. The article mentioned 'Death Wish' as the faulty ride which triggered the investigation, but made no mention of the manner in which the fault was discovered. And that was it. No attempt had been made to emulate the television news report's angle of a mystery hero saving the day.

  She moved immediately onto the local paper. She didn't have to flick through quite as far to find the story this time - and nor did she have to look quite as hard, the article taking up around a third of the page. The headline this time read: 'Near-Death Experience for Local Lass'. Kate's heart sank - this one seemed less promising. Again the article made mention of the possibly temporary closure of the park, but was mainly focused on the experience from Janey Lloyd's point of view. Clearly pressed, she described Kate's physical appearance in great detail. The article made mention of the fact that eyewitnesses - earwitnesses in this case - had heard another lady refer to her as Louise. It concluded by asking readers if they were Louise, or knew who she was. Clearly, the initial promise of a lifetime's entry to the park was not going to be fulfilled (at least not for some time), but the paper was keen to get more mileage from the story by unmasking the hero of the hour.

  Kate pondered exactly how damaging all of this could be. She had to concede that Sally calling her by a fake name had been an excellent stroke of quick-thinking and could possibly have saved her skin (not that she was about to admit that to her at this very moment in time). However, the combination of the perfect description of her being offered up and the fact that this was an exceptionality fortuitous piece of life-saving could possibly arouse Waddington's suspicions. She made a beeline for the cutlery drawer in the kitchen and took out a pair of scissors, brought them back to the recliner and began to remove the article.

'Good morning, Kate!'

Just the sound she did not want to hear. Kate looked up and feigned cheeriness. 'And good morning to you, Gordon!'

'What on Earth are you doing with that paper, dear?'

Kate looked down at the paper, then at the scissors, then at Gordon. 'I'm...well...'

'She's being a tight-arse, that's what!' Sally shoulder-charged her playfully. 'There's a voucher for fifty per cent off her favourite face cream, and she's cutting it out. There we go, skinflint, I'll tell him even if you're too ashamed to.'

Kate chortled. 'Rumbled! Rumbled. Egg on my face.'

Gordon laughed too. 'Goodness me, Mrs Jenson! Is this your way of subtlety informing me you're not earning enough?'

'Well...'

'You keep up the good work and we'll see what we can do. How does that sound? Now, do you think you two can manage without me for a little while? I need to run a few errands in town and I'll pick up some shopping while I'm there. Nigel is feeling under the weather so I've told him to get some more sleep. Not sure where Zak is, but he'll probably be back shortly.'

'We're FINE! Go on, you, sod off. Kate and I will keep things ticking over here.'

Gordon smiled and exited.

'Sal - thanks.'

'What are friends for? Listen, missus, I'd bloody hate it if I lost you. It'd be a total boys' club if you went. You keep me sane.'

'Do you think I'll be okay?'

'I don't know, Hun. Really, I don't. If there's such a thing as karma, maybe so. You did save that girl's life. Your intentions were good. You deserve it. He's none the wiser so far - you might just have got away with it. Now, we've got a bit of girlie time. I'm gonna knock this psychology textbook on the head and we'll sit around and talk about fit celebrities we'd quite like to shag. Sound good?'

'Sounds amazing.'

Unfortunately for both of them, this was relatively short-lived, and the day had something else in store.

Chapter Twenty-Four

Kate threw her keys onto the table and slumped into the living room armchair. She was emotionally exhausted, possibly somewhat shell-shocked, by the events that had transpired. It had not been a good day at the office. Kate had experienced what was, by a long chalk, her most graphic Vision. She had Envisioned a great many people's deaths by that point, and even witnessed some of them first hand when the rescue had failed at the very last moment. There was a sort of spectrum of graphicness, and thankfully most Visions were not overly disturbing to someone who was hardening to the process, as Kate was. People being knocked into the air after being hit by a vehicle - she could handle that. People slipping and banging their heads, dying in a pool of blood - she could handle that. But this - this was different. Disturbing. If Visions were like little snuff movies playing out in the Interveners' minds, this was the worst kind imaginable.

It was a workplace accident, a dozen miles away. The victim was a middle-aged woman. Probably someone's mum. Probably still someone's daughter. Probably someone's wife. Kate tried not to imagine the life stories of those people whose lives she was trying to save, as it added to the emotional investment of the deed. She didn't need that extra pressure. She much preferred to concoct such details after the Intervention had taken place - the journey back home seemed all the more pleasurable, all the more rewarding, as she pictured those people returning home that evening to hugs and kisses from their loved ones, all of whom were unaware of Kate's heroism. This time the death was so bloody and horrific, she couldn't help herself.

It was in an elevator. The woman was alone. When she pressed the button to ascend, she didn't realise her scarf was trapped in the lift doors. As the lift started to move, she was immediately pulled to the floor, and towards the door. The scarf quickly tightened around her neck. In another moment the pressure on her neck became so immense that it snapped. In another moment still the woman's head was severed, and blood gushed out of her body, filling the lift, around which her head rolled.

As the Vision ended, Kate burst into tears. It took her several minutes to regain sufficient composure to get herself into the Vision Room, where she was hooked into the Electric Chair by a now recharged and refreshed Nigel, still too shaken to operate the fiddly equipment herself. It could have been Alpha Male instincts and it could have been paternal ones, but he was adamant that Sally should step aside and let him take the reigns. He knew this was no ordinary Vision - and Sally knew she had to bow down to his greater experience. He was a Senior Intervener after all.

A fresh wave of anguished sobbing preceded her second viewing of this appalling accident - she really didn't want to see it again, and wished there was a way to ascertain the necessary information without replaying the scene. With only fifty-five minutes to go, the rescue was achievable, but not comfortably so.

Nigel drove - what choice was there? Kate now realised one of the reasons the Interveners carried out their rescues in pairs - there was the potential for the person who had experienced the Vision to be in such an emotionally broken state that they were simply unable to conduct themselves safely. Kate couldn't have driven: if she had, she would have been putting her own life and that of the other road users in danger. Nigel was her least favourite colleague and journeys with him could be painful - this time it was irrelevant anyway as Kate was unable to offer up coherent conversation. Her partner did not attempt chit-chat, and nor did he endeavour to make her feel better. Rather, he was efficient and pragmatic, going over all the options they faced when saving the poor lady.

Ten minutes short of their destination, Nigel and Kate found themselves stuck in traffic. A collision between a car and a lorry - presumably without fatalities, and if there were they had not appeared on any of the Interveners' radars - had spread across both lanes, leaving a trail of vehicles backed up behind them. Getting out was impossible. Kate desperately racked her brains for a solution, a way to escape, but nothing arrived. With a heavy sigh, Nigel killed the engine and the two of them watched the clock, Kate with fidgety agitation and Nigel with glib resignation. At the exact moment of death, Kate squeezed her eyes shut tight. The Interveners made it their business to get in the way of fate - this time fate got in their way.

Pete shouted from the kitchen. 'Hi baby! Dinner will still be a while yet. Cup of tea?'

'Oh God yes. Thank you.'

He appeared a few minutes later with an oversized 'World's Greatest Mummy' mug, a packet of chocolate digestives and a kiss on the cheek. 'You look like you need this. Hard day at the office?'

'Yeah.'

Kate closed her eyes. She could not muster up the energy to make up a lie about why her day had been so bad.

'Don't tell me it's Carol again – what's she said now? Or has Mr Big Shot been doing his usual trick of delegating all his jobs onto you?'

Kate yawned. 'Yeah. Something like that. Where's Lola?'

'She's over at her friend's house having tea. I'm picking her up at eight. Remember?'

'Hmm? Oh yeah, of course. I remember.' A lie.

Pete removed his apron and sat down on the chair next to Kate. 'Baby, listen. I've got something I want to talk to you about.'

This sounded serious. Was it the theme park incident rearing its ugly head again? Had she been rumbled? Kate's eyes shot open and she sat in a more upright position. What did he know? Maybe he had found out about the Interveners? About the night she spent in Zak's bed?

'What is it?'

'It's something I've been thinking about for a while. Something I think we need. As a family.'

'Come on, Pete, we haven't got all day. Spit it out.'

'Well, it's just that I know you've been working really hard, doing all this extra overtime, so maybe – and you don't have to say yes or no straight away – '

'For Christ's sake!'

'Holiday! Holiday. That was my idea. The school hols are coming up and I thought it might be a nice treat if the three of us went away somewhere.'

Kate relaxed back into her chair. 'Oh.'

'I've been shopping around on the internet while you've been at work and there are some real bargains out there. I checked the bank balance and we seem to be doing okay. And we haven't even touched any of my compensation money yet! Surely this is exactly the sort of thing we should be spending that on? So I was thinking maybe Florida? I mean, just imagine Lola's face as she's hugging Mickey or watching the parade!' Pete looked at his wife expectantly. 'This is where you're supposed to say, 'Wow Pete! What a great idea! Let's do it!''

'Honey, you can't just spring these things on me, you know. I mean, I'm going to have to check at work – it's a busy time, and everyone wants time off in the school holidays.' Not true in the case of her current workforce, of course.

'Can I take that as a maybe?'

'Just let me have a think. Go and check on dinner will you, please?'

'I'll take that as a maybe!'

'Tell me you haven't mentioned any of this to Lola, have you?'

'What? No, no, of course not.'

'Good.'

At Kate's request, the two ate their dinner on trays in front of the television, Kate far too tired to engage in conversation with her spouse. She lay down on her bed afterwards, in solitude, in silence, and quickly succumbed to sleep, not seeing her daughter until the morning.

Chapter Twenty-Five

Kate sat sheepishly in Gordon's office, the two of them drinking their usual morning coffee.

'What are you asking me exactly, dear? If you're *allowed* to go on holiday or if you *should* go on holiday?'

'Both I suppose.'

'Well, yes, of course you can go on holiday. This is no different to any other job in many respects – you have the right to a break. I encourage it. A refreshed Intervener is a sharp Intervener.'

'So how come you don't? You've been here every day since I started.'

'I don't have family like you do. You owe it to them. You owe it to yourself. Go. Go any time you want. Go tomorrow if you wish.'

'That's not the only reason you don't take holidays and you well know it.'

Waddington sighed and leaned back in his brown leather armchair. 'Come on, out with it. The reason you're reluctant to go away is because...'

'...is because I don't want people's deaths on my conscience. I'll be gone for ten days. Jesus, I've saved ten people's lives over the last seven days. What am I supposed to do – let a dozen people die just because I fancy a bit of sunshine and a cuddle from a man in a cartoon mouse suit?'

'I can't answer that. If you're looking for me to grant you some sort of impunity, you obviously have me confused with God. You could ask Him, of course, but I doubt you're flavour of the month anyway, messing with His grand scheme like you've been doing.' He placed both hands on Kate's shoulders and looked her in the eye. 'Whatever you do, it will be the right thing. Believe me.'

On what turned out to be a Vision-free day for the whole house, Kate found herself with plenty of time to ponder her dilemma, going back and forth on the issue many times. She talked it over with Sally, who assured her it was a 'no-brainer' – that she must learn to distance herself from the people being saved and not from the family she had.

She returned home that evening to break the good news to her excited husband, and together they informed their even more excited daughter.

Chapter Twenty-Six

Three weeks later, the Jenson family were in a taxi on their way to Heathrow. Pete and Lola were jubilant and fizzy, singing snippets of songs from Lola's Disney DVDs together. Kate could not bring herself to feign such emotions, blaming travel anxiety when quizzed. It was, indeed, a deep and almost crippling sense of anxiety she felt – anxious about the lives bound to be lost in her absence from the Intervention centre. Even an hour into the taxi journey, she still found herself debating where or not she should concoct a reason to have to get out of the vehicle and return home, allowing her husband and daughter to go on their holiday without her.

Could she survive without them for a week?

Yes.

Could they survive without her for a week?

Yes, undoubtedly.

Did they deserve such treatment?

No. Not at all.

She was doing it.

As she buckled up for the ascension into the air, Kate prayed she would not be subjected to a Vision on the plane. The hotel, the beach, Disneyland – these were all places she could easily mask the exertion of a Vision. It would be much harder on a plane – particularly if the seatbelt signs were on and she was unable to hide in the toilet. Her foot tapped vigorously on the floor, she chewed her lip and she was sweating lightly. A stewardess asked if she was okay, but Pete assured her that he would take care of his wife, who was nervous about flying. Kate did not thank him for her concern – and neither did she reciprocate the squeezed hand he was offering by way of support.

She relaxed a little as the flight went on, though the long journey across The Pond was an exercise in self-distraction for Kate, who used a romantic comedy, a political thriller, an episode of an American sitcom she had never heard of, a trashy magazine, her iPod and several stiff drinks to take her mind off what could possibly have been happening back at the Centre. She was well aware of the irony that many of these activities were the self-same as the ones with which she regularly engaged at the Centre in the first place in the vast expanses of time that often elapsed between Interventions.

The familiar rumble of the plane landing on the Tarmac was always a welcome feeling for Kate, just as it was for any other traveller, but never more so than this time. She had conquered the first battle: survived the journey without getting a Vision. Pete squeezed her hand once again, this time to convey a sense of congratulation that his wife had survived what had clearly been (for reasons different to those he believed to be true) a horrendous journey. This time she placed her free palm onto his hand and smiled.

There was little left to do that day other than eat, shower and catch an early night in preparation for a long and fun day of rides. Pete and Lola fell asleep almost as soon as their heads hit their pillows. Pete had spent the entirety of the long transatlantic crossing keeping his daughter amused, playing small magnetic versions of their favourite board games, helping her with wordsearches and making up bespoke variations of Lola's favourite Disney films, transposing the central characters with his daughter and her school friends. Not a wink of sleep was had by any of the three of them, and for Pete and Lola, the journey had taken its toll. Kate, however, was finding herself kept awake by an unwelcome second wind, gazing at the ceiling fan with wide, unblinking eyes.

She couldn't banish thoughts of her colleagues from her mind. It would be strange - hard - spending ten days and nights away from them. They had become like a secret second family to her. Gordon, with his paternal blend of sternness, praise and wisdom: Sally, with their lively banter and extended gossip sessions: even Zak and the sexual tension when the two of them shared a room. Christ, even Nigel had become an integral part of her life, quite in spite of his miserly ways. She couldn't help but wonder what was happening at the Centre at that exact moment, whether they were idling about the Mansion or involved in daring and heart-racing life-saving endeavours. Either way, at that moment she would gladly have joined them. Clearly, the next battle Kate faced was relaxing into the holiday.

The first full day certainly was a struggle for Kate. The gentle, tame rides favoured by Lola - slowly spinning teacups, elephants gradually ascending and descending - were doing little to scratch the itch she felt now she was away from the Interveners. She had become accustomed to danger - there was certainly an intoxication about racing against the clock to save another human being from certain death (not to mention a certain glamour behind doing so in an old, expensive car).

It was not that every minute of every working day was filled with high octane thrills - far from it. It could be days on end between rescue attempts, and when they came they were more often than not routine or bland. But what Kate loved - what she had evidently come to depend on - was the possibility and potential for excitement. Anything could happen, at any moment, and she loved living in that state of heightened anticipation. She doubted the holiday was going to thrill her in quite the same way - in fact, she was sure it wasn't. She wondered if temporarily abandoning her husband and daughter to go on some of the more grown-up rides might be a good way to ween herself off of the giddy thrills an Intervention could (potentially) provide. She hated that sort of thing, but the feeling of nausea and sweaty palms - the sensation of throwing oneself headlong into uncomfortable situations - would have felt oddly comforting. Meeting the Interveners had turned her stable and idyllic life upside down. Maybe a quick go on the Corkscrew ride on the far end of the park would have the same effect, however fleeting. At very least, standing near the rides and listening to the terrified screams of their passengers would be reminiscent of those of the victims and witnesses of the victims in her Visions and / or failed rescue attempts.

Kate knew these were unhealthy lines of thought. She knew she was being macabre. She knew she was being dark - and in the Sunshine State! She knew she was being grim - and in the so-called Happiest Place on Earth! She knew she wasn't being fair - not to Pete, not to Lola, and not to herself - but it was hard to shake that feeling. Queuing for over an hour to meet Mickey Mouse hardly helped matters, giving her ample time to stew and brood, and by the time the three of them were at the front of the queue, Kate was simply going through the motions, smiling on the outside but not the inside as she cosied up to Mickey, and failing to feel the sense of enchantment that she knew was expected in this scenario - the enchantment so plainly and obviously being experienced by her nearest and dearest at that same moment.

But the cravings gradually subsided the further into the holiday she got. The second full day was once again spent in the theme parks, but something felt different to Kate. She wasn't sure if it was a much better night's sleep or just that she'd finally started to unwind, but she found herself caring less and less about Intervening or the Interveners.

The third full day was when the holiday feeling really started to kick in. It was a beach day. She lay on the warm sand, becoming awash with contentment as the day passed. This time, it felt good to be with her little family unit - it felt right. She smiled as she watched her husband splash his - their - daughter with the warm sea water. Kate was blessed - not with psychic powers, which could just as easily be seen as a curse, but with a lovely and loving family. She saw that now, at long last.

It also now felt good rather than torturous to be so far from the Intervention Centre - the urge to save lives, she was now realising, carried with it a kind of addiction or guilty temptation. It was a drug of sorts, and this wonderful holiday felt like detox (although that was perhaps an odd choice of analogy considering the plethora of cocktails at her disposal).

She allowed herself a wry smile as she recollected the surreal experiences she had gone through as an Intervener. Drunken all-night house parties? Dangerous liaisons with attractive younger men? This was to say nothing of the job itself. None of this was Kate's life. Had it been fun, she asked herself? Hell yes. Did she want to continue the illicit secret second existence she had stumbled upon, or was it time to call it quits and devote herself to the warm familiarity of family life? Jack it all in when she got back and scour the jobs pages?

She looked into her daughter's eyes - so big and bright and shiny. They positively twinkled with an innocent and unbridled joyousness. How unlike the eyes of the old man she now called boss - themselves so haunted and jaded. She continued to stare as she sipped her Piña Colada, allowing the warm, glowing feeling inside her to replenish, recharge, revitalise her own soul. The young embodiment of life before her was the perfect antidote to the death that had surrounded her since stumbling into life as an Intervener.

She eventually put down her cocktail and joined her husband and daughter in the sea, splashing and giggling along with them.

*****

It was around the halfway point of the holiday that it happened - the moment she had dreaded. She knew it had to come at some point. The pains. The sweats. The intense feelings of dizziness. They were back in the park and it was during yet another unnecessarily long and snaking queue for a ride that Kate felt that familiar twinge. She immediately excused herself, saying she was getting hot and bothered so would sit this one out and go for a drink. As soon as she was out of view of her family, she sprinted to the nearest toilet and bolted the cubicle door, allowing the Vision to unfold and, ultimately, vacate her mind and body.

It was a whole different kettle of fish to her usual Visions. A rough looking neighbourhood - a ghetto Kate guessed it would be called - at some point in the night. A group of young men whom Kate would go to great lengths to avoid if she encountered them in real life, each with vicious looking dogs straining at their leashes. A gang? Possibly. This was a million miles away from her cosy, leafy, suburban existence back in England - or, at least, it was thousands of miles away. Then, a pimped up black car, with blacked-out windows, appeared and pulled up next to the men. The front passenger window was rolled down and with a single gunshot, one of the men was shot at close range in the head. A screech of tyres and the car was gone.

This was a no-brainer for Kate (fitting as the man in the Vision was also imminently about to find himself with no brain). She was in America. Doubtless there were Intervening Centres somewhere in the country, but she didn't know where or how to reach them. Besides, this was very clearly a murder attempt.

Rule Number Three - *You may not Intervene in murder scenes.*

She'd signed a contract! Even if she was able to locate the neighbourhood, there was not a chance in Hell she was going to get caught up in what was more than likely gang warfare. The unscrupulous looking young man with a bullet in his temple must have done *something* to deserve it, Kate reasoned with herself. They had obviously picked him out for whatever reason, and none of it was her business.

She decided she would go for that drink after all, enjoying a bit of personal space in the half hour or so she still had left before she needed to re-join Pete and Lola. A frosty-mugged beer and a chapter of her reassuringly predictable romantic comedy novel were all that was needed to regain the holiday feeling she had temporarily lost. The Vision - and lack of subsequent Intervention - did not plague her conscience one iota. Indeed, by the next day it was effectively forgotten as Kate's quest to regain domestic bliss continued apace.

The plane journey back to England was a pleasant one for Kate. She felt no anxiety whatsoever as she fastened her seatbelt; no hot or cold sweats as the plane climbed towards the clouds; no panicky thoughts as the hours up in the sky passed; no knotted stomach as the plane hit the Tarmac. She slept for brief snatches, as did Pete and

Lola, all three of them happily surrendering to the best possible kind of tiredness - the kind resulting from almost a fortnight jam-packed with activity and happy memories. She sat for long periods holding her husband's hand - not talking to him, not facing him, just smiling with her eyes closed. She helped Lola colour in pictures of the Disney characters she had met, and together they completed a scrapbook detailing their adventures to show off at school. Intervening had been deeply - addictively - satisfying, but in its pursuit Kate had forgotten exactly how great it felt to be a really good mum. Evidently, it was hard to do both things really well.

Now, though - now she was ready for the next set of adventures to begin.

Chapter Twenty-Seven

Kate didn't mind returning to work one bit - this wasn't like returning to an ordinary job. It wasn't a sudden change in gear from leisure and pleasure to fast-paced drudgery. On the contrary. There was, indeed, a likelihood that she would be doing no work whatsoever that day, should she be without a Vision and not be asked to accompany anyone on their Intervention attempt. And if that turned out to be the case, she might very well find herself reading magazines by the pool for hours on end. Hardly a shock to the system. If that turned out not to be the case? Even better. She would be doing something truly, truly great with her day - saving someone's life, possibly in a high-speed adventure. This truly was a win-win for Kate - no need for any post-holiday grumps here.

It was good to see her workmates - her friends, really. She was greeted with a round of enthusiastic hugs and compliments on her tan. The gang spent the first hour of the day drinking coffee, listening to her holiday stories and scrolling through the photos on her digital camera.

Chapter Twenty-Eight

Her months employed by Interveners Incorporated had certainly changed Kate. She had become more chilled out in many ways - rediscovered the fine art of relaxation. Her old job - frantic, intense, constant - was certainly not conducive to this, leaving her overly busy in the day and frazzled at night. This slower-paced lifestyle HAD to be good for her, she told herself. Visible evidence of this presented itself when she looked in the mirror. The rate at which grey hair was appearing was slowing down. Indeed, her hair generally seemed thicker, more full of life. Her skin seemed clearer and more glowing.

The physical changes were not all strictly positive, however. The hours upon hours of idling around, getting little-to-no exercise had taken a kind of toll on Kate, as had the three course lunches and her propensity to binge on sugary snacks while watching films on uneventful afternoons. Kate hadn't noticed it happening herself, but she had gradually gained a few pounds. Ten days in Florida hadn't helped matters, either. Arguably, it suited her - certainly no complaints were heard from Pete, who hadn't failed to notice (or appreciate) the fact that extra weight had been gained in his wife's bosoms. It was, in fact, Sally who broke the news to her (though it was Gordon who had urged Sally to do so. He had sense enough to delegate this task).

She did so with a skillful blend of jocularity and knowledgeable authority. She explained to her friend that Interveners had a kind of duty to stay reasonably trim and fit - whilst most Interventions were predictable and thus relatively relaxed affairs, some were more complicated. There were times when the team had to show high levels of dexterity and energy - sometimes (if the rescue was far away or complications had ensued between leaving the Mansion and arriving at the Scene) successfully Intervening meant running for their lives - or at least for the lives of their victims. She told her there was a very good reason they had had a gym installed - not just for the female Interveners to ogle Zak. It was the same reason, she explained, that fire stations had gyms.

And so Kate resolved to change the routine of her day, from thereon incorporating a strict hour of exercise into it - sometimes all at once and sometimes split into more manageable ten minute bursts. Whilst she did use the gym, it was not her favoured form of workout. She enjoyed following along with celebrity workout DVDs - and even more than this, she enjoyed leaving the Mansion with Sally and going for a run. The woodland scenery in the surrounding areas was nothing less than stunning, and upon returning to the Mansion, she felt truly exhilarated. She felt a greater sense of satisfaction knowing that she was getting paid to run than knowing she was getting paid to watch television chefs in action and trying to learn their tricks.

It worked. It took a matter of days for Kate to return to the weight she was when she first joined the Interveners - and not much longer until she was fitter and more toned than she had ever been in her adult life. Where before she languished around the Mansion, she now buzzed. She felt happy and confident, and soon an addiction set in to match that of saving lives. She still enjoyed the crisps, cakes, lavish meals and takeaways that were such a pleasurable part of her job - but she made sure these were balanced out by healthier pursuits.

Chapter Twenty-Nine

The months passed by. Kate had by now become increasingly ingrained in the Interveners gang and the mentality it brought. Chris had yet to be replaced despite everyone's best efforts, Kate's in particular – there had been a great many days in which she simply drove around with Sally, not even to attend an Intervention but just in the hope that an Intervener would appear on her Radar. She had yet to shake the guilt of being witness to Chris leaving, even though she knew it was a happy ending for him and even though she had no idea how she could possibly have stopped him anyway.

If anything, though, Chris's departure had helped Kate feel even more comfortable in her role, like they were more tight-knit now that their numbers had been reduced. Perhaps as a result of the extremely long hours they spent in each other's company – be it on a rescue mission or around the Mansion awaiting a mission – she felt very close to the people she worked with, increasingly regarding each of them not as a colleague, but as a friend. Even Nigel.

It was one afternoon that Nigel himself – who had been under the weather for a few days by this point – asked if anyone fancied doing his lottery run. He had booked a flight to Dublin as his latest prediction had been of the Irish lottery. Of course, he could have played the numbers from the comfort of his armchair via the internet, but Nigel enjoyed the excuse to travel to new and different places – plus as the most reclusive and least sociable member of the group (at least now in Chris's absence), he enjoyed solitude.

His request was initially met with silence, until Zak eventually ventured forth his services.

'Yeah, okay. Why not? I've never been to Dublin, and I do enjoy a pint of the black stuff now and again. Only,' he turned towards Gordon, 'do you think maybe we could shell out for an extra ticket? I'd like some company.'

Gordon nodded and smiled. Kate wondered whether Zak was going to ask someone he knew – maybe the brother they had heard so much about – or try to persuade one of the gang to go with him. She then wondered whether she would like it to be her or not.

On the one hand, though neither of them had ever spoken of it since and it appeared to have come to nothing – Kate still remembered them spending the night together after their drunken Chinese banquet. Could he be trusted? Could *she* be trusted?

On the other hand, she also remembered a magical weekend she had spent in Dublin with her husband to celebrate their first wedding anniversary. She had fallen hopelessly in love with the place and vowed to one day return. Okay, so this wasn't with Pete – but it was a freebie!

'Whaddya say, you lot? Anyone fancy a trip across to Ireland with the Zakmeister?'

Kate winced to herself at Zak's choice of nickname – it reminded her that he was, in fact, younger than her, and not even particularly mature with it. How could she have ended up in his bed?

Gordon ruled himself out straight away. 'Goodness me, no. I think I'll leave this one to the youngsters. I'm sure you'll have a much better time without me.'

Zak did not try to dissuade the old man.

Sally beamed enthusiastically. 'Yeah, go on then! I'm up for the craic! When's your ticket for, Nige?'

'The flight's tomorrow morning. You'd be back here for dinner then next day.'

'No way! Oh, sorry, Zak, no can do. I'm having my hair done tomorrow. It's my little treat and it's at one of those la-di-da salons where you have to book months in advance. There's no way they'd be able to reschedule.'

Zak looked pleadingly at Kate.

'I mean, I'd love to, but what would I tell my husband? Darling, I'm just hopping on a plane and spending the night in a foreign country with a handsome young man you've never met before to play the numbers in a lottery our psychic friend has assured us we'll win. Yeah. I'm sure he'll be okay with that.'

'I'm not hearing no! Come on, Kate, it will be fun! Just use your legendary truth-bending skills.'

Kate pondered for a moment. 'I mean, I could call it a business trip. It sort of is. I could say it's a conference. Maybe I could say someone has dropped out and my boss has strongly encouraged I take his place.'

Gordon wagged his finger at her with mock sternness. 'Young lady, I strongly encourage you to attend this business trip on account of your colleague being unable to attend! There. It's not such a big lie now.'

Kate threw her head back and laughed. 'Oh, God, what am I letting myself in for? Yes. Yes, okay, I'll come to Dublin.'

Zak made a fist and dragged it downwards, mouthing the word 'yes' as he did so. Kate winced again.

Sally looked at Kate and pointed her thumb towards Zak. 'He's a real ladies' man, so you keep an eye on him. He'll be all over those Irish women like a rash. Ooh, sorry, Zak, probably the wrong choice of words there!'

Nigel placed the lottery numbers – with the obligatory missing number – in an envelope and handed it to Kate along with the flight ticket. He wrote down the name of the hotel for Zak, who got straight on the internet to secure another plane ticket. As Nigel always chose to sleep in the lap of luxury, choosing the kind of large hotel rooms easily justified by his winnings, there was no need for an extra room to be booked.

Chapter Thirty

Kate spoke to her husband that evening as they lay in bed. He accepted her request with no attempt at resistance and with great pleasure for his wife (though, in actuality, it was not worded as a request and Kate would have done it even without Pete's approval).

And so, the next morning, Kate found herself on the short flight to Dublin with her friend and colleague. They were seated in different sections of the plane, Kate passing the journey by pretending to be interested in that day's newspaper and Zak by playing on his handheld games console.

*****

Zak whistled in appreciation as they entered the hotel room. 'Pretty swanky, eh? And check out the size of this four-poster bed! I'll bet you Nigel gets up to all sorts when he's on his lottery trips, judging by this. I mean, I'll bet you not all of the money he wins makes its way back to the Mansion, if you know what I mean!'

'Zak! Knowing Nigel, he probably just spreads all of his crossword puzzles out all over the bed. To him, that would constitute a wild weekend! If he's paying for the services of a lady of the night, it's probably just to help him out with 'four across', not getting 'one up'!'

Kate glanced around the room. It was, indeed, pretty impressive, but what pleased her most was that in addition to the four-poster bed, there was a separate bed in the corner of the room. Zak had promised in the airport that he would crash on the couch if need be, but Kate was glad it hadn't come to that.

Zak took a running jump onto the bed and sprawled out.

'Whoa, whoa, whoa! How come you get the big bed?'

'Er, cause it's my trip. You're my guest.'

'Precisely, and as the guest I think it's only common courtesy that you let me have the big bed. And don't make me invoke the 'ladies first' rule of thumb.'

'Right, well, Mrs Jenson, it's clear that we are faced with a pickle here and we have only two options. We can either share the bed or we can play Rock Paper Scissors to decide.'

'What? Are you five? Right, so be it. I'll play you at your own game. Rock Paper Scissors it is.'

Kate hadn't played the game since she was a child and the last time she had seen it played was when Lola had her friend over to stay. She still knew what to do, though, and played paper. Zak played rock. She smothered his rock with her paper using her hands.

'Ha! I believe I'll take the big bed, please!' She mimicked Zak's running jump and let out an exaggerated sigh of pleasure as she landed. 'My my my, Delilah, this *is* comfy!'

After freshening up, the two of them carried out the business element of their trip almost straight away, playing the numbers at the supermarket across the street from the hotel. Kate wondered to herself as she chose the final number whether it was, in fact, the one Nigel had omitted and allowed herself a moment of fantasy as she pictured herself running away with the money. A smile appeared on her face as she envisaged herself on a yacht some place far, far away with her husband and daughter.

That left the rest of the day – and night – for the two Interveners to do as they wished. Though it was a bitterly cold afternoon, they opted for an open-top bus tour of the city, finding that the whole of the top deck was theirs and as such spreading themselves out. They then went their separate ways for shopping and met up at the hotel. Kate got there first and drew herself a bath. Zak returned half an hour later.

'I'm in here! I'm having a bath!'

'Oh, great! Room for two in there?'

'Oi! Cheeky! There is room for two, and you well know it, but you're not coming in!'

'What? I'm just trying to do my bit to save the Earth. You know, water conservation and all of that. I'm an eco-warrior.'

'You're a lothario, mate, that's what you are.'

'Can't blame a chap for trying.'

When Kate had finished her bath, she got changed into the slinky black dress she had bought that afternoon, while Zak showered. He returned with a towel wrapped round his waist. The two surveyed each other, each feeling desires but not expressing them. Kate ignored the thoughts she was getting and put on her perfume and pearls, relishing in the act of getting ready for a night out. Other than New Year's Eve, it had been a while since she had done anything like that with Pete. Kate made a mental promise to herself that, just like New Year's with Pete, tonight was not going to end with sex.

'Make yourself useful and zip me up at the back, will you?'

Zak gladly did as he was told, enjoying the scent of Kate's perfume as he swept her hair to the side to expose the bare skin on the top of her back and bottom of her neck, thus avoiding trapping any of it in the zip.

'You know, I'm not used to pulling zips UP on the back of dresses - this is quite a novel experience for me!'

He performed his duty more slowly than he needed to. Kate noticed but didn't acknowledge this - nor did she mind.

'So then – where are you taking me?'

'You'll just have to wait and see!'

Zak linked arms with Kate and they left the hotel room, but she unlinked them when they reached the elevator and they stayed that way. It was, in fact, to the hotel restaurant that Zak took Kate, but it was a high-class affair, lit only by candle and with a violinist playing in the corner. As they ordered food, it was without regard to its costs, Zak paying for the meal using the company credit card entrusted to him by Gordon. He even managed to persuade Kate to share a bottle of champagne with him, even though she had secretly vowed not to touch the stuff after the state she had found herself in the last time she had drunk it – at the Chinese banquet.

It was a pleasant occasion. Kate couldn't help but feel relaxed, doubtless aided by the free (and free-flowing) alcohol. She had never enjoyed Zak's company quite so much. Though he often came across as somewhat cocksure and immature at the Mansion, she was seeing an altogether more tender side to him tonight. He allowed Kate to lead the conversations and showed great interest in what she had to say, openly encouraging her anecdotes about her family and Lola in particular. When they had exhausted that line of conversation, Kate asked Zak about his love life, and he regaled her with stories of doomed and mismatched romances, triumphs and heartbreaks. On more than one occasion, Kate found herself gazing into his eyes, not talking, not particularly listening. Just smiling.

'Let's see some of those legendary ladies' man skills in action, shall we?'

'What do you mean?'

'I mean – we're in Dublin, man! And we're frankly looking fabulous! Let's hit the town!'

'You sure? A woman of your age? We can go and find a bingo hall if you like!'

She slapped his arm. 'Hope you've got some better material than that up your sleeve young man!'

After stopping at a couple of bars along the way, unfazed by the high alcohol prices and each time charging it to Interveners Incorporated, the two of them eventually stumbled into a club. The music was far too loud for Kate's tastes, she was a decade older than anyone else she could see, and she could not pick out a melody in the thumping, bass-heavy noise being played, but she attempted to enjoy herself nonetheless. Zak wasted little time before making a beeline towards a pair of young girls, whispering something in the ear of the more attractive of the two before leading her onto the dance floor.

Kate sipped on her cocktail and swayed on the spot, attempting to engage in conversation with any woman or couple she could find, but it was a near-enough impossible task when the music was so loud. She eventually gave in, necked the remainder of the drink and moved on to the dance floor herself, spotting Zak with his tongue down the young lady's throat. She eventually disappeared, leaving Zak to dance alone. Kate left it a few minutes to see if she would return and, when it became clear she was gone, she danced towards her friend, shouting her words into his earhole.

'Hey you! Are you having a good time?'

Zak nodded. 'Yeah. You?'

'It's okay. I feel a bit old! She was pretty!'

Zak shrugged his shoulders and continued to dance, scanning the room as he did so.

'I tell you what,' he yelled over the incessantly repetitive beats, 'there's this really hot girl I've got my eye on tonight. Brown hair in a bob, about 5'4", smoking hot body, wearing a slinky black dress.'

Kate began to eye the crowd to see if she could catch a glimpse of the person he was talking about before the realisation dawned on her. She blushed.

'Zak, stop it. I'm really flattered, but I've got a family! A happy family! I can't carry on like that!'

'Oh, I get it, it's okay. You don't fancy me, do you?'

'Fancy you? Well, of course I fancy you! Half the girls in this club fancy you, I bet! You're gorgeous.' She touched his face. 'I just...'

'Look forget about it. I feel really silly now. How about we just have a dance?'

'That sounds lovely.'

And dance they did. They danced in the same way they had danced at the Chinese night; first separately and playfully. Then, as the early hours drew on, their bodies became closer and eye contact became more frequent; more lingering. When Kate found Zak's hand on her thigh, she did nothing to remedy the situation, and so before long the other hand followed suit. It was a natural progression that Kate reciprocated and soon their hands were no longer static, but rather moving up and down the sides of each other's bodies.

When the inevitable kiss came, it was impossible to tell who had initiated it. It was a kiss of passion and abandon. A kiss the likes of which Kate hadn't felt for many years. She couldn't deny she was turned on, and when Zak began to lead her by the hand out of the club some time later, the sense of reason she was able to summon up an hour ago had since deserted her. She knew what was going to happen and made no attempts to resist it.

*****

The two collapsed onto the bed and resumed their kiss, Kate pulling off Zak's shirt and he unzipping her dress before eagerly removing the rest of his own clothes. Without relinquishing the kiss, Kate slid out of the dress. Zak wasted no time in unclasping her bra. She wriggled out of her own panties. They stood there, totally naked, their bodies illuminated by the moonlight beaming through the open curtains. He marvelled at the sight before him – she might have been older than him, but Kate was pert, firm and shapely and she was stirring something inside of him that none of his recent conquests had managed to do. He felt wild with lust. He took her hand and twirled her slowly around, examining her backside as he did so – it was every bit as perfect and shapely as her breasts. She was everything he had imagined; everything he had hoped for, and then some.

And she, too, couldn't help but marvel. Where Pete's ascent / descent into middle age had started to leave him flabbier and saggier than the man she had dated, here was a sculpted specimen of a man, trim and muscular, and evidently totally ready for her. It was all he could do to stop himself throwing her around the hotel room and ravishing her. It was all she could do to stop yearning for the exact same thing. But they remained restrained, relishing the moment, relishing the anticipation, and this served only to stoke their desires further.

'God, I really wanted to do this that night at the Mansion,' he whispered into her ear.

'Me too. It was just wrong. And this – this is wrong. Just,' she moaned in a low whisper, *wrong.*'

'You make wrong sound so right.'

He pushed her gently onto the bed. Her heartbeat quickened.

Kate remained silent and oddly motionless as he caressed her breasts before she uttered the words Zak had longed to hear: 'Oh God.'

'I know, baby, I know. Jesus, you're hot.'

Kate pushed him off. 'No, it's not that, you idiot. I think I'm about to have a Vision.'

'What? Oh, for fuck's sake.'

Kate's body seized up and she went through the usual Vision process, except this time in a highly unusual environment, with an unusual set of circumstances. Zak watched her, unable to resist peering at the sight he had worked so hard and waited so patiently to see; her naked body. He rooted around for his jeans, pulling his phone out of his pocket and taking a picture of what, despite the obvious agony Kate was in, he considered to be a quite splendid scene.

After a few minutes of tenseness and perspiration, Kate flopped with exhaustion. The experience was not that dissimilar to a session with Pete after all.

'Are you okay?'

'Yeah. Well, not really. That was a really horrible one.'

Zak paused. 'You realise there's absolutely nothing we can do about it, don't you? I mean, it's not like you can just pop into the Vision Room and put the plates on. We're miles from home. Hell, I know there's an Intervention Centre in Ireland somewhere, but God knows where.' He smirked lasciviously and ran his finger up her inner thigh. 'So how about we pick up from where we left off?'

Kate brushed his hand off and pulled the covers over her torso. 'You really think I feel like having sex with you after seeing in the most vivid detail imaginable a family burning to death in a fire? That your idea of foreplay, is it, you moronic little ape? My God, you're something else, aren't you? Besides, there *is* something we can do. We can ring Gordon and ask him if he knows the address of the Irish Intervention Centre. And then if it's not too far away, we can get a taxi there. It's worth a shot.'

'Fine. Well, listen, you ring Gordon. Meanwhile, I've got some urgent business of my own to sort out, if you catch my drift. So, you know, screw you.'

'Well you certainly didn't.'

Zak stormed into the bathroom and slammed the door shut as Kate fished around for her mobile phone. She called Gordon, who answered on her second attempt. At first he was slightly disgruntled by the lateness of the call but soon changed his tone to a congratulatory one, proud that his newest charge was so dedicated to her calling. He confirmed to her that there was, in fact, an Irish Intervention Centre, but he seemed no more clued-up than his youngest employee about its exact whereabouts. He explained to her that, although the heads of each Intervention Centre were in possession of basic information about a limited number of other centres, they worked in isolation of each other, and the information was kept only for rare emergencies the likes of which they being presented with at that moment in time. They otherwise simply had no discernible use for each other. She hung on the line as he hunted for his address book, during which time Zak emerged from the bathroom wearing a towel and a scowl.

'That better, sugar?'

Zak looked to the floor and shook his head, still disbelieving at the anti-climax, so to speak, of the evening. 'Should have shagged that ginger dancer when I had the chance.'

'And so the real Zak re-emerges. Welcome back.'

He lay on the smaller bed and turned his back to Kate, pulling the covers over his head. Gordon returned to the phone and confirmed to Kate that there was a Centre which was commutable from Dublin, two and a quarter hours from their present location. Kate realised that this was a considerable distance and therefore meant her chances of Intervention were limited – what if the scene of the Intervention was *another* couple of hours from the Centre? Would she even make it on time? It was impossible to tell from her Vision the time of day the deaths were due to take place as it was indoors and the thick smoke and flames were obscuring any potential daylight. She was hoping it was going to be the next morning (by the afternoon, they would have missed their scheduled flight, and she was already desperate to end this unfortunate chapter). For all she knew, it could have been due to take place in the next few minutes. It was a risk she had to take.

She dialled the number she had scrawled onto the bedside notepad and waited, the nerves she might ordinarily have felt ringing a stranger at three in the morning drowned out by the alcohol in her bloodstream.

A kindly, lilting Irish voice eventually replied, which seemed to belong to an older lady. Kate explained her situation and offered profuse apologies for the lateness of her call – apologies which were immediately rebuffed by the person on the other end of the line, who explained that she had, herself, only just returned from an Intervention and had yet to attempt sleep. Kate told her to expect her in a couple of hours and ended the call with one more vain attempt at an apology. Her next call was to order a taxi, which was promised to arrive in the next five minutes.

Kate walked over to her colleague, who was snoring gently, and kicked him lightly on the back. 'Oi! Come on you! Get up! Duty calls.'

Zak opened his eyes narrowly and looked up at her, responding in a groggy voice. 'What? No. Sod off. Do this one yourself. I'm going to sleep. Come and get me when you're done.'

Kate pulled the covers off him. 'No you're not, you selfish little toad. You know full well it's too dangerous for Interveners to work alone, and this one's really bloody dangerous.' Her tone changed, becoming less vitriolic and more pleading. 'Besides, I need your help. I've got no idea how to stop this fire from happening. Please, Zak.'

Zak mumbled to himself as he pulled his clothes back on, before filling his mouth with chewing gum. He offered none to Kate, and nor did she ask.

It was a short wait in the foyer before the taxi pulled up and the two ventured back outside into the bitterly chilly night. Kate gave the address to the driver, who could barely contain his glee at the payload coming his way for such a long haul. Before he could ask any questions about why on Earth two people would travel from a hotel at that time in the morning to such an obscure location, Kate asked the driver if he would mind letting them sleep and waking them when they arrived. She realised the driver would probably take a deliberately longer route to elicit more money from them. The money itself she didn't mind – Interveners Incorporated would be taking care of that, whatever the eventual costs – but it did mean cutting into her rescue time. Between the cosy warmth of the cab, the lateness of the hour and the considerable quantity of alcohol consumed, the two Interveners had no option but to succumb to sleep in what was to be a matter of minutes.

*****

Though morning was approaching when they arrived at the Centre, the daylight was not; it was still dark, still very much like night-time. The sleep had sobered Kate sufficiently for her to feel like herself, like rational thinking was in her powers once more, even if she still felt tired and jaded. The Centre was, just as was the Mansion back in England, a magnificent and impressively large old building.

Kate knocked and was greeted by the same voice she had heard on the telephone. Just as she had pictured, the lady was much older than herself – though not, she surmised, as old as Gordon, and a sparkle was in her eyes, whereas Gordon always looked so haunted and vacant.

'Ah, hello, you must be Kate. And who's your handsome young friend, Kate?'

Zak perked up, pleased to receive a compliment after the knock-back he had received a few hours ago. Even if it was from someone old enough to be his grandmother. 'Hi! I'm Zak. I'm an Intervener, too.'

'Well, it's a huge pleasure to meet the both of you. You're the first foreign Interveners I've met for, ooh, probably thirty years now. Here, get yourselves inside and out of the cold. I've made you both a bacon roll. I hope you don't mind.'

'Thanks, erm – oh, I'm sorry, I've forgotten your name. How rude of me.'

'Helena.'

'Of course. Thanks, Helena, but I'd like to get on with trying to find out the location of the fire I Envisioned. I just hope I'm not too late.'

'Of course, dear, of course.'

'I'll take a bacon roll, please, Helena!'

Helena pointed Zak in the direction of the kitchen and ushered Kate into their version of the Vision Room. It seemed much more primitive than the one she was used to; a large, clunky helmet took the place of the small metal plates, and a simple keyboard replaced the more sophisticated dashboard of controls that so befuddled Kate. She awaited the mantra that usually preceded this part of the Vision process, but it did not come.

Within moments, the Vision appeared on the screen of an unconscious family – two parents in their thirties, two boys under ten – lying unconscious on the floor of a small house or flat, their bodies burning in a raging fire. Helena frantically typed code on the keyboard in an attempt to pinpoint their location and details. Because of the density of the smoke, it was impossible to identify the future victims, but eventually, she was able to discover the location – a village called Tipperton – and the time of the incident – it was one hour and two minutes away.

'It's miles away, my love. We're not going to make this one.'

Kate was crestfallen.

'Why the long face? I said we're not going to make it. I didn't say they're not going to make it. I take it they have fire brigades in England?'

'Of course! We just dial 999! It's so simple!'

'Simple, yes, but have you ever been in a situation before where you've used the emergency services?'

Kate thought back to the teenager falling down the stairs.

'Well, yeah, but just the once.'

'Just the once. Exactly. And, tell me, was it a last resort?'

Kate nodded.

'So you have to ask yourself why that is. Why don't we use them at every possible opportunity? The answer's quite simple – because then we're relying on another party. It's yet another factor which could potentially block the Intervention, and it's out of our powers whether that happens or not. We're going to go out there into my living room in a minute and ring the fire brigade, but then what? It's in their hands, not ours. And they might live; they might die. We'll never know. At least when you Intervene yourself, you have the satisfaction of seeing those people live on.'

Kate's crestfallen expression returned. They walked into the living room, where Zak was munching on his roll and chatting to a woman who looked remarkably similar to Helena – same height, similar build, but slightly younger-looking.

'Kate, I'd like you to meet Davina. I see you've already met Zak, Davina.'

'Hello there, Davina. Listen, I don't mean to be rude, but do you mind if we skip the introductions until after we've called the fire brigade?'

Helena chortled. 'You want to call them now?'

'Well, yes! The sooner the better, surely?'

'No, no. Not necessarily. See, this is another reason why we try to avoid external agencies if we can. When you Intervene, you usually know roughly how long it will take, and again, it's in your hands. You don't know how long it's going to take them to get there. You can't go ringing them yet – it's too early. Chances are, there will be no fire yet. On the other hand, you can't leave it until the last minute either. As I say, it's not the best option using the emergency services. It's pot luck, really.'

'I see. So when do you think we should ring?'

'Well, judging by the thickness of the smoke and flames, I'd say the fire had been going for a while in your Vision. It's really impossible to say. Just go with your gut. I personally think you've got a while yet.'

'I'll have that bacon roll if you're still offering.'

*****

'So you two are sisters. What a huge coincidence that you both turned out to be Interveners...isn't it?'

Helena and Davina looked at each other and smiled. Helena returned her gaze to Kate. 'You're joking now, aren't you? Of course it's not a coincidence! Have you a sister?' Kate shook her head. 'A brother then?' Another shake of the head. 'A son or daughter then?'

'I've got a daughter.'

'Grand. And does she have those big, beautiful brown eyes you've got there, Kate?'

'She's got brown eyes, yes.'

'What a huge coincidence!'

'Well, not really, I...oh. Oh God. Are you saying what I think you're saying?'

'Now don't panic yourself,' Davina said. 'It's not like eye colour or hair colour or height. It's not like you've a good chance of your daughter following in your footsteps. But there's a chance. More of a chance than your next door neighbour being an Intervener. Much, much more.'

Kate immediately recalled Lola's nightmare - her premonition of the hostage execution. She realised, even more than before, the gravity of that situation: the implications.

'Ah, but you look so sad now,' Helena said. 'So what if she does end up taking after her ma? It can't be all that bad, or we wouldn't be sat here having this conversation now at this strange hour.'

The kindly Irish lady's logic was hard to argue with, so Kate didn't try, but still it filled her with a dreadful sense of sadness, of guilt even, that one day her sweet and innocent little girl would be subjected to the world of death and near death experiences upon which Kate had stumbled. There was no turning back for Kate - that much was certain - but that didn't mean she wished the life on her own flesh and blood.

The four Interveners idled away the minutes comparing / contrasting their experiences of saving lives.

Helena glanced at her watch. 'Anyway, I think the time has come. You want to do the honours, my love?'

Kate thought for a minute. She was tired and deflated, and she doubted making a phonecall that would potentially save someone's life would change that. Besides, she didn't want her English accent to arouse any suspicions and thus jeopardise the Intervention - it would already seem suspicious, she thought, that the call was being made so far from the fire. So she left the duty to Helena. It was, Kate thought as she left, undoubtedly one of the least satisfying Intervention attempts she had made, though she was thankful the trip had ended with the possible saving of a life and not the possible ending of a marriage. Whether or not she had succeeded in saving the Irish family's life, she would never know.

The group parted company with a round of hugs and all manner of thank yous, which were more sincere than the half-hearted promises to keep in touch.

Kate passed the short plane journey back by once again flicking through the newspapers, this time even more distractedly than before, and Zak by playing on his handheld games console, his tongue sticking out of the side of his mouth every now and again, just as before.

Chapter Thirty-One

Kate shifted around on her chair. She had been back from Dublin for a couple of days now, but had yet to shed her ratty mood.

'For Christ's sake, is it really too much to ask for them to put some bloody adult chairs out? Two would be fine! You're telling me they haven't got two spare regular size chairs in this whole school? It's a joke!'

Though the classroom was populated only by the Jensons, Kate appeared not to be talking to her husband, instead directing her tetchy rant at the air in front of her.

Pete placed a comforting hand on her shoulder, which she immediately shrugged off. 'Honey, what's the matter?'

'Nothing!'

'Bad day at work or something?'

Kate at last met her partner's eye contact, doing so with a fierce and steely glare. 'I said nothing and I meant nothing! I - I don't know - okay?'

And indeed she did not. She couldn't put her finger on exactly why the prospect of sitting through Lola's parent's evening slot was proving so testing on her patience when a year ago it filled her with such pride and excitement. The two of them had listened to the gushing praise of their daughter's teacher with palms on each other's knees, every bit the doting parents and every bit the perfect couple. Now Pete's touch was a source of vague irritation and she couldn't wait for the whole thing to be over and done with. Her eyes darted around the classroom environment, though she was taking none of it in. Was it Dublin? Had the experience with Zak unsettled her? Was it guilt? There had been no penetration – she hadn't technically cheated on her husband, but she hadn't exactly been faithful either. She had stood there with another man, not a stitch of clothing between them, filled with desire. It hadn't been her conscience that had stopped her – if only she could say that had been true. Or was it something else about her trip to Ireland that had bothered her? Was it regret? Did some part of her still wish she HAD let her sexy colleague inside her? She looked at Pete. She loved him. Loved him in a way she could never love someone like Zak, or anyone else for that matter. But she found Zak insanely attractive.

Could she say that of the man on her left? That she found him insanely, wildly attractive? No.

Or maybe it was something else entirely that was putting her in a bad mood.

'Where the Hell is that woman? This really isn't very professional, keeping us waiting like this.'

'Baby, relax will you? She said she had to nip out. She said she wouldn't be long. And she hasn't been. It's been two minutes, tops! Why don't we have a look at Lola's exercise books while we wait?'

Kate practically snatched the Maths book in front of her, while Pete appeared to be treating her English book with the care and reverence of a sacred text. She flicked through the pages as one might an uninteresting and trashy magazine: Pete, meanwhile, was reading each and every word Lola had written, and each and every red inked response given, his smile unwavering throughout.

Kate tutted. 'I mean, Jesus, tick, tick, tick, tick, tick, tick bloody tick.'

'I know! What have I always said? Our little girl is one bright button.'

'That's NOT what I'm getting at, Pete. There's not a wrong answer in the whole book. So, yes, all right, she's clever, but she's also not being stretched or challenged. She needs harder work. I'm gonna say something.'

'No, Kate! No. Don't be 'that' parent. You do that and you're going to get her back right up. She'll probably end up taking it out on Lola. Lola likes her teacher, she's happy and she's doing well. Just leave it at that - please.'

Kate snorted, unable to argue with her husband but unable to admit to him that he was right. Without asking, she took the English book out of his hands and replaced it with the Maths book. She tried reading it. She tried and tried. It wasn't that she couldn't read the words - her daughter had, of late, developed a pleasing cursive style that belied her young years. They just weren't sinking in, instead just sort of dancing around the page, around her mind - she was finding it hard to concentrate. Her mind was elsewhere. Her emotions were always heightened and tense when she found herself in a situation that would be hard to get out of. A Vision would be hard to mask in this situation. She would have to excuse herself, say she was ill and needed to use the toilet - but how many times could she keep playing that card without rousing Pete's suspicions?

It wasn't just that, though. She had yet to master the ability to switch off when away from the Centre. Sometimes it seemed easy - a particularly gripping television drama and she quickly forgot she was ever employed in such a bizarre way in the first place. A really good back massage at her favourite spa and she couldn't care less who was dying, how and where. But sometimes - oftentimes - Intervening was all she could think about. The Visions she had had; the successful Interventions; the failed ones. They replayed *ad infinitum* in her mind. She couldn't help but speculate where she might be off to next - what kind of Intervention attempt awaited her. Young? Old? Bags of time to spare? Down to the wire? Too late? And often, when she found herself in a humdrum situation - a visit to her in-laws, a trip to the dentist, doing her online grocery shop - she craved the excitement of the Vision / Intervention process; yearned for the secret heroism of it all. This was exactly such a situation. She'd seen all of the Marvel films thanks to Pete and not once had she ever seen any of the heroes or their alter-egos attending a parent's evening.

'Sorry about that! I had to make a quick phonecall. Thanks for being patient.'

Miss Blackmore was a plump young woman with a round and welcoming face, a warm smile and a sing-song voice.

'That's okay! I'm Lola's dad, Pete, and this is her mum, Kate. Nice to meet you, Mrs Blackmore.'

'I can speak for myself thank you, darling.'

Pete shook his daughter's teacher's hand: Kate did not.

'It's Miss actually!'

'Oh, I'm so sorry! In that case, nice to meet you, Miss Blackmore!'

'Not a problem, honestly!'

'I have to tell you, Lola speaks very highly of you! We think she's made great progress since being in your class, so thanks for all your hard work.'

Miss Blackmore blushed and beamed. 'Awww! Thank you. That's very kind of you. She speaks very highly of you too, you know. My dad this, my dad that. Sounds like you do some really fab things with her - all those art projects and nature walks. I believe it's helping to make her the lovely, rounded young lady she's becoming, and that in turn is helping her to make that great progress you mentioned.'

Kate scoffed. 'Yes, well, he doesn't actually have a job other than being a housewife. Sorry, househusband. He has the time to spend with her and I don't. I'm the breadwinner, you see. I work my fingers to the bone and he takes away the Parent of the Year trophy.'

Not one of the Interveners - Kate included - would describe their lot in life as 'working their fingers to the bone', but neither of those two needed to know that. Her point remained that she was, indeed, the one who earned the money and that Pete was, indeed, very obviously Lola's favourite parent, unjust though it sometimes seemed.

'Of course, Mrs Jenson! I think it's fantastic that she's got two such brilliant role models. The way Lola tells it, you're a real high flyer. We'd love to have you in the next time we do Careers Day. We get lots of dads coming in talking about their jobs but hardly any mums. Do you think you'd ever be able to come in and talk to us about what you do? I think it would be really inspirational for our little girls in particular.'

Yes, that's what I'll do, thought Kate. *I'll pop in and tell your class all about how I lie around a mansion living in the lap of luxury for hours at a time with a group of other people who share my psychic gift of foreseeing people's deaths. Then, just occasionally, I'll actually do something vaguely akin to work by driving a fabulous old car around slightly altering the course of someone's day to keep them alive. Oh and I take home a shed load of money every month for doing this. Questions?*

'Yeah I'll think about it. Now can we get on with actually talking about Lola's education please?'

Miss Blackmore did not reciprocate Kate's curt, pithy tone but rather maintained her jolly demeanour throughout.

'Of course! Well, let me start by telling you she's one of our brightest stars, excelling in all subjects across the board. I'm sure that comes as no surprise. She's on our Gifted and Talented register in Maths, so we really have to ensure she's not just coasting.'

Kate let out a less than discrete snort / sneer, which neither Miss Blackmore nor Pete acknowledged.

'As for writing, she really has come on leaps and bounds, both in terms of the compositions and the punctuation and grammar. You can tell she's well-read, and that really feeds into her own writing. I love reading her stories - she's so imaginative, so articulate - but may I just voice a little concern? Please don't be offended.'

Pete shrugged. 'Please. Anything that will help us to help our daughter.'

'Well, sometimes - just now and again - her stories become sort of...violent. I'm worried she might be being exposed to content that's a bit too grown up for her, maybe on the television, maybe on the internet.'

Kate's body language changed. She started leaning in towards Misss Blackmore, and her tone became more aggressive. 'What do you mean by violent?'

'Well, let me give you an example. This is her Free Write book, where basically they can write about whatever they want. Listen to this one.' She flicked to a page marked out with a small pointy sticky note. 'It's just a normal story about princesses and castles, then all of a sudden we've got 'then the princess saw a man and another man out of the window and one man shooted the other man in the head. The other man falled on the floor and there was lots of blood around him.' I mean, that's not come purely from a little girl's imagination.'

Pete nodded, slowly and remorsefully. Kate tried her best to mask the sudden surge of panic coursing through her body. Just as she had been only a few days ago in Ireland, she was forced to confront the possibility that her daughter might also experience 'Daymares'.

'Is that it? Just one? I mean, crikey, have you seen some of the stuff that goes on in Tom and Jerry cartoons? Let's not start suggesting my daughter is some sort of sociopath or something.'

'Oh no, no, no, Mrs Jenson! Honestly, that's not what I'm saying. I just know you're both very good, conscientious parents and that you would want to know about it. Here, there's another one in the story. She's called it 'Puppy's Adventure', but halfway through she's put 'then there was a train coming and a old woman didn't see the train and it hit her. She flewed up in the air and her head falled off.' Pretty graphic stuff! I'm sorry, I didn't want to alarm you: just make you aware of it.'

Kate re-directed her aggressive stance towards her husband. 'I told you, Pete, you HAVE to monitor what she's doing more when I'm at work. I'll bet she's been on YouTube or something. You know what it's like: you're watching a Disney cartoon on it one minute, then five clicks later and suddenly you're watching an old cowboy gunfight or Top Ten Worst Train Accidents of All Time or something.'

'You're right, darling. I'm sorry. I suppose when I'm making dinner I'm so busy that she could be doing anything really. Well that's that Parent of the Year award being revoked!'

He chuckled. Miss Blackmore chuckled. Kate remained stoic, her thoughts now completely fixated on Interventions.

'Not at all, Mr Jenson! You're doing an amazing job, believe me.'

'Please. Call me Pete.'

He smiled. Miss Blackmore smiled. Kate did not. She huffed. 'Can we change the subject, please? I mean, quite literally?'

'Of course! Well as I'm sure you'll agree, Lola is quite the budding artist! Whenever she has a free choice, she goes straight for her sketch book. Here, have a look at some of her drawings - they're really rather good. Her fine motor skills are excellent.'

Kate took the book and looked at each picture in turn, though she had yet to divorce her thoughts from the prospect of her daughter having Intervener's tendencies. There was a seaside scene, with a cartoon sunshine wearing sunglasses, children playing on the beach and the waves crashing against the tall rocks. Only Kate didn't see rocks; she saw a cliff. And while Lola's drawing featured nothing of the sort, Kate saw a boy on top. The still and lifeless scene became animated in her mind and the boy fell from the cliff, just as the young boy had done in front of Kate's eyes all those years ago. Without realising, she began breathing more deeply and audibly through her nostrils.

She turned the page. This time a street scene, with houses comprised only of squares and triangles and that ubiquitous bespectacled sun. In Lola's scene, a kindly old gentleman - a Lollipop Man - was waving a man and a girl across the road (her artistic skills were sufficiently developed for it to be plainly obvious to Kate that the former was Pete and the latter Lola, as per their daily morning routine). As Kate's version of the scene came to life, the approaching car sped up instead of stopping, sending the old man flying up into the air and crashing down onto the pavement to his instant death. She had never seen that specific scene before, never had a Vision involving a Lollipop Man or indeed Lady, but she had already witnessed so many like it since becoming an Intervener. Sometimes the ending had been happier than the Vision; sometimes the prevailing circumstances had meant it was identical. She felt herself becoming hotter and started squirming uncomfortably.

Next up was a bonfire scene, probably drawn in November. Little swirls in the air had to be fireworks, and a group of revellers stood around the fire, smiling. But suddenly the fire started raging out of control. There were no fireworks any more and thick plumes of smoke appeared, knocking the little stickmen unconscious. Kate could feel a bead of sweat breaking on her forehead.

The next page was ostensibly the Jenson house, cut into a cross section so that all the rooms were visible. The woman who would be Kate was eating food in the kitchen, alone, with what looked very much like a wine glass on the table. The man who would be Pete was in the living room, screwdriver in hand, fixing something (possibly a toy). The girl who would be Lola was in her room upstairs, having what looked like a teddy bear's picnic. And there were stairs. Kate's mind raced back to the failed Intervention attempt in which the girl had fallen down the stairs. Before her mind had the chance to rearrange the sweet scene before her into the traumatic one in her head, she let out an inadvertent low moan and snapped the book shut, though several pages remained. She sat on her quivering hands and forced a smile.

A timer beeped.

'I'm so sorry, but that's all we've got time for! Five minutes really isn't enough, is it? I must move on to the next set of parents. But, of course, my door is always open if you ever need to pop in and chat! Really lovely to meet both of you.'

She stood up and stuck out her hand, which Pete shook vigorously with two palms and Kate once again ignored.

'Lovely to meet you too, Miss Blackmore!'

'Oh, you can call me Martine if you like!'

'Okay, well, bye Martine!'

Kate sucked in her cheeks. 'Bye, Miss Blackmore.'

Kate waited until they had left the building before unleashing her rant. 'God, what a bitch! Tell me how to raise my daughter again and I'll put you through the bloody window.'

'Eh? She was only trying to help. Anyway, I thought she was really lovely.'

Kate grinded her teeth. 'That much was plain to see, Flirty Bassett.'

'What are you on about? Look at me!' He grabbed her shoulders. 'Kate, look at me! I only have eyes for one woman, and they're looking at her right now. You know that. I honestly wasn't flirting. I'm sorry if I came across that way. I was only being friendly.'

He hadn't been flirting. Kate knew that. Perhaps she was looking to appease her own guilt over what had happened / could have happened / might possibly still happen with Zak - tarring Pete with her own brush. More likely she was just venting her frustrations and projecting her own anxieties onto him: a hard act to keep up in the face of such warmth and kindness. She squeezed his hand and nothing more was said on the matter.

Chapter Thirty-Two

Kate had tried her level best to ignore Zak since the Dublin incident - not an easy act to pull off when working in such close proximity to someone for so many hours in the day. The Mansion often seemed so lavishly enormous - but at that moment it seemed claustrophobically small. Only four days had passed since they had arrived back, but it felt much longer to Kate. Her inclination was to do something - anything - else when he walked into the room, and more often than not this was exactly what she did do. If he came in from the outside and sat in the living room, she vacated the living room and went outside, and vice-versa. And at all costs, she avoided being upstairs with him.

However, it wasn't that straightforward - she knew she couldn't just ignore him totally. That would have seemed suspicious. So now and again - always with one or more of the other colleagues in earshot- she would ensure she acknowledged Zak in some small way or spent some small amount of time in his company, painful though it could be.

Thankfully, many of Zak's favoured areas of the Mansion were ones Kate did not typically visit - he still frequented the Games Room even in the absence of his former sparring partner, Chris, honing his darts and pool skills alone, perhaps in the hope of a replacement joining the ranks. Kate actually enjoyed the previously jarring sounds of pinball and video games emanating from the room - partly because it meant he was somewhere she wasn't and partly because it was then that most Zak came across as a kind of man-child. Then that she felt the least attracted to him; then that she was most glad she hadn't had sex with him.

Of course, Zak also favoured the gym, and at those times her feelings were not so clear-cut. Dressed in his vest and shorts, he was hardly that far removed from the naked specimen that stood before her in the hotel room - an image she had failed to banish from her cycle of thoughts.

On this particular day, Kate had decided she could not stand to be around him as he stretched and posed in preparation for his next gym session. She took her coffee into the garden and chatted to Sally as her friend pulled up weeds. When rain forced the two of them inside an hour or so later, Gordon and Nigel were playing cards in the living room, but Zak was nowhere to be seen. Kate noticed the Vision Room door was shut.

Zak eventually emerged from the Vision Room, a hint of a smirk on his lips, a hint of a swagger in his step.

'Well, this one's a cinch. Teenage moron glued to his phone, too busy texting to notice he's crossing a road. You can work out the rest.'

'Indeed we can, Mr Winters! And who would you like to accompany you today?' asked Gordon.

Kate avoided eye contact. *Please don't pick me. Please don't pick me.*

'I'll pick the lovely Kate today, I think.'

Kate forced a smile. 'Yay.'

Zak's choice of transportation was the Mercedes. He fed the address into the navigation system.

Kate turned her back and curled up. 'I'm going to sleep. Don't wake me up til we're there.'

Zak said nothing. He still seemed to be sporting a self-satisfied grin, which Kate chose not to acknowledge. Before long, she really was asleep, and Zak made no attempts to wake her, even leaving the radio off.

The scenery rolled past. At one point, Zak ignored the navigation system's instructions to continue along the A road, pulling off instead at the next junction and heading towards the quiet country back roads. The electronic voice repeatedly imploring him to perform a U-turn filtered through to Kate's sub-conscious, and she awoke.

'Zak? What's going on? Where are you going? You're not attending a different Intervention, are you? Zak?'

His eyes were smiling, but he did not look at Kate. He calmly pulled over into the nearest lay-by, with neither vehicle nor human in eyeshot or earshot. As he killed the engine, the only remaining sounds were the occasional bird tweet and a light blustering of the grass and trees. He kept his gaze fixated on the windscreen.

'I must have you Kate. Ever since Ireland, I haven't stopped fantasising about you and that body of yours. In the back of the car, in that field - I don't care. I want you and I want you now.'

'Are you asking or telling me?'

'Telling you? It's not like that. I don't think it needs to be like that. I'm asking you.'

Kate's quickened heartbeat seemed to slow a little. Her panic turned to annoyance.

'Jesus Christ, did you even get a Vision back at the Mansion? Or was it some ruse to get inside my underwear?'

'I made it all up. I haven't had a Vision for ages now and I've got no idea when one's coming. All that time on my hands has just made things harder for me, if you see what I mean.'

He stroked Kate's hair, placing it behind her ear. She knocked his hand away.

'You cocky fucker. What happened - what nearly happened - between us was a mistake. One I don't intend to repeat. You think because you're young and single and good-looking, I'm just going to fall at your feet? I'm married. I've got a daughter. I'm not that easily won over.'

'So you're saying just try harder? This really doesn't seem like a 'no'.'

Kate rolled her eyes and tutted. 'Take me back to the Mansion. NOW.'

'I'll take you back, don't you worry. But I've got a little ace up my sleeve first.'

He rummaged around in his jacket pockets for his phone. After a few jabs and swipes of his thumb on the screen, he had arrived at his destination - a photo he showed to Kate, who immediately covered her mouth.

'Oh God. I feel sick. How did you - I mean, where -'

'Simple opportunism, Kate. I snapped it while you were having your Vision in that Dublin hotel bed. A little souvenir of the trip for those lonely nights ahead.' He laughed lasciviously, mirthlessly. 'Looks like you're having a bloody good orgasm, doesn't it? That's what I imagine when I'm looking at it anyway.'

'This is disgusting. I forbid it!'

'You forbid it? That's funny. You're not actually in control of this situation: I am. And believe you me, me wanking over a slutty-looking picture of you now and again is the least of your troubles right now.'

Kate felt her chest tightening and her pulse racing once more, though she knew it was not a Vision she was facing; it was something much more sinister.

'What are you saying?'

'I'm just wondering what Pete - the husband you're apparently so devoted to despite all the lies you tell him - would make of my photography skills. I'd tell him. I'd find out where you lived and I'd tell him. Not just about this, but about your new job - everything.'

'Bollocks to you. You're bluffing. I can maybe believe you'd tell him about me and you, and make up all sorts of shit, but I don't believe for one minute you'd tell him about the Interveners. You wouldn't be so daft. You wouldn't destroy our whole organisation for a few moments of passion.'

'Well if that's what you truly believe then you have nothing to worry about, do you? Just say no, right here, right now. Call my bluff.' Silence. 'Thought so.'

Zak began his drive back to the Mansion - a noticeable degree slower this time. Kate chewed over the complexities - or otherwise - of what was happening, speaking only when her thoughts were fully formed.

'So you're saying one quick shag and that's it? You'll leave me alone? You'll destroy that bloody picture and you won't interfere in my marriage?'

'I'm not saying it will be quick, but yes to the rest of it. I'll even sign a contract if you want. I just need to scratch this itch.'

'Nice choice of phrasing. How can I resist?'

Kate felt utterly frustrated. She had always considered herself a strong and powerful woman - yet here she was, at the mercy of someone she had once considered a happy-go-lucky simpleton. Maybe that was all he still was - and so she would try simple reasoning to dissuade him in a last-ditch effort to get out of the predicament. Simple flattery. She feigned a giggle.

'Zak! Sweetie! Let's not do this! Think about what you're saying - it's madness! A hunk like you is chasing after used goods like me when there are hundreds of naive young hotties out there with far better bodies than mine. I know, because I've seen you in action, that all you need to do is snap your fingers and - hey presto! - they'll be right next to you in bed, attending to your every whim. You don't really want me - it's just because you think you can't have me.'

'You're wrong. I actually do think I can have you. Sorry but I do. And you're wrong because I don't want them - I want you. You're just so God damn elegant and classy and intelligent. I can't resist you. Believe me, I've tried.'

Kate fell silent - disarmed and, frankly, stumped. Zak had evidently used the same strategy Kate herself was trying to employ - but while she was failing, he was succeeding! He really was outsmarting her! At its heart, this was sexual blackmail, but in actuality it wasn't nearly that straightforward. What Kate was fighting against was something most women in her situation would have killed for. The 'nightmare' was in fact strikingly similar to what she herself had daydreamed about when she started Intervening not so long ago. Zak propositioning her with sex in a country field was just the kind of thing she would picture as her eyes followed him around the Mansion on those long, Vision-free days. It still didn't seem like the worst thing she could imagine.

She took out her purse, and took from it a picture of Pete and Lola and wondered to herself if things would or could ever be the same again if she agreed to Zak's proposal. The answer came quickly.

'I'm sorry. I can't have sex with you.'

Zak remained calm. 'Take a look at your watch. I'm giving you exactly one week from now, to the minute, to give me a definite answer.'

Chapter Thirty-Three

Kate, inevitably, slept poorly that night, acting out different scenarios in her head, often multiple times, yet still not coming up with a satisfactory solution.

In one scenario, she gave in to Zak's demands, but not before signing the contract (the possible existence of which may or may not have been a joke). It was unnecessary for her to envisage the carnal act itself, less so for her to picture it in what she estimated (based on her husband's typical performance) to be in real time and (based on erotically charged movies she had seen) in graphic detail, but she did so anyway. The re-buttoning of shirts, blouses and trousers afterwards was followed by a business-like handshake and no more was said of the whole sordid affair. There was a neutrality to their relationship from thereon, which suited her fine. Kate liked this version of events, but what she could not then envisage was her relationship with Pete remaining unaffected. In her first draft of this part of the story, she lived with her guilty secret for many months, during which time it gnawed away at her. Each act of sweetness and kindness Pete bestowed upon her heightened her guilt until she felt physically pained; literally sick to the stomach. It tainted happy events - she pictured next Christmas, Lola's next birthday, the next family holiday, and in each picture she wore a forced smile, unable to escape the crushing gravity of what she had done to these two lovely human beings.

So she re-wrote the script. Same start; same steamy sex scene; different ending. This time she confessed to her husband what she had done almost immediately afterwards, bending the truth only slightly to say that Zak was a co-worker but not mentioning anything about Interveners Incorporated. The organisation would be saved -

but in this imagined scenario, at the cost of her marriage. Pete called her a whore, threw her clothes into a suitcase with the hangers still attached and forced her out of the house, vowing to fight for sole custody of Lola. Was it a happy ending? Definitely not. A noble one? She wasn't sure. She tried again to re-imagine the last part, willing herself to picture Pete forgiving her and life carrying on as per normal, but it was proving impossible. She glanced at her real-life sleeping husband and had to concede to herself that the abundance of love and affection this good man showed her was probably not unconditional. He loved her too much to forgive and forget any adultery - she was sure of that.

  Kate couldn't help but picture one more scenario involving her giving into Zak's demands before she moved onto all the scenarios in which she didn't. In this scenario, the sex was so amazing and their two bodies, their two souls even, connected so well that it didn't end there. The next day, Kate marched up to her new lover, tore the contract up in front of his face and they made love again. A long, protracted affair commenced and her family life crumbled. She had to admit that her thoughts were becoming far-fetched by this point and that she was fixating too much on what the sex would be like and not the consequences - an unhelpful line of thought with which to get carried away.

  So now for the scenarios in which she rejected him. In the first possibility that formed in her mind, it proved to be the right thing to do. She took great pleasure in telling him 'no', which she did unceremoniously, deflating his ego visibly. He sobbed an apology and pleaded for her to remain friends with him. He confessed that the whole thing had been a bluff - he never intended to track down Pete, and of course he would do nothing to jeopardise the livelihoods of his colleagues and friends.

  The second version of this story was not so pleasant. In it, Zak shook his head and grinned, telling her she had made a terrible decision and that now she would be forced to play the waiting game. A hellish existence for Kate ensued, every day spent on a proverbial knife's edge. Every day she would turn the key to her front door filled with a near-debilitating dread in case Zak had finally passed on the news to Pete. Every telephone ring was a shrill reminder of her destiny. In this scenario, she did not imagine an end point - Zak simply strung out her misery, which in many ways was worse. She became a nervous, paranoid shell of her former self.

  A highly likely sequence of events, she surmised, was this one: Kate rejecting Zak (again with great aplomb - she might as well take some consolation from the situation), and Zak almost immediately going to Pete with his news; certainly within a few days. He was too young and impetuous, she thought, to do it any other way, although she also had to concede that she apparently didn't really know the man at all, so who was to say? She was unsure what Pete would do first - perhaps he would aim a punch at Zak. She hoped he would. She realised, however, that if he did so, it would be a weak and ineffectual one which would be more than matched by what the younger and musclier Zak had in store by means of retaliation. More likely, she thought, Pete would retreat into a state of shell shock, unable to digest the news at first. That's how she would know the deed had been done when she returned home - he would be emotionally numb and unresponsive. This raised the question of what Kate would actually do when he found out. The first possibility she mulled over was just escape. Run away. Abandon Pete and Lola and not face her problems. Leave the Interveners and start a new life somewhere else, maybe accounting, maybe not. It was ignoble as hell, but at least it saved Pete the pain of having to face up to what he believed was his adulterous wife (and while that technically wouldn't have been the truth, it wouldn't have been far from it either). The second possibility would be to tell Pete the whole story, far-fetched though it seemed, and hope he believed her - and also that somehow he was able to look past the reams of desire and deception still involved. She WAS working for a secret organisation of psychics. She HAD got into bed with another man for whom, yes, she had had sexual feelings. She was sorry - she was so, so sorry. Her imagination did not stretch to a scenario in which Pete accepted that apology. She found it much easier to picture him ordering her out of the house and, the next morning, beginning divorce proceedings.

Or what if she did what had come so naturally to her for so long and attempted to lie her way out of the situation? She racked her brains for any explanation of why the naked body in the picture, every inch of which Pete knew and worshipped, was not hers. She toyed with some weak ideas about Zak creating the picture using Photoshop, but none of them really added up. What, then, of the Interveners part of the betrayal? In some ways this seemed the lesser of the two evils, but in others the greater - after all, this had been an ongoing deception, and neither accident nor mistake. Kate had been prepared to keep his from Pete for the rest of her life - he would undoubtedly be angry about that. Was there any way to lie about that? A long and protracted pause in her thoughts suggested not. Kate's best hope - everyone's best hope - would be for Pete to realise the greater good of the organisation and be prepared to keep its existence a secret. Pete was a fine man with decent morals - this seemed far from an impossibility. It would all depend on how bitter he was - if he felt the need for revenge on Kate, going to the press or, perhaps, the police would be a viable option. Then who was to say what would happen to Pete next? How Gordon would deal with the matter?

One thing was for sure - she was in trouble. A long and agonising week lay ahead.

Chapter Thirty-Four

Kate arrived at work bleary-eyed and sluggish, heading straight for the coffee maker. Her tired mind was swimming with thoughts. The best way for the day to pan out would be if Kate remained Vision free and nobody requested her accompaniment on an Intervention - especially Zak. It would be even sweeter if he had a busy day of Intervening in store. All she really wanted to do was get her head down, or at very least do some quiet reflection about how best to bring this nightmare to an end.

The downstairs part of the house had been empty when Kate arrived for work, but within a minute - before she had finished making her coffee - Zak had arrived and was ferreting around the fridge for some breakfast. Kate immediately felt tense and uncomfortable.

'Morning, Kate! Nice day today.'

Kate looked around to check that no one was in earshot. She kept her tone hushed just in case. 'Zak, I've been up all night thinking about your demands. You're going to be bringing a lot of pain into my life or my family's lives, whatever happens. So I'm urging you - just call it off. Please.'

Zak laughed jovially and closed the fridge. 'You could beg!'

'Excuse me?'

'You could get down on all fours and beg me to call it off. I can't promise I will, but it's worth a shot!'

Kate's anger swelled. 'Fuck you.'

'Now, now, you're supposed to be getting on my good side - be nice to me!'

'Oh, you're really enjoying this, aren't you, you little prick? This power you've got over me.'

'Not as much as I'd enjoy being inside you. And after that, it would all be over. You'd be free. So why are you making this so complicated? Why can't we just go upstairs to my room right now and get under the sheets?'

At that moment, Sally walked into the kitchen and made a beeline for the kettle. 'Morning, guys! What are you two chin-wagging about? He's not boasting about his latest conquest, is he?'

'The opposite, actually! He was just saying how he's having a bit of a dry spell with the ladies, how he must be losing his knack. Isn't that right?'

'Yeah, but you know me! I'll bet within the week I'll have bedded some hottie. In fact you mark my words.'

Sally laughed and shook her head fondly. Kate clenched her teeth and walked out of the kitchen with her coffee, which she took into the garden. Zak did not follow, instead heading once again to the gym. Sally, however, brought her mug of tea outside to catch up with her friend.

'He's like a walking hard-on that boy, don't you think?'

'Hmm? Yes, yes I suppose so.'

'You alright, babe? You seem a bit distracted!'

'Just a bit tired. Lola's got a really chesty cough, which kept waking all of us up, so I've had a bit of a broken sleep.'

'Bless her. Hope she's okay. Anyway, back to our young Adonis in there,' Kate winced, desperate to talk about anyone or anything else. 'I reckon he's developing a bit of a soft spot for you, you lucky thing.'

Kate sat upright. 'What? What makes you say that?'

'Oh that's woken you up I see! Well, I've been noticing the way he looks at you. He sort of looks you slowly up and down when your back is turned. Wish he'd do that with me. And he seems to be picking you a lot more to go with him on Interventions, especially since you two went to Ireland together. You've got to admit that.'

Kate let out a non-committal 'hmm' sound. She wondered whether she ought to tell her friend the whole story, ask her advice (though with how much she clearly lusted after him, she suspected Sally would consider the sex not just the right option, but quite a result to boot). She decided against it for now, changing the subject by offering Sally a game of Uno, but she put the idea on the back burner. A second opinion would probably be useful and insightful and of her two possible options, she felt more comfortable chatting to Sally about it than to Gordon.

The two ladies idled away the morning playing their card game of choice, affording Kate no real opportunity to peruse her options, but she felt none the worse for that.

The afternoon was more of a drag. The weather had taken a turn and Sally had decided she would use this as an opportunity to make a long distance call to her auntie in New Zealand. This left Kate with Gordon and Zak, who had tired of his posturing in the gym but still not felt inclined to return to a normal state of dress, flicking through the TV channels in his vest and shorts, his skin still glistening slightly from the workout. Kate knew this was a deliberate ploy. She ate away half an hour internet shopping for nothing in particular (and ended the session having purchased exactly that) before taking advantage of the spare room provided for her. She couldn't decide whether napping or thinking would be the better way to spend her alone time, but in the end the decision was made for her as she succumbed to sleep almost as soon as her eyes were closed.

A solid one it was too - a two hour sleep from which she awoke disorientated and her cheek bathing in a little pool of drool. It had been deep and dream-filled, the one freshest in her mind being the old recurring chestnut in which for no apparent reason she was forced to re-sit her final exams at university and, with even sparser logic, was forced to do so naked.

She mulled over how reasonable it would be to spend the rest of the shift hiding away in her room but conceded it would probably arouse the suspicions of Sally and Gordon, so she decided to make her apologies for her longer-than-expected absence and offered Gordon a game of Chess, which he accepted with glee. Before she knew it, her working day was over - and, not atypically in this choice of career, without a lick of work being done. She aimed a goodbye at the whole group so that she did not have to mention Zak's name and drove home, slightly pissed off with herself that not only was Zak's blackmail still ongoing, she hadn't managed to come any closer to a satisfactory solution, only now she was a day closer to the deadline he had imposed. She really had no idea what to do.

It was a pleasant evening and Kate's long nap had given her a surplus of energy she needed to burn off, so Kate suggested Lola fetch her scooter and go to the park with her while Pete cleaned up the house after dinner. The little girl was delighted but insisted her daddy accompany them.

Chapter Thirty-Five

The deadline was looming and still Kate struggled to focus on anything else. She was still determined not to give into Zak's demands but was still without a clue how she was going to deal with the aftermath of this.

It was a quiet afternoon at The Mansion. Nigel had chosen Sally to ride gunshot on his current rescue mission, leaving Zak, Gordon and Kate in the big old house. Each of them was engaged in a solitary pursuit: Gordon reading a novel, Zak playing on his X-Box and Kate trying to learn Spanish from a YouTube video.

Gordon went to the toilet. When he was gone, Zak put down his controller and started letting out low moans. His face was going red. He made his way to the Vision Room.

He returned at the same time as the old man.

'Vision, Zak?'

'Yeah, nothing exciting. Another poor sap getting hit by another car, blah blah blah. Not far away. Fair bit of time. Easy one.'

'Right, well you know the drill! You've a choice of two - and what a choice!'

Zak stroked his stubble and contorted his face to look as if he was riddled with indecision. 'I think I'll flip a coin this time. Heads I'll take Gordon, tails I'll take Kate.'

Kate forced an exaggerated act of cheerfulness and crossed her fingers, holding them in the air. 'Please be me, please be me!'

The coin clunked onto the wooden floor. Zak picked it up immediately and placed it in his pocket. 'It's your lucky day, Kate! It IS you!'

'Wow, you really should have let us check that coin, Zak! People are going to start talking about you and I! They're going to start thinking you're playing favourites!'

Begrudgingly, Kate grabbed her coat. Zak grabbed the keys to the BMW and they walked up the gravel driveway.

'Well Kate, like the old song says, get out of my dreams and into my car!'

Kate shook her head. 'Ugh.'

'You know what, Zak? I wouldn't even bother pretending to put the address into the Sat Nav, sweetie. Save your breath. I know full well you didn't have a Vision - I'm not an idiot. Just start the car and say or do whatever it is you need to say or do. But make it quick. One of us might actually have a Vision today.'

'Wow. You know me too well, Katie! Let's go.'

It was several minutes into the journey before Zak spoke. This time he did not stop the car.

'So - time's ticking. Any decisions yet?'

'The answer's still no. Get it into your thick skull. Get over it. Get a hooker. Get lost. Do something, because you're not doing me.'

'Maybe I'm not selling it well enough. You can choose the when, the where, the how. YOU'RE in control of this. It doesn't have to be seedy - although it can be if you like! I mean, we can check into a really nice hotel. I've been doing my research. There's this really lovely old place, about ten miles away from the Mansion, but right in the middle of nowhere. You know the deal - check in as Mr and Mrs Smith. There's a big open fireplace in each of the rooms. Just picture it - the candles would be lit. I'd slowly strip you naked and we could make love right there on the big thick rug, the fire warming our naked backs.'

Kate said nothing. Part of her wanted to tell him to shut up - part of her wanted to tell him to carry on, to paint each and every detail in her mind. She hated herself for it, but she couldn't help but feel a little turned on.

'Don't fancy that? The same hotel has a barn. We could do it right there in the hay. That float your boat?'

It did, but she wasn't going to give him the satisfaction of knowing that. 'Someone's discovered Mills and Boon.'

'Like I said, I've been doing my research. I really want this to happen, Kate. And I want it to be amazing - for you and me. You want to be wined and dined before we do the act? I'll do that. No problem. You want romance? You'll have it. You want me to buy you some really sexy lacy underwear so you feel special? Hell yes, I'll do that. You want the opposite? You want dirty, kinky, no-holds-barred shagging? I'll gladly make it happen. You've got a favourite position? Anything. You want me to do all the work while you lie back and think of England? Okay. You want me to put a bag on my head and dress as your husband? Fine.'

'Right, you're being ridiculous now.'

'I know I am. I'm just making a point. My point is, I NEED this to happen, and I'll do anything to make it so. Anything.'

Once again Kate sat in silence, and Zak let her. This time it wasn't purely a stubborn silence - in some small way, she couldn't help but consider the newly-worded proposal. She let each of the scenarios play out in great detail in her imagination. She desperately wanted to tell him no again, but the word was not forthcoming.

He was wrong, though, and well he knew it - he was very much still in control of the situation. Dragging her out into the back of beyond and putting sexy thoughts into her mind was a very deliberate ploy for him to regain control of a situation that was falling out of his grasp. To some extent his ploy was working.

'Right, you've had your fun. Take me back to the Mansion now.'

'Your every wish is my command. You know that.'

He turned the car around. Not a single word was spoken for the journey's duration. A smile remained on Zak's lips throughout. He delivered a half-hearted cock-and-bull story to his colleagues about his successful fake Intervention (including Sally and Nigel, who had returned from their actual Intervention). He did not attempt to engage Kate in conversation for the remainder of her shift.

*****

The afternoon dragged. Not a single one of them had a Vision. At times the Mansion could feel like a kind of holiday camp - and at times, it seemed more akin to a high-end prison. Today, it was definitely the latter. Nothing held Kate's attention for more than ten minutes at a time. Now more than ever, she was regretting ever agreeing to join the organisation in the first place.

Towards the end of the day, she received a text message from her husband. ***We need to talk when you get home.***

Kate's stomach sank. It was so unlike her husband to be that direct and blunt: so unlike him to be anything other than loving and affectionate, even in texts - sometimes to an extent that Kate found cloying or suffocating. No kisses on the end. No declarations of undying love. But how she missed that overbearing tone now.

It had to be bad news.

Not bad news as in a relative dying or Lola breaking a limb - he would have rung if that had been the case - but bad news as in the game was up for her where Intervening was concerned. What else could it be? Zak's deadline had yet to pass - so it couldn't be that! Could it?

She had responded to the message with a couple of tentative replies, neither of which received a response of their own. She found herself torn about what to do where the latter part of the afternoon was concerned: so often she lied to Pete, told him she was working overtime or that she was visiting a friend on the way back or returning some clothes - anything that meant she could prolong her day at the Mansion, where she would be perfectly primed to respond to any Visions (and where, failing that, she could idle away further hours with her new best friend Sally, whose company she often found more enjoyable and easy-going than that of her husband). The most convincing reason she could find for doing so was the exact same reason she had for NOT doing so and instead returning home at the usual time - that it would prolong having to face up to Pete.

Eventually she found her thoughts monopolised by what he might have to say and could think of nothing else, to the point where she was bordering on paranoia. She grabbed her keys, made her excuses (none of which involved the truth, because she knew there could be seriously bad news for the organisation on the horizon and didn't want to tell anyone as such) and headed home.

The journey seemed endless. Questions darted through her mind, none of which she could answer.

What exactly did Pete know?

What had he seen?

What had he been told?

Perhaps he'd been following her to work - stalking her. *Had one of the Interveners spoken to him?* Maybe he'd spotted her on a rescue attempt.

Her grip on the steering wheel was becoming tighter; her palms clammier. Her heart and head both pounded.

*****

She was home. She took a deep breath and forced a smile as she walked through the door. *Show time.*

'Hi honey! Everything okay? What was that text about? And where's Lola?'

Pete didn't look angry so much as he looked numb. His tone was measured. 'I've asked my mum to have her for a couple of hours. Sit down please, Kate.'

'Baby, you're scaring me. What's up?'

'Good day at work?'

Kate knew this was a trap. She knew her response would need to be as vague as she could possibly make it while she sized up the situation. Then she could take control, weave whatever lies she needed to weave to get out of whatever this was. 'Yeah, not bad, not bad. Had better, had worse.'

Pete nodded. 'Nothing out of the ordinary happen?'

'Nope!' Kate's voice was a notch higher than she wanted it to be. 'What's on your mind, Pete?'

'Be honest with me here. Look me in the eye and tell me that you've actually been to work today.'

Just what was he getting at here? Had she been found out? Almost literally a professional liar by this point, looking her husband in the eye would not be a problem. As yet, it wasn't even a lie. 'Yes, Pete. Of course I've been to work. Why wouldn't I have been?'

'Right, I'm just gonna come out and ask this: are you having an affair, Kate?'

Kate tried to mask her own nervousness and panic by feigning anger - an easy transition with the adrenalin pumping through her body as it was.

'What?! Pete Jenson, you'd better have a bloody good reason to back that up, because - I mean - God! How could you? How dare you?'

Pete retained his composure. 'Oh, I've got a good reason all right. My sister saw you today. At about 1 o' clock. In a car with another man. A dark haired chap in his twenties, she reckoned. Just outside Winthorpe. Said it was definitely you.'

She had indeed been found out. The man was, of course, Zak. Pete was wrong - they weren't having an affair, not technically - but she felt as if her secret world had been uncovered. At least it had if she couldn't lie her way out of it. She remembered the conversation she'd had with Gordon at her welcome party. Pete knowing about the Interveners could have potentially lethal consequences.

'Weird! You know what? It's probably that lady from the theme park on the news. Remember? My doppelgänger. She strikes again! She just happened to be in Winthorpe today!'

'No, Kate. It was you. Definitely you.'

'Well now, how can you possibly know that? Your SISTER thought she saw someone who looked like me, in a strange car - you didn't see it. She could have been mistaken. She was.'

Pete shook his head, by now fighting a losing battle to contain his own (very real) anger. 'Then how do you explain this?'

Pete took his phone out of his pocket and thrust it into Kate's lap. On the screen was a photo. A photo of her and Zak. She closed her eyes and sighed.

'So there we go. Apparently your doppelgänger wears exactly the same clothes as you're wearing at this exact moment in time. Fuck me, what a coincidence!'

Kate placed her hands on her husband's shoulders. 'Honey, listen. It's time for me to be totally honest with you.' Pete's eyelids were twitching and his right leg bobbing up and down. 'God, I really didn't want to have to tell you this. Please don't be mad with me. I didn't want you to find out this way.'

'Just say it!'

'Yes, that's me in the car. Of course it is. No point denying it, is there? And, no, clearly I'm not at work in that photo. That much is obvious. The man next to me?' Kate glanced around her for inspiration. A pile of brown letters on the side proved sufficiently inspirational. 'His name's Bill. Well, Billy. Billy has been helping me.'

'Helping you? Helping you do what?'

'Helping me plan your fortieth birthday.'

'You what?'

'Billy is a professional events planner. He specialises in birthdays and stag dos, that sort of thing. I got his details because they apparently used him at my place a couple of years ago - he does corporate events. You know, team building stuff. I know it's still eighteen months away, but I wanted to plan you something special. I know you're not into drinking, so I thought I would plan you something fantastic to do in the daytime, you and your buddies. I've spent the day with Billy and he's been taking me round some different places to show me what's available. Babe, I'm spoilt for choice. There's tank driving experiences, you can fly a light aircraft, the old classics like paintballing and outdoor laser tag, of course. You can do clay pigeon shooting - there's a firing range near Winthorpe that Billy was taking me to when your sister saw me. I'm probably gonna go for one of the combo packages for you, make it really special. It's not cheap, but you're only forty once!'

Pete squeezed his eyes shut and massaged his temples. 'Jesus, I really don't deserve this.'

'Of course you deserve it! You're such an amazing husband and such an amazing dad too. You treat me like a queen and Lola like a princess. Time for you to be treated like a king for once.'

'Oh, Kate, I feel like such a dick! I shouldn't have doubted you.' He kissed her cheek. 'You're amazing. Thank you.'

Kate laughed. 'God, look at me, I'm still shaking! Can't believe I've been rumbled! You just wait till I see your sister.' She shook her fist. 'Grrrrrrrr!'

'Well, it will still be amazing, whether or not it's a surprise. Kate, I think I need to show you something. I've got something to confess this time.'

He led her by the hand into their bedroom. On the bed was an open suitcase and inside it a selection of Kate's clothes and toiletries. The clothes were neatly folded and the toiletries placed in there carefully.

'I really did think this was the end for us. I'm sorry.'

'Well that's two Billies I've been with today - the events organiser and the silly one! Now what time did you tell your mum you were picking Lola up?'

'Seven. Why?'

She winked. 'Perfect. That gives us plenty of time for you to make amends!'

She pushed the case off the bed and her husband onto it. She removed her jacket, then blouse, then skirt, then bra. Pete still found his wife as wildly attractive as the first time he ever laid eyes on her - the site of her stood there bare-breasted in front of him drove him crazy. This, coupled with the relief of not losing the woman he loved, meant he was immediately turned on: no foreplay was necessary, and none attempted by either of them. Though more often than not Pete went on top, this time it was Kate who did so, removing first his clothes then finally the one remaining item of hers. She had enjoyed the sense of control she had felt as she wove her lie and wanted this to continue.

She inspected her erect husband. 'My my! Well I guess now it's my turn to feel a dick!'

No doubt about it, Kate felt exhilarated. She had thought on her feet, rescued herself (rather than a complete stranger) from the brink and it had felt oddly exciting. She channelled that energy into making love to her husband. Images of a naked Zak flicked in and out of her mind, uninvited but not entirely unwelcome either. Barely more than five minutes later they lay cuddling and smiling, and five minutes after that that Pete was in his dressing gown putting Kate's clothes back on their hangers.

She resolved from that moment on to wear a wig, or at very least a hat and sunglasses, on the journey to every Intervention attempt - a resolution to which she stuck. She worked too close to home to chance it. She had got away with it this time, but she knew she had to be more careful. This was to turn out to be a lasting contribution made by Kate to the timeline of the Interveners - her colleagues did the same from there on in.

Meanwhile, she had a fortieth birthday to plan. Not like she didn't have plenty of time on her hands to do so. She just had the small matter of resolving her little problem with Zak to get through first.

Chapter Thirty-Six

It was Friday. The group had always maintained many of the traditions associated with more conventional workplaces such as collections for special occasions, fancy dress days for charity and bringing in cakes for everyone else on birthdays. Fridays at Interveners Incorporated were Fried Fridays, the gang taking it in turns to make bacon sandwiches for everyone. Today was Kate's turn.

She smiled to herself as she fantasised about lacing Zak's roll with a little poison - that would at least be that problem solved. Though she did not usually enjoy cooking for her colleagues, on this occasion she was glad of the distraction. Focusing on not burning the bacon meant she was not trying - and failing - to think of a (sensible) way to get out of her predicament with Zak.

Nigel got a mid-morning Vision - a drowning at a beauty spot a hundred miles away - taking Zak with him for the ride, to Kate's great relief. Sally was cleaning the Mansion. Kate was watching a game show - or at least she was until Gordon got a Vision of his own and took Kate with him.

*****

'My dear, I've become a great student over the years of body language, and I can't help but notice something seems to be troubling you.'

'What makes you say that?'

'You're looking intently out into the middle distance at nothing whatsoever. You keep crossing and uncrossing your arms. And you've never been a nail biter. Now I firmly believe that one's own business is one's own business, so if you don't want to talk that's fine. But I also believe in that old adage of a problem shared is a problem halved. So if you want to talk, I'm all ears. I can't promise I'll have all of the answers, but I can promise I'll give you my full and undivided attention.'

Kate thought for only a moment before deciding that harbouring this awful dilemma was killing her. And Gordon was such a wise old owl - he would surely have something insightful to offer. Offloading on him couldn't hurt, she believed. She took a deep breath.

'Gordon, what I'm going to tell you will make you think less of me, I'm sure of it, but here goes. I've got myself into a huge amount of trouble.'

'I see. And would this trouble happen to involve young Zak, by any chance?'

Kate turned her head towards the old man, astounded. 'Yes. How did -'

'Like I say, I study body language and I can tell something isn't right between you two. He's impregnated you, hasn't he?'

'What? No.'

'Oh thank goodness. Although genetically speaking you two ought to produce one Hell of an Intervener. Anyway, I said I would listen and I'm interrupting. Please continue and I'll refrain from interjecting.'

'Well, I have to admit I've always found him a bit dishy, right since I started as an Intervener. Turns out it was mutual. Things spilled over when we went to Dublin and we ended up drunk and in bed together. Nothing happened because I got a Vision, but the dirty little bastard took a naked picture of me without me realising. He bided his time but eventually showed me the picture saying if I didn't sleep with him for real, he would go to Pete, tell him all about Dublin, all about the Interveners.'

Waddington bit his bottom lip and nodded before pulling into the side of the road and switching on his hazard lights.

'I see. Well this is rather a serious situation, isn't it?'

'Gordon, what's happening? Keep going or we might not make the Intervention!'

'One minute while we regain our composure is probably not going to change things.'

Kate could see Gordon's hands were quivering a little.

'Have you considered the possibility that he might sleep with you but still tell your husband? After all, now you'll actually have done the deed - what's stopping him secretly recording you in bed?'

Kate fell dumbstruck. She hadn't considered it. She had considered many possibilities - many, many possibilities - but not that one. She burst into tears and started hammering her temples with her fists. 'Fuck. Fuck, fuck, fuck, fuck, fuck. Fuck. Oh Gordon, what am I going to do?'

He took hold of her wrists. 'You're going to calm down. We're both going to take a sip of water and carry on with our mission. And we're going to think. Two heads are better than one.'

Not a word was spoken as they made their successful Intervention - a horrific would-be workplace accident in which a man was due to be locked inside a furnace. They managed to evade the death by Gordon pretending to be a delivery man, carrying an empty cardboard box into the reception with the company address on. Before anyone had a chance to realise the package was empty, Gordon had smashed the glass box on the wall to raise the fire alarm and the building had been evacuated.

As they entered the last mile of their return journey, Waddington finally spoke. 'Kate, I would like you to forget about your predicament tonight and sleep as soundly and as unburdened as you possibly can. I am going to take over now. If by lunchtime tomorrow, neither Zak nor I have had a Vision, I'm going to fake one and take him along with me. I'll talk to him, my dear. I'll reason with him. I'll make him see sense. I'll convince him of the terrible consequences that await him if he goes through with his plan - the lives that will be lost if our organisation becomes public knowledge. I'll be gentle with him if I need to be and firm with him if I need to be, but I'll sort it out, so please don't worry.'

Though nothing had actually changed yet, Kate felt instantly assured. The tight, nervous feeling in her stomach seemed to dissipate instantly and a smile appeared on her face. She leaned over and kissed the old man on the cheek. 'Thank you so much.'

Chapter Thirty-Seven
Kate felt a certain lightness of spirit as she drove to work. She trusted Waddington and was more than prepared to put all of her faith into him talking Zak out of the blackmail. When she greeted Zak in the living room, it was with a smile, albeit one cut with an element of self-satisfaction.

It wasn't long before Gordon was making his way to the Vision Room - way before the lunchtime deadline he had set, so Kate was unsure whether it was for real or not, but she knew what his next move would be.

'Zak, would you mind coming with me on this one?'

'No problem-o.'

Kate watched the two of them exit and as Waddington closed the door behind him, he shot Kate a wink.

No Visions for the female Interveners today, who idled away the drizzly day with a 'Chick Flick Marathon', grazing on popcorn (an absent Nigel was away on a money-raising expedition in the North East of England). The films were sufficiently fluffy and likeable to distract Kate's thoughts from becoming fixated on what was or was not happening between Zak and Gordon. Anything any more or any less demanding and she would not have been able to concentrate at all. She still drifted in and out, though, especially at those points when the films became overly predictable and when the scenes became raunchier, Kate finding it all too easy to interchange the male lead with Zak, and then the female lead with herself. Still, no second thoughts - she would definitely feel pleased when Gordon returned and informed her that it was all over, that he had dissuaded Zak.

It was just after two in the afternoon when the door burst open. Waddington stumbled through in a hysterical state, his breath shallow and tears streaming down his cheeks. Kate and Sally dashed towards him, supporting him at each shoulder and shepherding him to one of the sofas.

Sally spoke first. 'Gordon, what's the matter sweetie? What's happened? Where's Zak?'

Gordon looked into Sally's eyes, his own eyes glassy and vacant. More so than before. 'There's been a terrible accident. We were saving a small child from stepping onto a train track out in the countryside, but the traffic had been horrendous. We were cutting it really fine. I could hear the train coming. We ran as fast as we could but I couldn't keep up. Zak kept sprinting. He was running so fast that when he pulled the child out of harm's way, he couldn't stop his momentum and tumbled onto the track. He was struck by the train.' He burst into tears once again. 'It knocked him high into the air. I knew he was dead even before he hit the ground.'

The ladies joined in with his hysterical weeping and the three of them sat there, embracing, rocking, wailing, spitting out sentence fragments. When this eventually subsided, it was Sally once again who spoke first.

'Where is he now, Gordon? Where's his body?'

'I don't know, dear. I left the scene. I couldn't admit an association with him. Questions would be asked. Our whole organisation could be compromised. They'll discover his identity and no doubt track down his brother. His family will take care of the rest.'

'But won't someone have seen you, running with him?'

'No, no I don't think so. Only the boy, but he was small. He won't be able to recall me to anyone.'

Sally got up. 'Look, we can talk about all this later. I'll make us all a cuppa, eh?'

When Sally was out of earshot, Kate relinquished her embrace. She spoke in slow, broken whispers. 'Gordon, I need you to look me in the eye and tell me you didn't murder Zak.'

He obeyed the first of the two orders. 'My dear, how could you be so preposterous? So presumptuous? What happened today was a terrible, unfortunate accident.'

'Unfortunate coincidence, you mean?'

'I don't know what you're saying.'

'Don't play dumb with me, Gordon. You're better than that. This morning you're telling me my problem is going to go away and this afternoon Zak is dead?'

'Look, Kate, if you want to read more into this then maybe we call this a twist of fate.'

'Fate? The very thing we stop happening all the time? You think fate is on our side?' Kate eyed her friend in the kitchen who was pouring the boiling water into the mugs and so quickened her speaking pace. 'Did you even try to reason with him?'

'Yes of course. And he admitted the whole thing - told me that he was going to tell Pete everything but that I had talked him out of it.'

'And you were satisfied with that?'

'Not really. The boy was prepared to jeopardise everything - everything all of us have worked so hard for - just to get you in bed. No, I'm afraid he was not to be trusted.'

'So you did kill him?'

Gordon's tone sharpened. 'What I am saying to you is that a kind of justice was done today. You're a good person and your marriage was saved. We are good people and our organisation was saved, which means lots of lives - good, innocent people's lives - will be saved. Do you understand?'

'Tea's ready!' Sally wandered in, her eyes red and puffy but with a brave smile on her face.

'Thank you, dear.'

The three sat close together but no longer linked, this time in a prolonged reflective silence. Once again, Sally was first to speak, lifting her mug aloft.

'Hey, here's to a bloody good one. He lived a hero and he died being a hero. To Zak!'

Gordon and Kate raised their mugs and the three clinked together, but the toast they managed did not quite have the same vigour or sincerity as Sally's. 'To Zak.'

The remaining few hours of Kate's working day dragged by at an almost painful pace. Kate never found herself in a position whereby she was alone with Gordon again and therefore able to follow up her earlier questions, and she couldn't help but suspect that was partly by Gordon's design. It seemed disrespectful to their dead colleague to engage in any kind of leisure pursuit and Kate hoped and prayed she did not get a Vision - she was already emotionally spent and could not stand the draining feeling that would accompany the experience. So they all simply sat around, one, two or all of them bursting into tears periodically.

When 5 o' clock came, Kate held back before leaving the Mansion, switching on the local news on the television. Sure enough, Zak's story was the main one.

'A man has died after being struck by a train just outside of Harteston. The man has been named by police as twenty-four year old Zak Winters. The incident is being treated as unexplained but non-suspicious and his family have been informed. With further details, here's Linda Hargreaves who's at the scene of the accident. Linda, what exactly do we know about what happened?'

The reporter spoke from a cordoned-off scene next to the train track. 'David, at the moment details are sketchy but it would appear that Mr Winters tumbled down this hillside and onto the train track at precisely 12:32pm, at the exact time the freight train was passing by. We've been unable to get hold of any eyewitnesses, but police tell us that the driver of the train is inevitably in a state of shock so they're waiting for a suitable time to question him about what he saw.'

'Linda, can we say if drink or drugs were a factor?'

'Not as yet David, no. That's something that will be investigated, of course, but the toxicology reports will take some time.'

'And is too early to say whether or not this was suicide?'

'Well of course that's a line of enquiry that's being pursued, but at the moment that would be no more than speculation. We'll bring you further details as and when we get them.'

'For now Linda, thank you. Over a hundred jobs are to be -'

Kate switched the television off. Sally looked dismayed. 'And they never even mentioned his heroism.'

'I was just thinking the same thing,' Kate said. 'It's like it never happened.'

And then there were four.

Chapter Thirty-Eight

Kate found herself hugging Pete extra tight as she returned from work. His arms were emotional refuge. He asked why her eyes seemed so red and puffy - had someone upset her at work? She evaded his line of questioning by vague talk of hay-fever, though she was desperate to tell him the truth (or at least some of it) - that one of her colleagues had died unexpectedly. She needed - craved - his reassurance, his sympathy, his undivided attention. The only way she was able to get the comfort she needed was through wine, and lots of the stuff. That was also the only way she stood any chance of getting any sleep. She watched her daughter as she drank, glad that her family unit had survived unscathed. She was able to battle her emotions expertly, using each of her many toilet trips as an excuse to have a little cry.

Chapter Thirty-Nine

Once more, Kate found herself filled with dread as she drove to work, red-eyed from over-indulgence of alcohol, too little sleep and too much crying. She felt, in every way possible, exhausted.

As she arrived at the Mansion, she was greeted with the sight of Sally and Gordon breaking the news to Nigel, who had just returned from his fund-raising trip. Nigel was a glib man, and his emotional state was a consistent one - he did not react with any form of histrionics. Sally had her arm draped round him, though he was not reciprocating. He just sat there, gazing out into the distance, looking numb and dumbfounded.

A torturously uneventful day lay ahead. No one received a Vision. Such a thing would have been hard in many ways, as they were all so drained as it was, but the best possible turn of events in many others - the saving of lives would have been a much-needed counterbalance to the loss of Zak's. The show had to go on.

The Interveners had to go on.

The place felt deeply strange to Kate - eerie and ghostly in Zak's absence. Grief weighed heavy in every room - and for Kate and Kate only there was an added element of fear and mistrust. She was sharing breathing space with a murderer - she was sure of it.

Chapter Forty

The day of Zak's funeral had arrived. Sally sat on Kate's left, her shoulders occasionally bobbing up and down as she dabbed her crying eyes with her handkerchief. Gordon sat on Kate's right, evidently displaying no emotion whatsoever. His expression was somber, but then it almost always was. He simply stared out into space. Kate was, in both senses, in the middle, not crying but with the definite feeling that she could at any moment. Her throat felt thick and choked and there was an infrequent jabbing sensation in her stomach. She squeezed Sally's hand, but not Gordon's. Nigel had chosen not to attend the funeral at all, much to the great chagrin of his colleagues, though his reluctance seemed less to do with disrespect or indifference than a kind of fear that he might surrender to his own emotions. He would grieve privately, he told them, say his own goodbyes, and no one argued.

Kate wasn't listening as the vicar delivered a generic sermon. Much like the three Interveners in his congregation, he had obviously experienced a great amount of deaths in his career, albeit at a different stage - and like them he had become hardened to the whole thing. Like them, this was simply part of his job, part of his routine.

'At this moment I will ask if anyone here would like to say a few words. I understand it is a difficult time and you may feel unable to do so.'

Gordon looked around him and upon realising no one was going to deliver a speech got to his feet. He fixed his tie, cleared his throat and made his way to the microphone. Kate and Sally looked at each other, somewhat befuddled.

'Ladies and gentleman, I realise very few of you here know who I am. My name is Gordon. Zak was a friend of mine - a very dear friend indeed - who I met in the last years of his life. The last years of both of our lives really. There is something I would like to tell you all about Zak. A secret he held.' Kate's eyes bulged. What the Hell was Waddington doing? He wasn't - surely - about to reveal the identity of the Interveners? 'Zak was -' Gordon's voice broke and he took a moment to regain his composure, his audience totally enraptured. 'Zak was a lifesaver. And he was a lifesaver long before the dreadful day when his own life came to an end.'

Kate was dumbstruck. He really was doing this. *What was going on? Had Waddington become overpowered by his own sense of guilt? Was this his act of contrition? Forsaking the entire organisation to appease his own conscience?* The motives were irrelevant - all Kate could think about was how her lifestyle was going to change. She would revert back to the daily grind of accounting. No more heart-stopping heroics. No more chases in fabulous old cars to rescue people from the brink of death. Just reality. Just as it used to be.

'You see, folks, Zak saved my life. That's how we met. We both happened to be in the same pub one lunchtime and suddenly I found myself choking. That bag of pork scratchings could have been the death of me.' Kate saw a little flicker of a smirk appear on the corner of Gordon's mouth. If anyone else had noticed it they would have thought it as result of his fond reminiscences. But Kate saw it differently. 'There was absolutely no one else around: no bar staff, no other customers. Just Zak and myself. Quick as a flash, he was straight over, performing the Heimlich manoeuvre, cool as anything. It was almost...almost like fate.'

What exactly was he playing at here? Kate wondered. Was this just a game to him? Just a joke? Who was he toying with here - the church full of mourners or Kate herself? She was as certain as she could be that Gordon deliberately killed Zak, and equally certain that Gordon knew that Kate knew. This brazen display of lies felt to Kate like rubbing salt in the wounds.

'Zak prolonged this old fella's life. Not just by saving it that day, but enriching it with his friendship in the days, weeks, months and years that have followed. What a terrible injustice that I stand here today on the day that we bury that beautiful young man. Thank you, Zak. Thank you and goodbye.'

Gordon returned to his seat to a gentle smattering of applause, but not from Kate. She couldn't even make eye contact with him. There had been no need for him to deliver his eulogy - no one had specifically asked him to. No one had expected him to. If, indeed, Gordon really was Zak's killer, it was the ultimate act of disrespect and arrogance. The man next to her was an actor at best, a remorseless killer at worst.

*****

And so the time had arrived for Zak's coffin to be lowered into the ground. Though she had tried her hardest not to do so, Kate couldn't help but look at the grieving faces around her. A handsome young chap cocooning a lady in her middle ages, both of them weeping openly, simply had to be Zak's brother and mother. An almost overwhelming sense of guilt washed over Kate. She, herself, had not murdered Zak. Nor had she been responsible for the emotional and sexual blackmail which had (unjustly) led to the end of his life. That was all Zak. But if she had never walked into that Mansion in the first place - dismissed the invitation as the work of nut-jobs or pranksters and just carried on with her ordinary life - none of this would have happened. Zak would still be out there, young and carefree, alive in so many ways, bedding anything that walked. She had witnessed many untimely deaths but never before rued her existence as an Intervener quite so much.

She began to sob. She could no longer be part of what was happening. She slipped away from the assembled throng and returned to the car, where she waited for Gordon and Sally to return. When they eventually did, she pleaded with them not to attend the wake, saying she simply didn't feel up to it. She found herself emotionally spent and slept through most of the journey back to the Mansion.

Chapter Forty-One

Zak was gone. Kate's biggest - or at least most immediate - problem was gone (though seldom did the removal of a problem ever feel so achingly painful). Potentially - and Kate had to remind herself of this, which she did almost to the point of obsession - the biggest threat to the very existence of Interveners Incorporated was gone. A fifth of the remaining Interveners staff itself was gone. But something else was gone, too. A sense of vitality, of exuberance and energy, was gone - not just in terms of the absence of Zak himself, but also that of Sally in particular. The grieving process had diminished her, subdued her. Where she was fizzy before, she was now flat. Her banter - so frequent and flowing before - was now infrequent and forced. She clearly felt Zak's absence more keenly than did the other three (and to her - as well as Kate - a certain air of sexiness had also gone from the Mansion). Possibly she was somewhat shell-shocked. Either way she wasn't herself.

The Mansion was quieter. Not just a fifth quieter, but more so. The Interveners spoke less to each other, and did so in softer, more polite tones. Sometimes they simply sat around, not doing anything at all. Not engaging with each other, not watching the television, not doing crossword puzzles, not doing any of the pursuits designed to keep their brains sharp in the lulls between Interventions - not knitting, not learning Spanish, not attempting to play the old Mansion piano, not studying Law. Rather, they gazed into space, their inactivity soundtracked by the ticking of the grandfather clock. Each of them knew – or in Sally's case thought they knew - what each of them was thinking. At times like that, the Mansion seemed ludicrously huge and empty. With both Chris and Zak gone, the pool table remained unused, the balls permanently ready and waiting inside their triangle. The video games consoles gathered dust, and the remaining Interveners seldom played poker. It was yet another room that was all but untouched in what was starting to seem like a place of needless opulence and space.

Interventions were always a welcome change of pace and focus from what could at times be a morbid workplace, and regardless of who had experienced the Vision, the other three desperately but secretly hoped it would be their turn to act as the plus one. The grief - the gravity of what had happened - seemed to ease in the fresh air outside of the Mansion, and even more so the further away they travelled.

It wasn't that Zak was never mentioned. When his name came up, it was in a fond and reminiscent way - *do you remember the time Zak did this? Do you remember the time Zak said that? Zak always used to love such and such*, and so on and so on. Most often it was Sally who spoke of him in that way. Kate refrained from such talk as she would have found her own hypocrisy unbearable - how could she speak of him in such a rose-tinted way when his final days with her were so dark and sinister? When, in some small but undeniable way, his death was of some relief to her? Her skills as a liar were not in any doubt, but lying to herself was another matter entirely. Occasionally, it was Gordon who spoke of him in that dewy-eyed way - an act Kate would find so repulsive that she would simply have to leave the room and make a cup of tea or use the toilet. *How dare he?*

Yes, the aftermath was difficult. Difficult for everyone, in different ways. But, true to the old adage, time was a healer. The mood lightened as the weeks and months passed. The banter gradually returned. The joviality gradually returned. Kate's trust of Gordon even gradually started to return. Not since the first time she had asked him, on the very day of Zak's death, did the question of whether Gordon actually murder him ever crop up again. She just assumed he did. Of course he did. Yet there was always that small - oh so small - element of doubt in Kate's mind. Zak's death was evidently never treated as suspicious by the police - so maybe, just maybe, it really was an unfortunate accident. If

Gordon really was Zak's murderer, he seemed to be getting off scot-free - so maybe he wasn't! Kate found that doubt a necessary tool in working so closely with Gordon and tolerating him. As time passed, she went from being certain he did it to near-as-dammit certain to almost certain and finally to fairly certain. And that worked for her just fine. No need to prod and poke.

Her increasing trust of him went hand-in-hand with her increasing affection towards him. She'd liked Gordon the first time she met him, and she'd liked him more and more pretty much every day since. She had somehow managed to convince herself, as time passed, that what had happened – what had potentially happened – didn't need to change that. And if he really had murdered Zak, Kate had to concede that he had at least done so with the best intentions - with the company's future and Kate's marriage in mind. Both were still intact. The world deserved that. The company deserved that. Kate deserved that.

Chapter Forty-Two
It was just Kate and Sally in the living room of the Mansion late that morning. Gordon and Nigel were on an Intervention.

Kate looked at her friend and smirked. 'Sal, we're good friends, aren't we?'

Sally beamed. 'Of course we are, chick!'

'And we can tell each other ANYTHING - right?'

'We always do!'

'And ask each anything - right?'

'Yes! Yes, yes, yes. Obviously.'

'Great. In that case I need to ask you - what the bloody hell is going on with your boobs?'

Sally blushed and shifted around. 'What do you mean?'

'They're ruddy huge all of a sudden! I'm well jealous! Have you had a boob job or something without telling me?'

She laughed. 'No babe. I really haven't. I've just invested in some really good bras, that's all.'

Kate eyed her with mock suspicion. 'You'd best not be fibbing to me, young lady!'

'I'm not. Anyway, how's about a cuppa and a brain dead chick flick?'

'Sold.'

Chapter Forty-Three

Equilibrium eventually returned to the now truncated Interveners staff - they adapted to life as a foursome, and before long it became hard to remember a time when this wasn't the norm. Equilibrium returned, too, to Kate's family life. As her emotional state stabilised, so too did her marriage. She found herself less prone to mood swings, less snappy with her husband, and more devoted to him. She hated to admit it, but Zak's absence was a blessing of sorts.

One day, however, Kate awoke with a strange feeling in her stomach, which she immediately dismissed as period pains and loaded her handbag with paracetamol.

The feeling only intensified as she got to work. She found herself feeling distinctly out of sorts, and it wasn't going unnoticed by her favourite and most intuitive Intervener.

'You okay, babe? You look a bit pale.'

'Yeah, I'm okay. Okay-ish, anyway. Think it's just time-of-the-month stuff. You know how it is.'

'Well, in that case Doctor Baxter prescribes sitting around the Mansion all morning doing sod all. You know, just for a change.'

'Thanks for the offer, but I'm on the cleaning rota today. Those toilets aren't gonna scrub themselves, you know.'

Kate stood up, but Sally immediately pushed her back down onto the sofa. 'Sit down, you daft cow. I'm doing it today. You can do mine next time I've got a debilitating hangover.'

'Deal.'

'And if it gets any worse, just let the boss know. He's really good: you know that. He'll let you go home without question.'

Kate didn't feel bad enough to be away from the Mansion and the opportunity to save lives. And so she idled away the morning, sometimes doing nothing more than watching disgruntled young couples sweating over televised paternity tests and sometimes doing nothing at all, but either way doing it on the giant sofa. Sally laboured away getting the Mansion spick and span, as promised, while Gordon and Nigel said not a word to each other as they played long, thoughtful and multiple games of chess.

It was just after lunchtime that it happened. The pains became sharper, more frequent, and she felt more and more light-headed. Soon her whole body felt encapsulated by the physical agony. She was having a Vision. But just as she wasn't feeling the normal succession of sensations, this wasn't a normal Vision. It was altogether something more intense, more terrifying.

It was an office scene. Inside the office, four women and a man going about their business. Could have been any office, anywhere. Then all of a sudden the door was kicked open and a wild-eyed young man wearing a backpack stormed in brandishing a gun. The women screamed. The man was pleading something inaudible as he advanced with great trepidation on the gunman, his hand gestures a cross between surrendering and gesturing for the gun to be put down. Before he had the chance to come face to face with the assailant, the gun was fired and the bullet landed right between the man's eyes. The eyes themselves had rolled to the back of his head before he had even hit the floor. Cue further screams. It was within a matter of ten seconds that four further muffled thuds were heard - the gunshots that led to the immediate deaths of the women. A further gunshot and the gunman himself was dead, this time self-inflicted.

Kate came to, by this point drenched in sweat and shaking uncontrollably. Sally was by her side, holding her hand.

'God, mate, I've never seen you like that before. Let's get you in the Vision Room pronto.'

Kate couldn't muster up any words and allowed herself to be led, then to be hooked up to the machine. She could barely watch the scene being replayed, though her friend did, white-faced and open mouthed.

'So now you know why I looked like I did. Holy shit. Come on, let's get the address, quick.'

'What? No! Absolutely not!'

'Excuse me?'

Sally was panicky. And angry. 'I said no! You signed a contract. Number Three - *You may not Intervene in murder scenes.* And this, Kate, is very obviously a murder. In fact it's a murder-suicide, so you'd be breaking two rules.'

Kate matched every bit of vitriol she was receiving, and the two of them continued their exchange in this fashion. It was the theme park incident all over again. 'So what are you going to do? Just let those poor, innocent people die? Rules are meant to be broken. I thought you had more about you than that, Sally.'

'Yes. As a matter of fact, yes I am going to let them die. And actually rules are not meant to be broken. There's a perfectly good reason you're not meant to attend murder scenes, and you well know it. I'll be damned if I'm going to sit back and let you get shot by some maniac with a grudge.' Her anger had spilled over into tears. 'Newsflash - you're not actually a superhero. You're not invincible. You get shot, you will die. I care about you too much. We NEED you too much. Now please, please. Forget about it and go home. Go shopping. Do something, but do not attend that Intervention. It's out of your reach.'

Sally leaned over to unhook Kate from the machine - a gesture that was immediately rebuffed as Kate freed herself from its confines, glaring at her partner throughout.

'I'm not going to mention this to Nigel. And I'm definitely not going to mention it to Gordon. He would sack you immediately if he even suspected you were contemplating this.'

'Gee, thanks. You're all heart. I know the contract says this, that and the other, but I also believe it's just words. I think Gordon would actually approve when he found out.'

'Kate, I'm going to tell you something now that will shock you. You won't like it and you're not to repeat it. Remember about five years ago, that awful knife attack in that secondary school in West Yorkshire?'

'God, yes, of course I do. All those innocent lives lost. Such a tragedy.'

'Indeed. And Gordon foresaw it all. He foresaw it but he chose to do nothing about it. Not because he's chicken shit, but because he's got his head screwed on. Now tell me again that you think he'd pat you on the back for trying to Intervene today.' Silence. 'Yeah, thought not.'

Sally slammed the door of the Vision Room behind her as she left.

Kate refused to go home. Initially she was too shaken up, too full of pent-up aggression to get herself home safely. When that had subsided, she was too stubborn to be told what to do. She remained on the couch, sulking, pretending to watch grudge-filled ex-couples exchange insults in front of a live studio audience. She wasn't actually in possession of the tiny concentration levels required for even that task, instead still obsessing over her Vision.

The minutes passed, painfully slowly. She had no idea whatsoever how long the victims had until their lives came to an end, if indeed they hadn't already. She flicked on the news. Conflicts in the Middle East. A Premier League football manager sacked. A disgraced politician forced to resign. But no mention of a fatal workplace shooting spree. Which meant, potentially, there was still time.

About an hour had seeped away (seeming much more like ten) when Gordon made his way into the Vision Room. Kate wondered if he was possibly seeing the same horrendous Vision she had. Evidently not - he walked out shortly afterwards relatively perky and grabbed his coat and keys.

'Nothing too exciting. Old lady slipping on a grape in a Tesco about forty miles away. Easy. Now then, eenie-meenie-miney-mo - I choose Sally, go go go!'

Sally's eyes widened. 'Are you sure, Gordon? Don't feel like you have to. You can go with Nigel if you like. I won't be offended.'

'Nonsense! He and I have spent far too much time together of late. And it's been several days since you and I had a spin together. It won't do you any harm to be separated from your Siamese twin over there for a bit.'

Kate looked at Sally. Her darting eyes suggested she was desperately thinking of something to say.

'I...I...I've got a bit of a headache, Gord. Honestly, probably best I stay here.'

'Headache? No problem. We'll get the top down on the old girl and blow the cobwebs right away. You'll be right as rain in no time. Come along!' He grabbed her by the hand and led her towards the door. 'I'll start to get offended if you keep turning me down.'

'Erm, yes. Yes, of course. Nigel, do me a favour will you, hun? Whatever you do, make sure Kate does not leave the sofa. She needs some rest.'

The two ladies exchanged narrow-eyed glances. Nigel nodded and returned to his broadsheet.

Kate kept the twenty four hour news channel on. Still nothing. Part of her knew that she was simply torturing herself by watching, but she couldn't resist. And all the while that the victims were still ostensibly alive, Kate couldn't rule out going to their rescue.

She looked at Nigel. What would his reaction be? Would he side with Sally, agree that there was no way in the world she was to attend this Intervention? Or beyond that glib exterior, was there a sparky rebel, an outlaw desperate to shine? No, she decided. He was just a miserable bastard. He'd tell on her for sure. If she was to make this Intervention

- if - it would have to be alone. She'd already be breaking two rules. A third couldn't make matters any worse.

Kate felt like she was in some cartoon or old Western. Nigel was the sleeping jailer, sat there on his rocking chair just outside her cell. She was the prisoner, scheming for a way to get the (metaphorical) oversized ring of keys from his belt so she could unlock the cell and be free from this prison.

She could simply leave. Tell Nigel her condition had worsened and needed to go home. Then get in her own car and Intervene. The only problem? She didn't know the address. She would need to find a reason to be in the Vision Room, without arousing Nigel's suspicions. Occasionally - though not often - Nigel would have an afternoon nap. That would have been the perfect opportunity for her to strike. She could play the waiting game, but time really wasn't on her side.

That's when the idea came to her. She knew, from previous cleaning duties, that Gordon kept sleeping pills in his top drawer. She fetched them.

'Cup of tea, Nige?'

'No thank you.'

'Oh, go on. I'm having one. I insist.'

'Fair enough.'

'Sugar?'

'As always.'

A spoonful of sugar helps the medicine go down, went the song in Kate's head. She made the tea then crushed three pills with her thumb and forefinger, allowing the contents to drop into the mug. A heaped teaspoon of sugar and an extra-brisk stir followed. She brought the mug over, with a Rich Tea biscuit for good measure, as per her colleague's preference.

If time seemed to be digging its heels in before, it was nothing compared to the painfully slow process of waiting for Nigel to doze off. But, eventually, he did just that. Kate waited a few minutes until he was snoring loudly, then gave him a little jab with her elbow to be sure.

Success.

She tiptoed gingerly into the Vision Room and hooked herself up. She saw the Vision play out for a third time - only this time the colours on the screen seemed more vivid. The voices were more audible. The pleading man could now be heard saying,

'Patrick, I'm sorry. It was out of my hands. Please, put down the gun. We can help you.' The shot to his forehead - and the ones that followed - seemed less muffled, this time leaving more of a crisp, ringing sound. The screams that filled the scene seemed shriller, sharper, more chilling, more real.

But Kate was on a mission and was determined to remain focused and unperturbed. Her adrenalin levels were high and she was going to put them to good use - do something unthinkable, something strictly forbidden. She gathered the vital information, choosing not to commit any names to memory (partly because it was unnecessary information and partly because knowing the names would only add an extra layer of guilt if and when she heard them again on the news). No, she needed to know only two things. The scene? Only twelve miles away. The time? A minute short of half an hour away. She could make it. Hell, she would be back with bags of time to spare before Gordon and Sally returned. They would find her back on the sofa watching crappy daytime television quite as if nothing had happened, blissfully unaware of the ultimate act of heroism that had occurred that afternoon. All being well, of course.

She crept out of the door with absolutely no idea of what she was going to do. All she knew was that she needed to be somewhere, and she needed to be there post-haste. Her Sat Nav seemed bog standard compared to the ones in the luxury cars (suckered to her windscreen as it was), and the act of physically typing in the address rather than speaking it aloud seemed annoyingly time consuming.

She hadn't even got out of the gravel driveway before she realised she needed to turn back. In her panicky rush, she had forgotten a key component of the rescue process - the wig. She hastily reached for the nearest one, a curly, shoulder-length ginger hairpiece.

She tried to formulate a plan as she drove, but her thoughts were wild and random. She was determined, but ultimately very scared. She was about to come face-to-face with an actual gunman - thinking straight was proving nigh-on impossible. How the Hell was she going to disarm him? This wasn't like most Interventions. Altering his path slightly or stalling him briefly was going to change nothing: this was a man with a plan, a purpose, and he was going carry it out. This one needed something bigger, bolder, better. Her only real hope was that something - something - would come to her in the heat of the moment. That, much like in the theme park, her brain would thrive on the pressure and, right at the last minute, something brilliant would come to her. If it didn't, she would be waiting outside an office as a murder took place inside, knowing all about it, practically an accomplice.

She tried so hard to Envision a successful resolution - driving away buzzing with her own victory, hoping that if she thought of it enough, it would somehow happen. That picture was vague and fleeting. Much clearer and more lingering was the image of Pete and Lola weeping over her grave. Perhaps she had seen her family for the final time. Perhaps this was her last day on Earth. Perhaps her own death was due within the hour. More likely than both of these scenarios, though, was the one in which she drove away alive but a failure, with a secret she would have to carry inside of her forever more, knowing she should have stuck to the contract.

The journey was fluid. She couldn't be totally sure, but by the time she pulled up in the office block car park, she couldn't recall a single red light. It was quite possible that if she had, she had gone through it. Either way, she was here and she had six minutes to spare.

Six minutes to think of something.

Six minutes in which she considered turning around, but then changed her mind, at least a dozen times.

Six minutes in which her thoughts only seemed to be getting cloudier, busier, more muddled. Louder somehow. She felt in no way in control of this situation - the situation was controlling her, and she was no longer accountable for her own actions. Would she have to kill him? Was that the only way to stop him, whilst still keeping herself safe? Somehow try to murder him with his own weapon? Was that morally okay, to kill a person in order to stop others being killed? She just didn't know any more. At that moment, she no longer seemed to possess a moral compass.

Why hadn't she thought to ring the police? An anonymous tip-off. Her time with the Interveners had made her wary of the law, from whom the identity of the organisation had to be kept a secret. But in this instance, it would have been absolutely the right choice to make.

Then, out of the corner of her eye, she saw him. The gunman. Getting out of a car. Her blood ran cold. She found herself paralysed by fear. The young man was still a fair distance from the entrance. He seemed to be talking to himself, perhaps giving himself a pep talk. Geeing himself up for the bloodbath that lay ahead. He was walking around in circles as he did so.

So this was it. Do or die. The only trouble was, Kate still had no idea what to actually 'do'. She was in too deep and she knew it. She just watched him, her eyes unblinking.

The spell was broken by her own ringtone. Sally's name was flashing up on her phone. Was she back? Did she know Kate had left the Mansion? She considered letting it ring, but suspected this would only worsen the situation. She killed the engine, leaving a near-silence. She took a deep breath and cleared her throat.

'Hey Sal.'

'Hey you.'

So far so good.

'Just wanted to say sorry if I came across as a bit of a bitch earlier on. I just care about you so much.'

'Honestly don't fret it. Where are you?'

'Just heading back now. About an hour and a half away I reckon. I hope you're taking it easy. You still at the Mansion or did you knock off early?'

The gunman's pacing stopped. He started heading towards the entrance of the building.

'Erm...yes, that's right.'

'Eh?'

'Sal, I've gotta go. I think Nigel is having a Vision. Bye.'

It was action time. A fresh wave of adrenalin surged through Kate's body. She almost forgot about the wig once again, opening the car door before realising she needed to alter her appearance. She dashed towards the gunman, whose weapon she presumed must still be in his backpack. She had a plan – of sorts.

'Patrick?'

He turned around, startled and confused. She had absolutely no idea what her next move would be. All she knew was that a man carrying a loaded gun was looking her in the eye.

'Patrick? Oh my God, it is you!'

'What? Who are you?'

'You don't remember me, do you? No wonder really - you were only tiny the last time I saw you. I used to babysit you.'

'Did you? You're right, I don't remember. Now if you'll excuse me, there's something I have to do. Sorry.'

Kate desperately tried to appeal to the young man's sentimental side, hopefully entice him from his murderous state. She was hoping to disarm him - not literally, but emotionally.

'You were such a sweet and lovely young boy, you know. I'm sure you still are.'

'Nope, things change. Once again, I really need to go. Nice to meet you. Now please, PLEASE get out of my way.'

'Wait! Do you...do you work here or something?'

'No, but I used to. Until they fired me and ruined my life. Left me in a right mess, knee deep in debt. Anyway, see ya.'

'Oh, no way! They did? Don't suppose I can talk you into coming for a coffee with me? You can tell me all about it. Might do you good. A problem shared and all that.'

What am I doing? Kate wondered to herself. She was inviting a man she knew full well was harbouring a murderous weapon - and a grudge - to Costa. She started shaking. He looked at her. Looked as if he was considering her proposal. Ordinarily, this small amount of stalling time would have been enough to secure a successful Intervention – but this was anything other than an ordinary situation. Nevertheless, she felt a small twinge of hope. Then he shook his head, utched up his backpack and continued towards the entrance.

Kate sprinted back to her car and muttered under her breath. 'Right, you leave me no choice, you little bastard.'

She started the engine and with a screech of wheels headed in his direction. By the time she hit him her car had only reached twenty miles per hour - not enough to kill him, not even enough to knock him out, but enough to knock him into the air and send the backpack flying. Kate immediately got out of her car and seized it, then proceeded to make as much noise and commotion as she could whilst running away from him; she emitted primal screams of fear. A security guard came running in her direction.

'This man! He had a gun! Please help!'

The guard grabbed the would-be killer and locked him in his grip as he called for back-up on his radio. The man did not struggle – he was much punier than the one gripping him, and such an act would have been futile. As another guard appeared on the scene, Kate handed him the backpack, which he opened.

'Holy shit! There's a bloody gun in here! Paul, you keep hold of him and I'll call the police.'

Kate beat a hasty retreat to her car, which now sported a dinted bonnet. As she reversed away, she didn't dare look into the young man's eyes. Her attention was diverted by the site of several staff at one of the first floor windows, their hands either covering their mouths or pointing at the unfolding drama (or both). She recognised them all too well.

A final screech and Kate was gone. It was a good ten minutes into the journey before her heartbeat was anywhere near its resting rate and she was able to gather her thoughts.

There had to have been CCTV in the office block car park - right? Where isn't there nowadays? The remotest possibility that there wasn't was all Kate had to cling to. If, by a gigantic stroke of fortune, there wasn't, she had to hope and pray that no one had taken note of her car registration. The police were definitely going to want to speak to the lady who ran over a gunman in her car.

But she had done it. That was all she knew for now; all she needed to know for now. She had saved the lives of five innocent people. She had managed to stay alive herself. She would Intervene again: see her family again. All of this could only possibly be amazing news. So why did she feel so utterly terrible?

She knew full well why: this was the beginning of a whole lot of trouble for Kate. Again.

*****

As she arrived back at the Mansion, Kate was relieved to see that the car Gordon and Sally had taken was still out. Better still, as she crept through the front door, she could see Nigel was still sound asleep, almost as if nothing had happened. Perhaps, she told herself, she was in luck. She collapsed onto the giant sofa and switched the television on. Before she knew it, she too had drifted off, the sheer adrenalin of the day and the subsequent comedown knocking her clean out.

The sound of the front door opening some time later startled her awake. She wiped a globule of drool from her mouth.

'Well, well, well, Gord, check out this pair of Sleeping Beauties! Hard day at the office, eh?'

Nigel came round. 'What? Oh, I must have dozed off.'

Sally went to sit with her friend. 'You feeling better, babes?'

'Erm, yeah! Much better thanks.'

'What happened to your car?'

'What?'

'Your car! It's got a bloody big dint in it!'

Kate sat up. 'Right. Well. Listen, Sal, I've got a confession to make. I know you told him not to let me go, but when Nigel was asleep I took a quick spin out to Boots to get some tablets. On the way back, I was travelling down that winding country lane and I hit a deer. I think I might have killed it. Ha! Didn't get a Vision of THAT unfortunate sod's demise!'

'Oh, you poor thing!'

'Meh. I'm doing better than the deer. Anyway the tablets have sorted me right out but I must have dosed myself up good and proper. I was out like a light.'

'Good.' Sally looked around. The two men were engaged in conversation about the supermarket rescue. She spoke to Kate in hushed tones. 'We've had the radio on all the way back. No news of any shootings as yet. You'd have thought it would have happened by now. Surely most offices will be shutting soon.'

'I know! I was thinking the same! I mean, is it possible I could have got crossed wires or something?'

'Well, it's not unheard of. You remember Gordon's story about the death that turned out to be just a play? This could be a similar thing. You could be picking up on something that's not really a death at all.'

Kate laughed. 'You know, I'll bet there's some nerdy teenage boy playing Grand Theft Auto in his bedroom somewhere nearby and I picked that up!'

'Well, who knows? Fingers crossed. Let's have one last look at the news, then I reckon cake and a cuppa is in order.'

Kate's nerves became frayed once again. The news story being played out, which they'd tuned into halfway through, was still the one about the sacked manager. Kate waited with baited breath.

'Dramatic scenes in South Heatherley today as a man carrying a loaded gun was apprehended outside an office block. Police are trying to ascertain the whereabouts of a woman in a black Nissan Qashqai who hit the gunman with her car. He is being named locally as twenty-two year old Niall Baxter. Our correspondent Brianna Knightley has more.'

Sally looked at Kate. Kate did not look back.

'Ian, I'm here with Jeffrey Murphy, the security guard who managed to restrain Mr Baxter until the police arrived to arrest him. Mr Murphy, you're being hailed as a hero for your part in the proceedings today. What can you tell us?'

'I'm no hero. The hero here today is the quick-thinking lady who ran the scumbag over. If it wasn't for her, they'd have been carrying bodies out of that building in a bag, let me tell you. I remember the lad. Used to work here. I had to escort him off the premises when they sacked him, cause he was kicking off. My theory is he'd come back to get his revenge. And, like I say, he would have succeeded if not for that lady.'

'And what exactly can you tell us about her, Mr Murphy?'

'Not much, my love. Not much. No one actually saw her run him over, me included. She'd gone before anyone could speak to her. God knows why she took off like that.'

'What would you say she looked like?'

'Erm, probably late thirties. Slim build. Small-to-medium height. Attractive. Oh yeah, and she was a redhead. Curly hair she had. Yeah, that's just about sums her up.'

'Mr Murphy, thank you. We'll have more on this story as it develops. Back to the studio.'

'Former Manchester City manager Philipe Dellagio has emerged as the front runner to succeed sacked -'

Sally turned off the television. 'Kate, you stupid fucking cow. What have you done?'

Kate burst into tears. 'I don't know, Sal! I'm sorry! I'm so, so sorry!'

Chapter Forty-Four

And so it began again. The feeling that the world had a searchlight, and that Kate was desperately dodging it. The feeling that she had tried her very best to help, but that she had somehow very possibly caused more damage than good. The feeling that she was about to get found out, and that the consequences of this would be dire.

Explaining the dint to Pete wasn't hard. She didn't have to rack her brains to come up with the requisite lie - she was driving down a country lane on the way back home, she hit a deer, she was okay, bit shaken up, doing better than the deer, etc. No need to over-complicate matters. He didn't mind one bit, and was just glad his wife was unhurt.

Unlike the incident at Huntingley Manor, which was a relatively small and insignificant story, this time what had happened at the office blocks was all over the national news - the lead story on all of the channels. How Kate prayed for a politician who couldn't keep his dick in his pants or a beloved recently deceased celebrity to come along and steal her limelight. Still no CCTV evidence of proceedings had emerged - yet. The only footage that had emerged was a very grainy mobile phone video which started after Kate had made her getaway. Still no one seemed to have noted the number plate of the Qashqai. Kate and Pete watched the news with great fascination - Pete, like the rest of the nation, intrigued by the mystery redhead who had prevented the possible massacre. Confused, like the rest of the nation, by why she felt the need to flee the scene. She probably panicked - that's what Kate told him. Or maybe she was driving without insurance and didn't want to get into trouble - that was the next theory she offered up to him. He seemed to find these suggestions equally plausible. At no point did he make the connection between the continual mentions of the black Qashqai which knocked the would-be assassin over and the fact that Kate's own black Qashqai suddenly sported a large dint. Why would he? He hadn't married a redhead. And the woman he had married was at work, to the best of his knowledge.

Once again as she lay in bed, Kate had some thinking to do - a plan to formulate. Fingers to cross. Luck to ride.

Somehow, though, she felt different this time. The more she pondered the situation, the more confident she felt. She had broken a golden rule when she rescued the girl at the theme park - and she'd got away with it. Gordon was still none the wiser. She'd faced the prospect of her marriage ending head on - felt totally down and out, utterly defeated. But she'd been victorious, and this time Pete was none the wiser. Maybe - just maybe - she was invincible. Untouchable. So what if Gordon did find out, anyway? He could dock her pay - no problem. She had amassed considerable savings in her secret account during her months as an Intervener. She'd dip into those if need be. Was he going to sack her? No. No way. No matter what Sally said. He couldn't possibly afford to lose another body - times were growing desperate enough now they were down to four. He needed her much more than she needed him.

She knew exactly what she was going to do when she saw Gordon in the morning. A little smile spread across her lips as she drifted to sleep.

Chapter Forty-Five

Kate was breezy as she opened the door of the Mansion.

'Morning campers!'

Her colleagues chorused their greetings. Sally held her eye contact longer than did Gordon and Nigel. Kate shrugged. She poured herself a coffee.

'Wow, how about that woman who knocked over the gunman, eh? Christ, what a hero! We should try and track her down to join our ranks. Whaddya reckon, Gordon?'

Sally's eyes widened. Kate smirked. She was doing to Gordon much the same as he had done to the group of mourners - deliberately and brazenly drawing attention to what had happened in a bid to deflect any possible attention off herself. She had learned from the best.

'It's quite a story, dear, that's for sure. Quite a story indeed. Except, of course, she prevented a murder. That's obviously something we stay clear of here, isn't it?'

'Oh yeah, I mean, obviously. I'm just saying - that chick had some guts, didn't she? And she was quick-thinking. All the makings of a great Intervener, I say.'

Sally couldn't resist chipping in. 'I think she was really stupid, to be honest.'

Kate folded her arms and tilted her body in her friend's direction, still smiling. 'Do you now, Sal? Why's that then?'

'Well, I mean, she put her own life at risk, didn't she? By all accounts, she sounds like she was about your age. I'll bet she's got a family too, just like you. And this woman - this stupid, stupid woman - was prepared to put all of that in jeopardy. She could have died. I'm amazed she didn't.'

'Yeah, you're right. About the age thing I mean. And she's about my height, too. And my build. Hey, she could be my long-lost twin or something! What do you think, Gordon? Nigel? Don't you think this woman could be my long-lost twin or something?'

Kate was finding her own little (dangerous) game amusing to the point of exhilaration.

'She was ginger,' replied Nigel matter-of-factly.

'Well, I know that, Nige! I'm just saying, other than that, this chick could have been me. And no offence, Sal, but you're talking bollocks. She was a hero, nothing more and nothing less. Hats off to her.'

'Oh, none taken, hun! None taken. That's just your opinion, and everyone is entitled to one. Let's just hope they find this lady. Maybe then she'll get exactly what she deserves. The recognition, I mean.'

Only one Intervention took place that day. The Vision was Sally's - a brightly-dressed motorway workman being hit by a passing lorry which had careered off the road, squashing him against a tree. A higher-risk endeavour than the usual fare, this was sorted out by Sally pretending to break down fifty yards short of where the man was working - as she switched her hazards on, the workman came over to see if he could help. Magically, the car roared back into life the very first time the workman turned the key. She thanked him in as long and profuse manner as she could possibly muster up in a bid to hold him for as long as she could. The timing was exquisite, the execution masterful - the lorry still careered off the road, just as he had started to make his way back to his place of work, but the damage was minimal. No one was killed or injured. He returned to the car and this time it was his turn to offer long and profuse thanks - did she realise she had just probably saved his life? Secretly, she of course did - although she knew that there was no 'probably' about it. She also knew not to milk his thanks or dramatise what had happened in any way.

A remarkable act of saviour - but also noteworthy and unusual was the fact that Sally had not chosen Kate to be her partner. She still felt cross with her for being so remorseless and cocksure. She instead took Gordon, partly so she could make Kate sweat a little, hoping she would wonder if Sally was spelling the beans. She wasn't about to do that, of course, and Kate knew this full well. She spent a quiet day at the Mansion, periodically checking the news for any developments. There were none, and the story was already starting to blow over by the time she left for home.

Chapter Forty-Six

The days passed. Media coverage of the incident at the office blocks very quickly diminished. It faded, too, from Kate's thoughts - both in terms of the glory (which she was refusing to allow Sally to deny her) and of the possible consequences. Further Interventions - both her own Visions and the ones to which she was party - pushed what had happened further and further from her mind. Evidently, they had the same effect on

Sally - their friendship healed naturally, without either of them offering up or demanding an apology. In the first several days after the incident, every knock on the door - either her home door or the Mansion door - quickened Kate's heartbeat. She half-expected the police to be on the other side. This never happened, and life - such as it was - resumed.

It was soon a different matter that Kate felt she needed to address.

'Gordon, I don't wish to alarm you, but where the Hell's Nigel?'

Sally chortled. 'Why's that, babe? Missing him?'

'Well hardly...but don't you think it's all a bit strange?'

Gordon shook his head and placed a reassuring palm on Kate's shoulder. 'Your concern is duly noted, dear, but worry not. He's in Scotland, remember? On a lottery mission.'

'Yeah I know that. I do remember. But he does seem to have been gone for ages. I've never known him disappear for more than a couple of days, three tops. How many days has it been this time?'

Sally looked skywards as she did the calculation in her head. 'Five.'

'Shit. Something's wrong here, guys, I'm telling you. Something's happened. Call it instinct if you like.'

Sally and Gordon did not share Kate's evident sense of panic. Gordon, indeed, was smiling. 'Kate, Nigel has been a colleague and friend of mine for decades, but let's all be honest here - the man's a bit of a drain. He treats the job with no little amount of disdain. I'll wager he's having a strop. He's done it before. A few times as it happens. He'll be telling himself he's had enough of it all. Then he'll decide he's missing the whole thing - missing us too, but he wouldn't admit that, even to himself - and he'll come back. No one will mention anything - please promise me that - and business will be resumed.'

'He's right, sweetie. We'll just have to cope as a three for a bit.'

'Well I hope you're right! But don't you think he's been acting a bit off lately? A bit weird?'

'Nigel?!? Weird?!?! Nigel acting normal would be the strangest thing of all.'

'Yeah, I know, I know. But I'm telling you, something wasn't right. He was being guarded and moody even by his standards.'

'Kate, please. You're reading too much into this. Honestly, you must forget all about it.'

'I will - but can't you just put my mind at rest first? Give him a quick ring?'

Gordon and Sally erupted into simultaneous peals of laughter. 'Babe, Nigel is old school. He doesn't own a mobile phone. Possibly partly for this very reason - he likes his privacy. He doesn't WANT us to reach him. Like Gordon says - just leave it.'

Leave it she could not, or would not. Something was definitely wrong, and she regularly checked the news - nationally on the television and any Scottish news she could find on the internet. She was still - despite their reassurances - certain something had gone wrong somewhere along the line. It wasn't a psychic feeling - just a gut feeling.

He was the first thing she thought about when she awoke - and the last thing she thought about at night. His absence plagued her thoughts in every bit of down time she had at the Mansion. It wasn't that she loved and adored him the way she loved and adored the other two. But she cared. She had worked with him for so long now - how could she not?

She tried again the next morning.

Chapter Forty-Seven

'Morning Sal! Any news from Nigel yet?'

'Actually yes!'

Kate bolted upright. 'Really? Oh my God!'

She smirked. 'Yeah he rang to say tell that silly bitch from work to stop fretting about me. Reassure her that if roles were reversed I probably wouldn't even have noticed she was gone, for I am a grumpy, selfish old git.'

Kate laughed. She was probably right. About the not caring bit that was.

Chapter Forty-Eight

Kate was the proverbial dog with the bone.

'Right, so I know we're not worrying about Nigel, but...I'm worried. It's been a week now. What if he's dead in a ditch or something? Should we let the police know?'

'And what exactly are we supposed to tell them? Please help us. Our friend Nigel is psychic. He lives here in this Mansion where a bunch of other psychics live and work. Only we haven't seen him for a while, since he took off on one of his regular money-making missions. Oh, I forgot to mention he's also psychic where the lottery numbers are concerned. Any questions?'

'Point taken. But still - you don't think he's done anything silly do you?' asked Kate.

Sally shook her head. 'You mean suicide? I doubt it. He's a bit of a curmudgeon but I wouldn't say he was depressed or anything. No, I don't think we need to be putting his face on any milk cartons just yet.'

Chapter Forty-Nine

Sally and Kate were starting their working day in the usual way, flicking through the morning papers over coffee. Sally jolted.

'Holy shit, Kate. Take a look at this.'

She tossed the newspaper at her friend, who read the headline aloud. 'Lucky Local Lottery Bonanza.'

'Son of a bitch!'

Kate continued to read the article. 'Nigel Beeston, 65, of Barker Crescent, scooped a whopping £10 million on this week's National Lottery draw. Nigel says he will give up his job as - get this - an emergency services operator, where he has worked for the last thirty years, and treat himself to a Caribbean cruise. *'I never married or had kids,'* Nigel tells us, *'so who knows - I might even stay out there!'* God - so many lies in one paragraph!'

'So that's where the little shit's been! He's not AWOL or dead. But he's bloody gonna wish he was if I ever get my hands on him. Gordon! Gordon, get in here.'

The old man ambled down the stairs. 'Whatever is all this commotion?'

'He played all the bloody numbers! That git!'

Gordon slowly drew in a lung full of air through his nose, the bridge of which he massaged, his eyes closed. 'Damn. Damn, damn, damn. I knew this day would come. I knew the greed would get the better of him eventually. I just knew it. I'm amazed it's taken this long.'

Kate was growing increasingly indignant. 'We need to track him down! I mean, where does this leave us?'

'Apart from high and dry? Well, it's quite simple. We have plenty of money stockpiled. We can continue to live the life we lead for a good while yet. And I can continue to pay you both the wages you are receiving. Alternatively, if we tighten our belts - cut down on the extravagant meals and endless supplies of alcohol we seem to get through, we could probably make the reserves stretch even further. A little more austerity, that's all we'd need.'

'And after that?'

'After that we do what so many other groups of Interveners are forced to do - we work part time. Or we Intervene part time - whichever way you want to look at it.'

'What, even you?'

'Yes dear, even me. I'd probably join all those silver tops hobbling about down at the hardware superstore. If I can put up with the rigours of Intervening, I'm sure I can point folk towards the laminate flooring aisle.'

'And while you're doing that and I'm ploughing through someone's accounts, and Sal's doing whatever the Hell she can to cobble the pennies together, all those calls for Intervening are going to go unheeded?'

'Yes is the simple answer. Inevitably more people are going to succumb to their deaths but we'd have to put in damage limitation strategies. Bend a few rules - Intervene alone if necessary. And if we can find shift work, the old house might not be vacant as often as you think. This is all a long way off yet. The thing is, we've plenty of collateral here. Those beautiful machines outside are a luxury. We can start selling them off - I mean, we don't need more than two at the minute anyway. Even those we can downgrade. All the antiques and paintings in the house can start to go. Why, even the Mansion itself can go - perish the thought, I know, but there's no reason in the world why we can't run this operation from some two-up-two-down. It will be a long time before we're living on the breadline.'

'I suppose,' said Sally. 'But still - what a bastard!'

'No arguments here,' replied Gordon.

And then there were three.

Chapter Fifty

Working life continued for Gordon, Sally and Kate - what choice did they have? At that early stage, they had yet to make any changes to their comfortable and luxurious lifestyle - they still cooked and ate the most expensive and delicious of foods, treated themselves to luxury possessions whenever they were internet shopping and kept putting petrol in their fabulous cars. The fine wines stayed cold and the Mansion stayed warm.

But the way they were spending their working days had started to change. Where before it wouldn't be unheard of for Kate and Sally to pop down to the nearest village pub for lunch, or to the salon in town for a spot of pampering, now no one left the house unless they were on a mission - and likewise no one was left alone in the house unless the other two were on a mission. It just wouldn't have been fair, or practical.

There was no denying that Gordon's personality was slowly changing. His friendship with Nigel had been a very reserved, very restrained, very old-fashioned, very British affair. But they had known each other and worked closely together for decades. Inevitably, though he was still extremely angry, he was starting to miss Nigel, who was, after all, the only Intervener even remotely close in age to Gordon. Sally and Kate tried as best as they could do include Gordon in their conversations and activities, but he was something of a third wheel. He seemed to be losing some of his sparkle, and he napped more than before, perhaps partly so he could leave the two ladies to their friendship without him spoiling it.

This was one such occasion. Kate was cooking under Sally's watchful tuition as Gordon slept. She was, as she had vowed to be, getting better and better as a chef, and felt the need to celebrate.

'How's about a nice glass of Chardonnay to go with the exquisite lunch I've rustled up?'

Sally winced. 'No thanks, chick.'

'Stop the press! Sally Baxter refusing alcohol? It's never been known!'

'I know! I know. I went a bit overboard with the vodka last night and I'm feeling a bit fragile, that's all.'

Kate narrowed her eyes. 'No you didn't.'

'Sorry?'

'No you didn't have too much vodka. You didn't have any vodka. You were with me last night. I stayed late and we watched the Big Brother final together, totally sober. Remember?'

Sally looked down at her feet. 'Oh yeah, so we did. I guess you'd call that...baby brain?'

Kate took a moment to process the news being delivered to her. 'Oh. My. God! You're kidding?'

Sally shook her head and smiled apprehensively. They embraced.

'So you weren't wearing really good push up bras? And when you've been puking in the morning, it's not because you've had - what did you call them - 'monster hangovers'? You're pregnant, you lying cow!'

Sally bit her lip and nodded. 'I've been dying to tell you. I just wanted to wait until the scan. You're still the only one who knows apart from the fella. I haven't even told my mum yet.'

'And was it...'

'Planned? Nope. But I couldn't be happier. We couldn't be happier. I'm going to be a mummy, Kate! Can you believe it?'

Kate's beam dropped. 'Hang on, what does this mean for us?'

Sally rubbed her hands up and down the tops of her friend's arms, her uneasy expression a mixture of smiles and frowns. 'I'll come and see you ALL the time. I'll bring the little one with me. It's not the end.'

She brushed Sally's hands off her. 'When?'

'Excuse me?'

'When? When are you leaving me? Leaving us? Leaving here, I mean? When are you going to stop being an Intervener?'

Sally paused. Not because she was pondering her response, but rather because she was dreading delivering it. 'Probably next week I think. Maybe sooner.'

'What? Why so soon?'

'I can't go on doing this job with a child inside me! In all the years I've been an Intervener, I've never had so much as a scratch, but I take that risk every single time I go out there. I put my own life on the line to save others. I've been a couple of seconds away from being hit by a car as I've saved someone else from being hit by it. I've stood right near the edge off tall rooftops to stop children falling off of them. I've stopped fires from starting knowing full well that if I failed I could be engulfed myself. God, in my last Intervention, I sat only yards away from where I know a bloody big lorry was going to career off the road! I cannot in all good faith go out there and put my unborn child's life in jeopardy.'

'So you'll just let other people die? You'll just ignore your Visions?'

'Yes, Kate! Of course I will! You make it sound like that's even a choice! Of course my child will come first.'

'And presumably that's a dig at me, is it?'

'What? No! Honey, no! Lola's older. It's different.'

Kate shrugged. 'So what will you do? For money I mean? You'll be back when the baby's a bit older...won't you?'

'Well, Simon doesn't do too badly – he can pick up quite a good wage doing long-distance hauls in his lorry. We're not exactly going to starve. I mean, I know I could come back. I know Gordon would want me -'

'And I want you!'

'- but in all honesty I think this is it for me. This is a sign, a turning point, SOMETHING. It's time for me to move onto a new chapter. Something that doesn't involve people dying. I fancy being a teaching assistant, something like that. I still want to help people, but just in a different way.

The two sat in silence as Kate comprehended the news and Sally allowed her to. When she eventually spoke, Kate's tone was softer and more accepting.

'So you're gonna leave me with Old Father Time, are you? Just me and him left now. No more girly chats. No more shopping trips. No more talking about celebrities we fancy. No more hanging out with my best friend.'

'I'm really sorry.'

'Don't be, sweetie. I mean it - don't be.'

They hugged again.

Sally broke the news to Gordon later that day. He, too, reacted with a blend of delight and dismay. He, too, was fond of Sally, but it was the practical implications of being down to two Interveners that immediately struck him more than the realisation that the big house would seem considerably emptier and more lifeless without her. He knew it would place more pressure on Kate and himself: knew they would have to step up the search for new blood to join their ranks.

Nevertheless Sally's farewell - which came only a few days later, at Gordon's insistence - was a fond one. A small token party was thrown by Kate on Sally's final afternoon (not the raucous kind Kate first encountered upon arrival at the Mansion, but rather an alcohol-free affair with balloons and bunting and finger food). Assorted presents were given - but none more generous than the year's wages handed to her by Gordon as a thank you and gesture of goodwill. Almost as generous was the promise that, should she wish, she could resume her post at the drop of a hat at any point in the future, without question and without condition. None of them envisaged this being a probability; it barely seemed a possibility.

And then there were two.

Chapter Fifty-One

As the days as a duo passed, Kate and Gordon quickly acclimatised to their new set-up. Their relationship, though never as electrifying or fun as the one she had had with Sally, was never strained and the two exchanged not so much as a cross word. She held him in enormous veneration, always amazed that someone of his advanced years was still doing a job as demanding as Intervening often was. The mistrust she had felt for him after Zak's death was now long-gone, all but forgotten. And he treated her with great respect, great dignity, great affection. He became increasingly strict on his insistence that Kate only work her set hours and not be tempted to pop to the Mansion during the night or at weekends, even though this meant he was alone for long periods. He was adamant that she should do her best to preserve her family life. He assured her he would resist the temptation to attend Interventions alone, though she didn't believe he was sticking to it.

It was on a bog-standard mission to rescue a middle-aged man from being knocked over and killed by a speeding car that Gordon seemed to be conducting himself differently.

Saving the gentleman from his untimely death was not a problem - it seldom was in this sort of Intervention. Of the plethora of choices before them (each and every one low risk, each and every one of them as good as guaranteed to work), this time Gordon chose to play the sweet, befuddled old man, who had become separated from his wife. He'd remembered her instructions should this happen to meet at the nearest bus stop, he assured the man, but had become disorientated and could no longer recollect how to get there. What Kate could not work out (and Gordon simply smirked when asked and tapped his nose) was why he felt it necessary to don a fake moustache and flat cap. Sprightly though the real Gordon was, he was, after all, an octogenarian (his milestone birthday having taken place a week earlier). He could easily have passed as the elderly chap he was portraying. He was an elderly chap!

Kate looked upon the scene with a further degree of confusion - only a few seconds' worth of contact with the potential victim was enough to save them from the incident or accident foreseen in the Vision. Waddington was really making a meal of this one. She'd watched the speeding Land Rover disappear out of sight quite some time ago, and yet there Gordon was, still stalling the man. *Just what was he up to?* Had he, himself, not seen the car go by? Perhaps. Maybe he was erring on the side of caution - but it was definitely unlike him. Maybe he was simply enjoying a spot of amateur dramatics and wasn't ready for it to end.

The man had already directed Gordon to the nearest bus stop. Yet he appeared to be telling the helpful, seemingly random passer-by (whose slightly bored looking expression suggested he wished to get away but was too polite to do so) something akin to his life story, as attention-starved pensioners are so often inclined to do. But Gordon was not attention-starved. He was, in fact, despite some recent declines in his vigour and increases in his fatigue, a busy and lively man with an important job to do. This procrastinating was potentially very dangerous - the longer they spent away from the Mansion, the less likely it was that they would be able to get to any further Vision scenes that might happen to appear to either of them that day. Gordon knew this.

Enough was enough. Kate marched up to them. 'Dad! What's going on here? Have you lost mum again?'

'Oh, hello dear! Yes, I'm afraid I have. I think this doddery old gent's finally losing his marbles! But the lovely young man just here was helping me out.'

'Right, well thank you sir. Much appreciated. I'll take it from here.'

'Yes, thank you very much for helping this silly old timer!'

Gordon leaned into the man and embraced him. This was quite unlike the real Gordon, who had an old-fashioned stiff-upper-lip sort of personality. He barely made any physical contact with Kate, the lady with whom he spent at least eight hours a day, at least five days a week (usually much more since they had become a duo). Why was he hugging a stranger? The man himself looked uncomfortable and gave him a trio of pats on the shoulder to get acknowledge the gesture. He then made his way across the road that was supposed to be his death scene and disappeared out of sight.

'Come on then, Hugsy Malone, what the Hell was all that about?'

'Wait until we get to the car.'

Gordon shook off his alter-ego's hobble and resumed with the fluid, determined stride of a man half his age.

When they arrived and were seated, Gordon took off his moustache and removed from his pocket a black wallet. Kate knew immediately it wasn't his. She gasped.

'Did you steal that from that man? Is that what you were doing when you hugged him?'

Gordon beamed. 'Yes, I did! And yes it was. It was practically hanging out of his back pocket. I noticed it in the Vision. Folk really should be more mindful of their possessions. There are some very unscrupulous sorts about.'

'Okay. Why? Why did you take it?'

'To prove I could still do it!'

'STILL do it? What are you talking about? Are you a thief now all of a sudden?'

'No, dear. Not now. But I was before. And very likely I will be again.'

'Eh?'

'Let me ask you this, Kate. What's your life worth? I mean as a monetary value?'

Kate found herself slightly irritated by this indirect line of question. 'Don't be so daft. I can't put a price on my own life.'

'Precisely. And let's say I offered you - ooh, I don't know - five million pounds. Five million pounds which would go straight to your husband and daughter in exchange for your life. Would you take it?'

'No!'

'No. Of course you wouldn't. What I've done today is save a person's life, and all I've done is taken a small payment in exchange for doing so.' He flicked through the notes in the wallet. 'A payment of £110. Here you were rejecting five million pounds for your life and all it's cost this chap is £110 to save his. Absolute bargain!'

Kate found herself stupefied. 'Gordon, I don't understand...'

'This is how it used to be. Nigel was such a blessing to our organisation, especially when the National Lottery came along and we realised he could predict the numbers. That was a game changer. It allowed us to Intervene full time.'

'I know, you've told me this many times. But I thought you said you took on part time jobs.'

'That we did. But that only got us so far. We were living on the breadline. Barely making ends meet. We had to do other things too - things to supplement our income. I became really quite skilled at the old-fashioned art of pickpocketing.'

'I mean, I sort of see the logic. I suppose. But we're not in dire straits. Not yet. We've still got a fairly big chunk of the lottery reserves left. Haven't we?'

'There's some money left. Not much. I didn't need to take the wallet today - indeed, we're going to swing by the police station on the way back to the Mansion and you're going drop it off. What a day for that fellow! His life saved AND his lost wallet returned!'

'So why did you?'

'Like I said, to prove I still could. To get back in shape for when the day comes that I need to steal something from every victim I can. It would be helpful if you could do the same.'

Kate waved her hands defensively, defiantly. 'No. No way. I'm not pickpocketing.'

'You don't have to. Remember when you had to break into that girl's house? The one who fell down the stairs? Well, next time you find yourself in someone's house whose life you are saving - for it will surely happen again - you should collect a little memento on your way out. A piece of jewellery, an iPad - anything you can grab quickly then sell on.'

'Oh Gordon! Please tell me this is a wind-up!'

'I wish it was. Truly I do. Listen, I can see you don't feel comfortable about taking someone's possessions. Well it's the twenty-first century now. There are other options we could look into. I hear those cyber criminals lead a very lucrative life - you know, the ones who hack into people's bank accounts and such. You must have had to be quite computer savvy in your old line of work - I bet you could learn the tricks of the trade really quickly.'

Kate felt totally conflicted by this prospect. She didn't mind being a liar to facilitate her role as a lifesaver - but to be a criminal! To be a thief! This was a different matter entirely.

'I'll think about it, Gordon.'

'Promise me you will. We need to start preparing for the future, my dear.'

Chapter Fifty-Two

Kate was still reeling from Gordon's earlier bombshell as she drove home - how could she possibly become a criminal? She really didn't think she had it in her. Clearly, Gordon had the capability to shift personalities. Kate had the capability to LIE - and she did this often, and well - but not to turn into someone else completely. She couldn't keep switching from hero to villain like that. Could she?

Her thoughts were already all over the shop when she walked through the door - but things were about to get much worse.

Pete was stood in the middle of the living room, arms folded. He didn't even give his wife time to say hello.

'Kate, I think our marriage is over.'

Kate gazed at him, open-mouthed. 'What? What are you talking about?'

'I've been thinking. A lot. For a long time now. And I've finally plucked up the courage to say it. You're not the woman I married. I don't know WHO you are any more.'

'Okay, I -'

'I haven't finished talking. You're different now. You're secretive and guarded. And to be perfectly frank sometimes it feels like you would rather do anything other than spend time with your husband and daughter. There's always some task that apparently desperately needs tending to after hours in the office. Or there's a group of you meeting for drinks. You're not bothered about us.'

Pete looked at his feet.

'You finished?' He nodded. 'Right, well listen to me now. You're wrong. I do love you. I do love Lola. And you're also wrong because actually, mate, you're not walking out. And I'm not either. And you know why? You can't afford it. You're unemployed. I'm the fucking breadwinner in this household. You depend on me. So if you want to go out there and try your hand at finding a crappy low-paid job that doesn't involve manual labour - the only thing you're trained to do, let me remind you - then go for it. Fill your boots. Don't come crying to me when you can't make ends meet and want me back.'

Pete was stunned, punch-drunk by his wife's display of ferociousness and arrogance – not the response he had anticipated. He wanted to call her every name under the sun, but she was right. He didn't have the financial means to support himself and Lola. And what court was going to give him the level of custody he wanted anyway? It was hard enough for dads to win that kind of battle anyway - harder still when the mums were in such a comfortable financial position.

Yep, she was right.

He had no more words. With a huff and a slammed door he was off and making his way to the spare room, where he would sleep on the sofa bed that night.

Kate poured herself a large glass of wine and slumped into the armchair. 'Shit.'

She pondered her situation. It was true to say she had changed. Of course she had – her whole life had changed, immensely. Immeasurably. How on Earth could being an Intervener not have an effect on the kind of person she was, how she conducted herself and what – who - her priorities were? If only Pete could know that she was a dedicated life saver – he would surely revere her heroism, cut her some slack. She wondered – but only briefly – if she should tell him. This would clearly be a huge gamble she realised - too much was at stake, including (if her suspicions about Gordon murdering Zak and the conversation they had had about what might happen if Pete did find out) her husband's life. She would rather be a divorcee than a widow – that went without saying.

So that begged another obvious question – ought she to leave the organisation? She was certain this would give her marriage a fighting chance, but at what cost? What was she supposed to do – simply ignore the Visions, just as she had before her path crossed with Gordon's? Just leave Gordon to it? How on Earth was she supposed to sleep at night knowing people were dying and she had the power to stop them – but she was simply letting it all happen? The marriage would be intact – her sanity, maybe not. And on a purely selfish level, she enjoyed her job, more than she had ever enjoyed any other job she had held – for all the stretches of boredom, for all the traumatic near-misses, she would hanker after it all. No doubt about that.

Kate's next thoughts were practical ones – what would she do if she had to move out? What if Pete was right – what if the marriage was over and there really was no way back? It wasn't as if Kate didn't have the means to buy a house of her own. The surplus of wages she had received on top of her previous salary, which was going into a secret account, had by now turned into something far greater than a rainy day piggy bank - she had amassed considerable savings. She had resisted dipping into the account to fund impulsive and expensive purchases for fear of arousing Pete's suspicions. She had never come up with a plan for what to do with the money but liked the idea of a nest egg which might pay for Lola's university education and the beginning years of her adult life – she would simply concoct a story about a long-lost relative bequeathing her the money in a will or some similar nonsense. However, she was now faced with the possibility that it could be used to pay for a house of her own. There was enough in the pot to pay for one outright. And not just any old house – one worth more than her current house.

Of course if she was so inclined, she wouldn't even need to buy a new house – she had a place of residence ready and waiting for her. A magnificent place where she already had her own bedroom. If she lived in the Mansion, she could devote herself fully to the process of preventing accidental deaths. It would just mean not living with Lola –

going from being a hardly shining example of motherhood to someone who was not really a mother at all. Lola could never, ever visit the Mansion.

As Pete's snoring permeated the walls, Kate drained her wine glass and fell asleep on the armchair, neither of the Jensons spending the night in their marriage bed.

Chapter Fifty-Three

Unbeknownst to each other, as morning turned to afternoon, Kate and Pete were engaging in much the same activity – house cleaning. This was part of Pete's daily routine. He kept the house immaculate. When Kate arrived home, without exception the worktops gleamed, the floors were spotless and the smell that greeted her was a blend of freshly-cleaned rooms and dinner cooking in the oven. In the early days following Pete's departure from his job, Kate would find herself thrilled by this on a daily basis and bragged about it to her colleagues and friends. She made sure she thanked him, profusely, every single night. She hadn't lifted a finger to do housework since (at least not in her own home) – not loaded a washing machine, not ironed a blouse, not packed a lunch. However, as time passed, she inevitably started to take all of this for granted. Pete neither received thanks any more nor craved it – it was just a way to pass a chunk of his day. He could have had no idea that his wife's high-paid job also involved her donning marigolds to scrub toilets.

When the Interveners were at full strength, cleaning was done on a rota system, daily. Of course, their immense funds could easily have afforded them the luxury of a cleaner, but this was simply not a possibility – the Mansion was too curious a place for an outsider. The thought of some stranger hovering about the Vision Room with a feather duster in their hands was a ludicrous one. None of them really minded, for much the same reasons Pete didn't mind – it passed the time. The long, Vision-free days didn't seem to drag on quite so much when cleaning the old place up (and because of the enormity of the Mansion, it did take up the whole day). Other rotas existed too, such as cleaning the pool, cooking, shopping and so forth. However, now they were down to a skeleton staff, the rota system had gone. There was simply no need to clean every day – most of the rooms were untouched for days on end now. The two of them simply mucked in whenever either of them deemed it necessary, as Kate had on that particular day.

The cleaning was intended to serve a dual purpose – it was also supposed to take her mind off what was happening with Pete. It didn't. Scrubbing food splats from the inside of a microwave only requires a tiny amount of brainpower and concentration, and so Kate's thoughts were wandering. So were Pete's.

Pete was still angry. Angry that Kate had adopted such a callous tone when confronted with the possible end of her marriage. He had expected – wanted – weeping and remorse, Kate begging for forgiveness. Her response was far removed from that. She had been fierce, fearsome, unapologetic, and this only confirmed Pete's thoughts that they had come to the end of the line.

Kate was sorry. Sorry that she had been so horrible to Pete. She wished she could turn back the clock. If she had another chance, she would shut up and listen to him – let him pour his heart out. Let him say his piece – at the very least he deserved that.

As he hoovered the living room carpet, Pete wondered if he could live without Kate. Part of the problem was that oftentimes, he appeared to be doing exactly that already. Her long shifts meant sometimes he was barely seeing her at all. Sometimes even when they were in the same room, they might as well have been a million miles apart. They had become disconnected.

As she ran a microfibre cloth around the giant plasma television screen, Kate wondered if she could live without Pete. The answer was yes. It wasn't like she would never see him again – they would still have to work as a team to raise their daughter. Nor was it the case that she didn't have the skills or the mindset to live alone. She was every bit the independent and strong twenty-first century woman.

As he scrubbed the grouting in the shower, Pete wondered if he *wanted* to live without Kate. The answer was no. Not at all. He didn't want Lola to grow up being bounced around parent-to-parent, house-to-house. He still idealised the notion of a nuclear family. Not just that, though – it wasn't as if his attraction to Kate had died. It still burned, undiminished. That the two would never make love again was something akin to unthinkable to Pete. More than all of this, though, he still loved her and cared about her.

As she dusted the antique grandfather clock, Kate wondered if *she* wanted to live without Pete. The answer was no. She could but she didn't want to. Her heart still melted when she walked into the room and saw Pete on the floor helping Lola decorate her doll's hair or playing Buckaroo. He made Lola happy, and that made Kate happy. He made life easier for Kate, and that made her happy too. Did he stir her loins in the way that Zak had? No, but it wasn't like their sex life was dormant.

As he polished the kitchen table, Pete mulled over an apology – whether he should offer one and if he should what it would consist of. What did he have to be sorry for? Perhaps for threatening Kate with the end of their marriage before they had had a chance to discuss the issues. He shouldn't have done that – that was what he told himself. This element of guilt quickly festered and multiplied.

As she polished the silverware in the kitchen, Kate mulled over her own apology. Whilst secretly the opposite was true in so many ways, in lots of ways she had much to be sorry for. Perhaps she should concede that she hadn't been a particularly good wife / mother – make promises (and not simply lip service, either) that she would try to do better. Maybe the argument was exactly what she – what they – needed.

Her thoughts were interrupted by a clatter. A small, thick envelope dropped through the letterbox with the rest of the post, addressed to 'Gordon, Kate and Sally'. As the former was napping and the latter long gone, Kate took it upon herself to open it. The postmark read Anguilla. Kate's thoughts about Pete quickly disintegrated. Inside was a wedge of fifty pound notes (a hundred of them, Kate later discovered), covered in bubble wrap, and a note:

Dear friends,

I'm sorry about what I did. Sincerely, I am. But everybody deserved to retire at some point and I felt my time had come. I don't wish to be like you, Gordon. I don't wish to be Intervening until the day I die. I was growing more and more tired - physically and mentally.

I hope you feel you can accept my gift. I will be sending the same amount every month. It should go some way to covering your wages and upkeep. I'm sorry I didn't send any sooner - I thought it would be better if I let the dust settle a bit. I knew you would be angry with me and that you would reject my offer outright. Hopefully that's no longer the case. If it is, please donate the money to a charity of your choice, or simply burn it. Either way my conscience will be eased knowing I have at least tried to help.

I realise you probably don't want to hear this, but it's paradise here. For the first time in a very, very long time, I am at peace with myself. There aren't many people here, and the island itself is very remote, so I haven't had a single Vision as yet. When that day comes - for it will come - I fully intend to ignore the Vision. After all these years, I have played my part. I aim to see out my days somewhere in this part of the world.

Don't come looking for me as I will be moving on soon, and I will keep doing so until I have found the place I know I want to call home.

Gordon - thank you for your many years of friendship. Kate and Sally - please remember that Intervening is a part of your world. It isn't your whole world. Or at least it shouldn't be.

Goodbye everyone,

Your friend Nigel.

When Gordon found out about the gesture later that afternoon, his initial reaction was one of contempt and fury. As he calmed down, he began to see the situation for what it was - an opportunity. An opportunity to continue the pursuit of saving lives without resorting to desperate or underhanded measures - theft, fraud and corruption were all possibilities once the previous stockpile of lottery winnings had run dry (and by Gordon's calculations, that was likely to happen within the next twelve months). This way, they could live comfortably and sleep better at night. Moreover, without the need to take on part time jobs, more lives would be spared. Gordon still wasn't prepared to accept his old friend's apology, but he was prepared to accept his money.

The working day had ended fabulously for Kate. The actual day - not so. Kate had returned home to find the house empty, and a note on the fridge which simply read: 'Need time to think.'

Chapter Fifty-Four

The days and weeks rolled by with Interveners Incorporated down to a skeleton staff of just Kate and Gordon. Kate had made many appeals in the initial days following Pete's departure for him to return home. Whenever he did, it was without Lola, and with the express intention of talking things through. Talking always turned to shouting, and this situation only worsened. Kate grew more and more accustomed to living without Pete, and before long they came to the mutual agreement that Pete and Lola would move back in, and Kate out. She moved into the Mansion more or less full time, but rented out a small flat, which she pretended was her real home, staying there whenever she had Lola over. She continued to support her daughter and estranged husband financially. Not that she had ever found herself stretched since joining the Interveners, but she could comfortably afford to keep up both of these sets of payments, particularly as Gordon had increased her wages in recognition of the extra hours she was devoting to the organisation. Strictly speaking they should have doubled, but even with the reduced numbers on the payroll, the supply of money was far from endless.

Kate and Gordon became increasingly good at using the time they did have together in the Mansion, striking a well-honed balance of being in each other's company and, for the sake of their longevity, being out of it. For the latter, Kate spent a healthy proportion of her time in the gym and took over Sally's gardening duties while Gordon developed a new and consuming interest in genealogy, eager to find a blood family among the dead that he hadn't had for so long in the living. Oftentimes they would alternate an afternoon nap and of course menial acts like television watching were still a feature of the day even for intelligent folk like these. They didn't share many programmes, however, Kate favouring the daytime quizzes and Gordon never giving up hope of developing a psychic connection with horse racing so that he could further boost their income, just as Nigel used to (while his continued donations were generous, they still did not equate to the extravagancies of the Interveners' heyday). For that reason, television watching was yet another separate activity on all but extraordinary occasions when something piqued both their interests.

Not that they weren't good at indulging in shared activities. In Sally's absence, Kate found the necessity to find - or make - common ground with the old man, and this she did. She shared Gordon's great passion for Chess and no day ever passed without a game. Most days involved three, the two players becoming more evenly matched as time passed and therefore one winning the first game and the other the rematch, leaving the need for a decider. Gordon always showed visible delight if his protégé defeated him, while Kate was not quite that dignified, never able to hide her own disappointment if she lost. Scrabble was another shared favourite, and any other board games which they felt were stopping their brain cells from dying were welcomed. They enjoyed completing the cryptic crossword from the newspaper together, Gordon sometimes finishing it as best as he could before handing it over to Kate and sometimes the other way round. Sometimes they sat side-by-side and completed it together. Gordon's knowledge of the world before the latter quarter of the twentieth century was as impressive as Kate's knowledge of the world after it, and together they made a formidable team. Answers were often accompanied by supplementary facts and background information, which the other party would do their best to absorb and retain.

One of Kate's favourite activities, however, was a passive one - she loved to listen to Gordon's stories from his long and illustrious time as an Intervener. Her routine was always to make herself a cup of tea and curl up on the sofa as she listened, gazing up at the white ceiling which became a kind of canvas onto which she projected the images forming in her mind. He regaled her in slow, deliberate tones and that was just how she liked it, finding the experience a highly soothing one. She was just as thrilled by hearing old stories as she was new ones - she was particularly fond of the story of Gordon's removal of what would have been a lethal banana skin which would have caused Prince Philip to slip down a marble staircase in the early seventies. He assured Kate that, whilst clearly a potentially great tragedy, there was a slightly comic element to his demise. He bemoaned the fact that, for such an act of heroism, by all rights he should now be Sir Gordon Waddington, but such was the clandestine life of the Intervener.

Expert though they were at spending their free time, they both always looked forward to one of them getting a Vision - not so much for the Intervention itself, which was mostly routine and mundane, occasionally tragic if a complication had ensued, and seldom as satisfying as Kate had found it in the early days. No, it was the escape from the Mansion they really enjoyed - a ride in their Jag, the one remaining guilty pleasure from the fleet, always with the top down on a warm day. They had a fair system in operation when it came to the car stereo, each of them taking control for fifteen minute chunks. Gordon would favour stations where heated political discourse dominated, throwing in his own opinions with the same vehemence as the ones being shared. Kate, in contrast, seemed increasingly drawn to the local commercial pop music station - while she was too old to be part of their demographic, and only really enjoyed a small amount of the already limited number of tracks on rotation, the vitality and youthfulness of the station was a useful way to offset the fact that she spent the entirety of her working day with a very old man. Kate did not enjoy Gordon's radio time and did not engage with the debate, but nor did she ever complain. Gordon, likewise, did not enjoy Kate's radio time and tried his level best to zone out from what he considered to be an insufferable din, but he never complained either.

Intervening as a duo had its problems and limitations. There were times on the road when the other person got a Vision. If it was the person doing the driving, he or she pulled over at the first hint of a Vision coming (a sudden cold flush of blood, a woozy, swimming sensation and a tingling of the fingertips were all warning signs worth paying heed to). He or she would simply buckle up in the passenger seat and let the Vision play out. Mostly this would happen without any communication taking place between Kate and Gordon. Depending on how far away their current mission was, every once in a while there would be a positive ending to the situation - they would always go that little bit faster on the way back and do their level best to locate and attend the new Vision, but Kate had learned to detach herself from the content of the Vision knowing full well how unlikely it was that the victim would survive. If that victim happened to be a child, or worse still a pregnant woman, so be it. Rule Number Five clearly stated that rescue missions were not to be abandoned in favour of other Visions. There was no room for priority or hierarchy.

One afternoon when the two of them were out tracking down the victim from one of Gordon's Visions, Kate got a Vision of her own. They continued on their current mission - what choice did they have? - then hotfooted it back to The Mansion. To their great dismay, the screen in the Vision Room displayed a set of flashing zeroes in lieu of the usual countdown timer, indicating that the victim had already perished. This was a pivotal moment. From then on, they decided the benefits of Intervening together were outweighed by the potential risks.

This presented challenges of its own. In Gordon's absence, Kate would find the Mansion desperately and dispiritingly dull. Likewise, the journeys to and from Interventions were often soul-destroying experiences, for Kate in particular. She missed the company, the camaraderie. She took to listening to audio books to stave off the boredom. Sometimes they did so and sometimes they did not. Monotony was a very dangerous thing indeed where Kate's mental state was concerned. She would replay the potential death towards which she was travelling *ad infinitum*, and the emotional gravity - the burden - of what she was doing would intensify. Sometimes she would arrive at rescue scenes frazzled and consumed by wild thoughts. On one occasion (her millionth rescue of a pedestrian being hit by a car), for reasons unbeknown even to herself, she found herself arriving at the scene and spotting her victim, but then deliberately procrastinating, leaving it until the very last second before blocking her victim's path as per the original plan. Was it God complex? Bloodlust? Boredom? She knew not.

Chapter Fifty-Five

Gordon had an exciting development to share with Kate - a potential game-changer, no less.

'My dear, I have excellent news. I know life with an old git like me must be hard for you, and I know you miss Sally - well all of that might be about to come to an end. I may have located a potential new recruit.'

Kate turned the TV off and tried her best to repress an excited smile. 'New recruit?'

'Yes. She appeared on my Radar a few days ago when I was running some errands in town. I followed her around for a while to see if the signal remained strong, and it did. I got on the same bus as her and followed her all the way back to her house.'

'Wow! Creepy!'

'Here's her address. We're going to do this one differently. No letters, no invitations - I'd like you to meet her, face-to-face and use that persuasive charm. She's about your age I'd say. Hey - maybe it's that long-lost twin of yours who ran over the gunman!'

'Shit! Really? That sounds a bit intense. When should I go?'

'Well you can stew on it for a few days, really let that apprehensive feeling you've got fester and multiply, or you can jolly well get those car keys right now!'

Unable, as always, to resist following Gordon's orders even when she had reservations, she was changed, made up and on the road within ten minutes and following the computer's directions. She couldn't shake her good mood, her good inkling, as she sang along to the short burst of eighties pop hits on the radio station. She was there within fifteen minutes.

She sat in her car to regain her composure - there was no doubt that she felt a good degree of excitement at the prospect of someone joining her and Waddington at the Mansion - and moreover that she was about the same age as Kate. A potential new best friend to share the extreme levels of boredom and excitement that made up her time as an Intervener. One more time, she went over in her head what she would say, how she would begin by explaining that what she was going to say would seem strange, but that the exact same thing had happened to her not so long ago. She would ask her if she got the painful and vivid images in her mind, seemingly out of nowhere. She would explain that she, too, was psychic and that the technology existed to pinpoint the location of those real life scenes. She would explain how she had become a hero, saving hundreds of lives.

She would ask her to accompany her to the Mansion, either right away or at a time that suited her, to see this strange miracle in action.

She glimpsed the figure of a lady in the upstairs window. It was time. She checked her make up in the vanity mirror and readjusted her trouser suit. She was quivering as she knocked on the door. The lady answered. She looked about Kate's age, but more bedraggled, more frazzled. She did not reciprocate Kate's smile.

'Yes?'

A voice called from somewhere in the house. 'Mummy! Evan won't share his Lego with me!'

Kate glanced towards the end of the hallway, where she could see three young children charging about in a scene of mayhem. She looked at the lady's hands, specifically at her bare ring finger.

'What do you want? I'm kind of up to my neck in it here!'

Kate hesitated for a second. 'I've come to talk to you about Jesus.'

The lady tutted and closed the door on Kate, who walked rather glumly back to the car and drove back to their workplace in silence.

She put her arms around Gordon's shoulders. 'Looks like it's going to be just you and me for a while, old man. She just slammed the door in my face.'

'Ah well, give her time, my dear. You've just delivered to her the strangest news of her life. She may need a little time to come around.'

'Yeah, maybe. Back to the Mansion for a cup of tea?'

'Of course. Of course.'

Kate smiled and squeezed Gordon's knee.

Chapter Fifty-Six

For Kate - as well as anyone else who shared or had previously shared her odd profession - being an Intervener had the capacity to be both deeply predictable (like most jobs, including her former one, which now seemed a lifetime ago) and totally surprising. The lion's share of her rescue missions were repeats by this point - variations of previous Interventions. They were comforting insofar as she knew what she was doing, and was able to execute her duties with confidence. Every now and again, though, something totally different and unique and surprising would crop up. She loved those ones even more - loved flying by the seat of her pants.

What she did not expect this far in was for the process of actually receiving the Vision to seem or feel any different. She was wrong. The Vision she was encountering now seemed different to the others she had had, not just since joining the Interveners, but before she even knew of the company's existence. There was an intensity to the scene - an urgency. It burned the inside of her head; physically pained her and, upon its completion, left her feeling more drained than any Vision had ever done before, even that of the shooting scene. Yet there was also a vagueness about it. It bewildered and confounded her. She could not decipher the images, which were blurry and indistinct, almost as if she were looking at them too closely.

She turned to Waddington, awaiting his accompaniment to the Vision Room. He let his palm rest on Kate's hand. His eyes - so often filled with vacancy – now seemed somehow pleading.

'No, my dear. Not this time. You take this one alone.'

She gazed at him disbelievingly - he knew there was no one else around now! He - he of all people - knew that you sat in the Vision Room in pairs unless it was impossible to do so. He had taught her that, for Christ's sake! Shaking her head, she darted towards the Vision Room and attached the plates. She was adept enough at using the equipment at this point to be able to pan around and zoom in and out of the scene - and so she zoomed out, until the scene and victim were all too clear - and all too familiar.

An elderly man, evidently sleepwalking, fell to his death from a two story window.

There was no mistaking that the window belonged to the very house in which she was situated. No need to locate this one. No mistaking, either, that the man with his eyes closed whose life was ending with a blood-splattered crash to the concrete beneath him was, in fact, Gordon Waddington. An icy shiver ran down Kate's spine and her heartbeat seemed first to stop then to quicken. She watched in stunned silence, but felt compelled to rewind and replay the scene, just to be certain. It was definitely Waddington - that lithe frame, the long, craggy face, the waves of grey hair - and his demise was just under three hours away.

As her initial disbelief subsided, a wave of relief overcame her - this was going to be the easiest Intervention of her career! For the very first time, her victim was allowed to know exactly what was happening, know that his life was about to be saved. All she had to do was tell him! She re-entered the living room with a twinge of excitement, where

Waddington was slumped on his chair, his elbows and forearms resting on his thighs, his head hung low. He did not greet her entrance with eye contact, or indeed any recognition at all.

'Gordon, what I'm going to tell you will shock you, so brace yourself. It's amazing news, in a weird sort of way. Gordon?'

Waddington did not move. Unperturbed, Kate continued with her news.

'Basically, the person I just saw in my Vision - well, it was you, Gordon! So - ta-dah! I suppose tonight I'm your guardian angel!'

Still no response. Kate waited, but in the end could not resist finishing her bombshell.

'You are - well, were, really - going to die in your sleep tonight. Not from a heart attack or anything like that, thank God, but by walking - sleepwalking - through your bedroom window. So I insist that tonight you sleep on the couch. We'll lock the doors upstairs and maybe we could think about moving your room tomorrow? Maybe turn one of the downstairs rooms into your sleeping quarters? I mean, you were lucky tonight, cause I was here, but you might not be so lucky next time!'

Waddington finally showed a reaction to Kate's news, letting out a snigger pitched somewhere between saddened and incredulous but still not raising his head.

'Lucky, yes. That's me. Gordon Waddington. Luckiest bugger in the world. Blessed with this amazing gift. Ha. Lucky, yes.'

Kate fumed, darting towards the old man and prodding his shoulder.

'What the Hell?! I just saved your life! Why are you being like this?'

Waddington looked up. His eyes were red and his cheeks streaked with tears, none of which he was attempting to wipe away. Kate suddenly felt disarmed.

'Kate, sit down. Please.'

She obliged. As she stared at him, this broken old man, the realisation sank in.

'Oh God. My Vision. You weren't sleepwalking at all, were you? You...you were killing yourself!'

He nodded very slowly. Suddenly it was she who was crying – deep, unrestrained sobs.

'Kate, I'm a very old man. I've lived a long and now full lifetime carrying this blessing, this curse, around with me. A lifetime of saving people, but also of almost saving them, of witnessing first hand their horrible deaths. People's fathers and grandfathers, mothers and grandmothers. People's husbands and wives. People's sons and daughters. *Children.* Tiny, helpless little children dying in front of my eyes, for God's sake.' A fresh wave of tears streamed from his eyes. 'I'm tired, my dear. So tired. I'm physically tired, more so than ever before, but I'm also tired of my lot in life. And I want it all to end.'

'And that's it? That's why?'

He hung his head. 'No, there are other factors here too. Kate, I did murder Zak. Consider this my deathbed confession. You knew that, though, didn't you?'

She said nothing.

'I did what I had to do. I stand by that. I was protecting you – protecting the organisation. But it's been a Hell of a cross to bear, let me tell you. It's funny, though. When he died, I actually envied the poor bastard. I was glad for him that he didn't have to suffer through another fifty years of this. And who knows when I will come to my own natural end? For all I know, I could have another ten, even twenty years of Intervening. I can't do it. I just can't do it. I'm giving up. Just like Chris did. Just like Nigel did. Just like Sally did. Just like countless others did before you joined us.'

Once again they sat in a ruminative silence, which Kate eventually broke. If there was no stopping Gordon, then there were things he needed to know. She couldn't let him go to his grave before she had finally shared her secrets.

'If we're confessing our sins, I need to tell you something myself. I saved a girl's life at a theme park once. Sally was with me. Only I really cocked up. I went a bit far. I nearly blew the cover for all of us. I was on the news and in the papers and everything. I didn't want to let you down. I got scared. I'm so sorry, Gordon.'

'I know.'

'You know I'm sorry?'

'I know what you did. I saw the news report.'

'Wait - how come you didn't punish me?'

'Because - it was an honest mistake. And because - you were my favourite, Kate. I didn't want to drive you away.'

Kate smiled. She felt the confidence to confess to him her ultimate sin. 'And there was something else. I did something I really shouldn't have done. I got a Vision of a murder scene and...well, I knew I shouldn't have done it, but I Intervened. I saved the day. I'm...sorry.'

Gordon looked away from her. 'That one I didn't know about. You shouldn't have done that. You *really* shouldn't have done that. I can't condone that sort of recklessness, even with my dying breaths. Kate, you were stupid. You need to promise me - promise me - you won't ever do such a thing again. Don't ever put your own life in jeopardy. You're not just an Intervener - you're someone's mother. Promise me.'

Fresh tears streaked Kate's face. 'I promise, Gordon. I promise you I won't do it again.'

He let her cry. She eventually spoke. '*Shit*. I mean, Christ. No. *No*. I can't - *you* can't. Gordon, please no.'

'I've thought about this long and hard and I'm afraid my mind is made up.'

'But what about the contract you made me sign? You know the rules! Number Two - *You may not Intervene in suicide attempts.*'

'I'm asking you as a friend - as a dear, dear friend, as the only thing even close to family I've got in this world - to make an exception. Turn a blind eye. Bend the rules one last time. I beg you. Put this old horse out of its misery.'

'Exactly. That's what you're asking me to do. By letting you die, you're asking me to kill you. I won't be the one that does it, but I'll have blood on my hands.'

'I know. I do know that. I was rather hoping you wouldn't be around tonight, for that very reason. Blissful ignorance and all that. But I've been planning this for quite some time and vowed that tonight would be the night, no matter what. My deadline, so to speak, has arrived. I sincerely do not wish for you to feel guilty. You must consider it a mercy killing.'

'And what - that's it? Have you even thought about me at all? I'll be the only Intervener left here! I'm supposed to run this operation all by myself, am I?'

'Yes. You are. In all my years as an Intervener, you are the most talented, most capable, most intelligent, most conscientious, most human, most *humane* colleague I have ever had. You are more than capable of continuing our work alone. If I didn't think you were, I wouldn't be doing what I'm doing.'

'Oh gee, thanks, that makes me feel great. I'll remember that as they're lowering you into the ground.'

Waddington ignored her. 'And you will find more Interveners. There have been times when I have been forced to work alone. Just be patient. You'll find them. They'll find you. Here.' He reached under the sofa and handed Kate a large folder, thick with paper.

'Everything you need to know about Interveners Incorporated is here. Details about the house, instructions for operating and repairing the computer, Marco's phone number as a last resort if you can't do that, and other contacts you might need, whatever circumstance you might find yourself in. It's all here. You'll also find instructions on what to do after my death – what you'll say to the police, the people you'll need to inform and my wishes for my burial, the kinds of flowers I'd like and so on. Needless to say, it will only be you in attendance, but I'd still like a nice send-off. There's a small poem in there I would like you to read, if you'd be so kind.'

Kate placed her fingertips on the folder but did not take it. Waddington retained his own grip on the other side and the two of them sat there, joined by the folder. Eventually, he pushed it towards her and relinquished his grip.

'Oh, Gordon,' Kate whispered, softly and sadly, letting another tear run down her cheekbone.

'I'm going to leave you now. I won't be doing what I'm doing for a while yet - well, you knew that already, didn't you? But I'd like to be alone with my thoughts. Goodbye, Kate. Good luck.'

The two of them hugged, tightly at first, then long and lingering. As they released themselves from the embrace, their hands dropped into each other's. Kate squeezed her eyes shut tight in an attempt to halt the flow of tears and she looked down, cloudy-eyed, as Waddington removed his hands and made his way up the stairs and out of view.

She collapsed on the sofa and sobbed loudly and incessantly. It was the best part of an hour before she was able to regain her composure. She got up and walked towards the fridge, resolving to do what she had done so many times since joining the Interveners – get drunk. This was, however, the first time she had done so alone in the Mansion. She grabbed the first bottle of wine she could see and poured a large glass, drinking hearty gulps from it. It didn't take long for a familiar and very welcome fuzziness to kick in; it blunted (perhaps blurred) the pain, though no amount of alcohol was going to stop her from thinking about Gordon. It was taking all she had not to run up the stairs, throw her arms around the old man and say one more goodbye.

However, her thoughts seemed to become lighter in tone after the first bottle of wine; she began to reminisce. She pictured the first time she met him, their first handshake – her first cautious steps into this strange new world. She remembered back to her welcome party and the buzz of new friendship. She remembered her very first

Intervention - the old lady who she saved from being run over. Then every successful Intervention from that point onwards seemed to replay in her mind, one at a time, and she recalled who had accompanied her on each one. She remembered endless warm afternoons out in the garden with Sally. Suddenly, the big, empty room seemed spirited. Zak came back to life. The Games Room - all-but deserted for so long - suddenly became the joyous mixture of sounds it used to be. Clinks and clonks; whizzes and whirs; pings and pongs; celebratory cheers and grunts of frustration. It hummed with life and laughter. Kate became lost in her own happy memories, and was only awoken from her reverie by a loud thud outside. She glanced at her watch, nodded to herself, then reached for the bottle. She found she had no more tears to cry as she continued to drink herself to sleep.

And then there was one.

A heartfelt thank you for reading my novel (and special thanks to Beth for her meticulous proofreading skills!) As a self-published author, your feedback is invaluable to me. So if you could spare a moment to leave an honest review on Amazon and / or Goodreads, I would be really grateful! This helps me to 'spread the word'. If you haven't already read my debut novel, 'Baby One More Time', please do! My third book is already well underway, so please follow me on Facebook and Twitter for updates:

https://www.facebook.com/craigtilstoneauthor/

https://twitter.com/craigtilstone

Thank you once again for helping my dream to come true.

Craig

Printed in Poland
by Amazon Fulfillment
Poland Sp. z o.o., Wrocław